A Bride

SEWS WITH LOVE

IN NEEDLES, CALIFORNIA

Barb,
I thank you to
the DCHS!

Erin Vetsch

A Bride
SEWS WITH LOVE

IN NEEDLES, CALIFORNIA

ERICA
VETSCH

BARBOUR
PUBLISHING

Print ISBN 978-1-61626-741-4

eBook Editions:
Adobe Digital Edition (.epub) 978-1-62029-556-4
Kindle and MobiPocket Edition (.prc) 978-1-62029-555-7

Cover design: Faceout Studio, www.faceoutstudio.com

Published by Barbour Publishing, Inc., P.O. Box 719, Uhrichsville, Ohio 44683, www.barbourbooks.com

Our mission is to publish and distribute inspirational products offering exceptional value and biblical encouragement to the masses.

 Member of the
Evangelical Christian
Publishers Association

Printed in the United States of America.

Dedication

In memory of the brave men and women of the Great War who served in the US and abroad. And to the memory of the thousands of Harvey Girls who provided hospitality and service to soldiers and passengers of the AT & SF railroad.

Acknowledgments

The author would like to thank Mary Ann Bucher and Faye Ricter of the Dodge County, Minnesota Historical Society for their assistance with the history of World War One veterans of Dodge County. It was at the DCHS Museum that the idea for this story was born after seeing a vintage WW1 Red Cross signature quilt. Very special thanks go out to my sister-in-law, Linda Ambrose, for all her help in creating our own Red Cross Signature quilt, embroidered with the names of over 300 Dodge County WW1 Veterans. Both quilts are on display at the DCHS Museum in Mantorville, Minnesota.

Chapter 1

There is nothing so stubborn and exasperating as a headstrong Irish daughter."

"You only bring up my Irish half when I'm suggesting something you don't like. If I please you, you claim my Norwegian side." Meghan set her jaw, determined to stand up to Papa.

"How do I know this isn't just another one of your wild schemes? Like the mail-order candy or the door-to-door sewing notions? Remember how those ended? Flying high only to fall to earth with a thud after a few weeks." His huge boots clomped as he paced the sitting room floor, drowning out the sound of rain pattering against the windowpane as a late spring storm blew through. "You always start out with the best of intentions, child, but you don't think things through. Always you think you can whip the world, but you take on too much and come crashing down."

"It won't be like that. I was a child then. I didn't know what

I was doing." Meghan Thorson poked the logs in the fireplace, sending a shower of sparks racing up the flue. "I won't be trying to start my own business. I'll be working for one of the most reputable companies in the country. And it's only for six months, not forever. If I don't like it, I can come home then. But I will like it. You'll see. You're the one who has been saying I need to find something to occupy my time, something that would help the war effort and keep me out of your hair. This job will definitely keep me out of your way. Needles is more than fifteen hundred miles from here."

Papa stopped pacing, stroked his reddish-blond beard, and studied her with somber blue eyes. "And how long will it be before I get a letter saying you hate it out there and you're coming home?"

"You won't get such a letter from me."

"Couldn't you find something closer to home? I thought you would get a job here in Mantorville, or even over in Rochester. California is too far away."

Mama's knitting needles clicked, a sound as familiar to Meghan as her own breathing. "You hoped it would be in Rochester so you could have an excuse to drive your new motorcar over there." She barely looked up from the sock she knitted. Socks, socks, and more socks. American soldiers in the trenches in France needed socks, and Mama's knitting needles never stopped.

I pray over every pair as if they were going to Lars himself. They are all my sons in that way, all those soldiers. And I know their mamas are praying for them as well. Mamas of soldiers knit and pray.

"I don't want a job close to home. I want to stand on my own two feet, do something bigger, travel, and"—she spread her hands—"I don't know how to explain it. I just know I need to do this. I knew it as soon as I saw the advertisement in the *Tribune*."

Mama sighed. "She needs to go. She's gone in her heart already." *Click, click, click.* "I'm surprised we were able to keep our little sparrow in the nest this long. She's always desired to fly. This is her chance." A faraway look invaded Mama's expression, softening her face in the firelight.

But Papa was not softened. "Mary Kate, I thought you would have agreed with me that Meghan should stay here. With us. She's too young to leave home." He thrust his hands into his pockets and stood square before Mama's chair. "She is barely more than a child. Not old enough to go so far away from home."

Mama's red lashes flicked upward from her yarn, showing eyes so green they seemed to glitter—the same eyes she'd passed on to Meghan, along with her red hair and freckles—and according to Papa, her Irish stubbornness.

"Look at her. She's twenty years old. When I was eighteen, I set out on a wonderful adventure. I sailed away from Ireland to America. And I met a handsome Norseman on the boat who swept me off my feet and carried me away to his new home in Minnesota." She grinned. "By the time I was twenty, I was already a mama to Lars."

Papa's brow scrunched. "That's different."

"Is it? I think it is very much the same. Let her have her adventure, Per. She's young, and there is so much strife in the world right now, so little for a young woman to be excited about. Who knows, perhaps she'll find a strapping, brave young man to call her own like I did."

Jabbing the poker into the coals, Meghan protested. "Mama, that's not why I'm going. Working for The Harvey Company means I will get to see more of America than this little corner. I'll get to meet lots of people and have a steady job that pays well. I want to be busy just now. I want to feel like I'm doing something important. Serving people, especially soldiers, in the restaurant will be my way of helping with the cause. The woman who interviewed me for the position said hundreds of soldiers pass through their eating establishments on their way to the war."

Papa made a gruff sound in his throat. "But it's so far away. If I had known you were going to apply at The Harvey Company while we were there, I never would've taken you with me to Chicago."

Meghan left her spot beside the fireplace and stood on tiptoe to kiss his cheek above his full beard. "Well, I'm glad you did take me. Seeing Chicago was a real treat, and so was getting this job. The interview nearly scared me out of my shoes, but I lived through it, and they hired me. Please, Papa, give me your blessing. It's only for six months."

He enfolded her in a bear hug, resting his chin on top of her head. "The women in my life will be the death of me."

She squeezed his waist and pulled back to look up into his face. "You know I wouldn't be going if I didn't think this was what God wanted me to do. It feels right."

His eyes narrowed. "Be careful how you throw that around, child. Many a foolish thing has been done in the name of God. And many a thing we *want* to do has been justified by calling it the will of God."

She bit her lower lip. Was she being headstrong and impulsive?

It wouldn't be the first time. But she wanted this so badly. And it did feel right.

He tweaked her nose and let her go. "When do you have to leave?"

Meghan whirled and pounced on the letter that had come that day. "I'm to report to the offices in Chicago in three days. They'll provide the uniforms, the training, and the transportation to my new job."

"You will be homesick within the week," Papa predicted, crossing his arms once more. "You've never been away from home, and you love Minnesota. Your Irish and Norwegian heritage has given you a need to be surrounded by green, growing things. The desert won't feed your soul the way the fields and forests of this land do."

"I will miss you and Mama, but seeing different places and meeting new people is part of the fun. It wouldn't be much of an adventure if where I'm going turns out to be exactly like here."

"And you are sure you will be safe? You'll have someone to look after you?" The doubt-clouds returned to his eyes.

She rushed to reassure him. "All the girls must live in a dormitory, and there is a strict curfew, and there are lots of rules. Your little girl will be just fine."

"Will she?" Papa's mouth twisted, rueful and wry. "Lots of rules and my Meghan have never gotten along too well."

Mama chuckled and loosened more yarn from her skein. "That's a plain truth. How will you do following rules and behaving yourself?"

"I can do it," Meghan boasted. "I'll be the best Harvey Girl that company has ever seen. By the time my contract is up, they'll be begging me to stay."

"Needles, California, coming up!" The dapper conductor, brass buttons gleaming in two bright rows down his navy suit, rocked his way along the aisle as passengers stirred and began removing belongings from the overhead racks.

Meghan turned her attention to the window, eager to get a glimpse of the town that would be her home for at least the next six months, but she was on the wrong side of the train.

Empty wasteland swept by, punctuated by clumps of cactus and scrub. Jagged, rocky peaks and rounded piles of sand thrust upward into the sky, and occasional sparse green patches showed where someone was trying to scratch out a living in this inhospitable landscape. They had crossed over the muddy Colorado River which flowed sullenly, as if the heat had sapped its energy and the sand had choked its will to move.

"I knew we'd be living in the desert, but I didn't realize how stark it would be."

"It doesn't look much like Illinois. It's terribly hot, and it's only May. What must it be like here in July?" Natalie Daviot, a Springfield native, dabbed her temples again and nudged Meghan's arm. "Are you nervous? I sure am."

Meghan shook her head automatically, paused for a moment,

and crumbled, nodding. Though they'd only known each other a few short days, she and Natalie had become instant friends. Neither had ever been away from home before, and they'd grasped onto each other like a lifeline in the huge, bustling depot in Chicago where they had been met by someone from the Fred Harvey Company to begin their employment as Harvey Girls.

Meghan was grateful to have Natalie with her, because instead of the customary four weeks of training in one of the Kansas Harvey House Restaurants that they'd been told to expect, they'd been whisked away on the train to fill vacant spots in Needles, California, that had suddenly opened up. They'd had no time to become acclimated, to make new friends, or to get their bearings. Instead, they'd had a brief orientation meeting, been measured for uniforms, and been all but tossed onto a southwest-bound train.

"Okay, so we're nervous." She sat up straight and squared her shoulders, lifting her chin to a confident angle. "But we won't show it. We're capable, independent, intelligent women employed by the Fred Harvey Company." Which sounded so much more impressive than she felt. And yet, the glow of accomplishment and pride at being hired by such a prestigious company remained. The company's high standards were well-known, and the pay was better than anything she could've expected to earn back in Mantorville. Not to mention the bonus pay Harvey Girls received for working in Needles during the summer. For the next six months, she was a Harvey Girl, subject to the company rules and expectations, and the recipient of the respect her new black-and-white uniform would command.

Natalie fanned herself with a folded newspaper. The air in the car had grown progressively warmer until someone had finally relented and opened a window. The trade-off for air circulation was the smoke and soot from the engine blowing in the window and coating everything with smuts and smudges. Still, it was better than suffocating.

"I'd be pleased to help you with your bags, ma'am." A gravelly voice had them both looking up. A scruffy man in a battered cowboy hat stood in the aisle. Sunshine had tanned his skin to leather and etched deep lines around his eyes and mouth. Those eyes lit with admiration as he looked at Natalie, and though Meghan couldn't blame him for staring at her friend's blond loveliness, she couldn't help but feel a prick in her heart. Her own wavy, red hair and pale, freckled skin never drew that kind of admiration. What would it be like to have men falling over themselves to assist her? What would it be like to be classically beautiful and capture every man's eye when she walked into a room? Not that she really wanted to be the center of attention like that any more than Natalie did. But it would be nice to know she *could*.

"That's most kind, thank you, but I'm sure we can manage." Natalie showed not the slightest interest in him, just as she had ignored the advances of every man they'd encountered on the journey. The hopeful stranger touched the brim of his hat and turned away.

Natalie leaned her head against the seatback and closed her eyes. Her profile reminded Meghan of the cameo Papa had given Mama as a wedding gift, delicate, regal, beautiful. The sadness in her new friend's eyes seemed only to add to her beauty. It made Meghan want to protect Natalie, to reassure her that everything would be all right. Was it simple homesickness, or did Natalie carry other burdens?

The train slowed and lurched to a stop, causing all the standing passengers to grab seatbacks to steady themselves. The conductor opened the door, and like a gopher trying to squeeze out of a too-small hole, folks crowded through. Not until the car had half-emptied did the girls file out of their seats and reach for their bags in the overhead racks. Meghan searched their seating area for any stray belongings.

"I need to see about my trunk." Natalie dug her luggage ticket out of her bag.

"The conductor will direct us." Meghan gripped the handle of her case, her only piece of luggage. With the company providing room, board, and uniforms, she had chosen to pack light. If she needed anything in the future, she could purchase it once she got paid. The thought of earning her own money, being able to buy the things she wanted, made her squeeze her hands together and bite her lower lip. No more asking Papa every time she wanted something from the mercantile. Twenty-five dollars a month, plus tips, room, board, uniforms, and travel vouchers. And a bonus on top. That was nearly as much as her brother made as a soldier on the front lines in France, and she wouldn't even be risking her life in a placid little railroad town like Needles.

She followed Natalie toward the end of the car. When they reached the door, the smart little conductor greeted them with a broad smile and a quick pattering tone that fascinated Meghan. He never seemed to pause for breath, and the words blurred together into one long sentence. "You the two new Harvey Girls I was told to expect? You look the type. This here's the back of the hotel, but you can reach the lobby through the center doors. You want to see Mr. Stock, the hotel manager, or Mrs. Gregory, the head waitress. Someone will direct you. But you'd do well to wait until after all these passengers are fed and back aboard the train before you bother them. Passengers have first priority, and the hotel staff will be busy for the next thirty minutes or so. If you have other bags, you can walk along to the baggage car. One of the bellhops will be gathering the hotel guests' luggage, and he'll see that yours gets to your room. That will fill some of the time. Good luck, and I'll probably be seeing you." He flashed a quick smile before hurrying to help other passengers disembark.

Meghan stepped down onto the sidewalk and got her first glimpse of the El Garces, the jewel in the desert crown of Fred Harvey establishments along the Atchison, Topeka & Santa Fe Railroad line. The heat hit her full force as she emerged into the sunshine, but she couldn't take her eyes off the imposing concrete structure throwing back the sun's rays from its blazing white exterior. She screwed up her eyes and shaded her brow with her hand.

"More pillars than the Parthenon." Though the building was impressive, she wouldn't really call it beautiful. Large, imposing, and a trifle daunting, but not particularly appealing. Majestic palms stood in little patches of emerald grass along the sidewalk. Surely the grass must take daily watering to keep it so green in this dry heat.

Two stories high, the hotel stretched out before her to either side like a royal palace. Pairs of pillars marched across the hotel on both floors, supporting wide porches that must help shade the rooms and keep them cool. Or as cool as one could be in the desert. Iron-railed balconies cantilevered from the second-floor loggia in graceful scallops.

Beyond the hotel and spreading out on either side, lay the town of Needles—a straggly conglomeration of wooden, adobe, and brick buildings popping up between clumps of grayish-green brush and yucca. Electricity and telephone lines crisscrossed limply over the streets, and a jumble of automobiles and wagons lined the roads. Everything seemed to shimmer in the heat, and the few folks on the sidewalks moved slowly. Most curiously, Indians stood before the hotel with baskets, pottery, and blankets for sale, their faces solemn, patient, and long-suffering. Was it the heat or their nature that made them so stoic?

Meghan tightened her grip on her valise handle and headed toward the front of the train and the baggage car. The sooner they tracked down Natalie's trunk, the sooner they could get into the shade. She had expected to be battling a damp, sweaty feeling, but a dry breeze evaporated any perspiration instantly. She moistened her lips, only to find them dry a moment later.

They had to wait in line at the baggage car as cart after cart of luggage and US Mail and supplies for the hotel came out first. Finally, one of the workers was free. Natalie turned over her trunk ticket to the dark-skinned man with flashing, white teeth. "Shore enough, ma'am. I'll get your luggage over to the hotel with the rest.

One of the bellhops will take it to your room." He accepted the nickel Natalie placed in his large, big-knuckled hand.

"Let's get out of this sunshine. I'm wilting." Natalie tilted her head so her hat-brim would shade her face. Meghan's own hat, a small sailor-style, offered little protection. Heat prickled her fair skin. Her face would probably be as red as an apple by the time they got inside. If she wasn't careful, she'd walk around with a red, peeling nose for the next six months. Sunshine always deepened the despised freckles covering her face. Not all the lemon juice in the world would lighten them if she spent much time out of doors here.

A large sign emblazoned in white letters near the lobby doors directed the way to the lunch counter, and another on the other side pointed the way to the dining room.

Natalie put her hand on Meghan's arm and stopped her in a thin patch of shade cast by a straggly tree. "We might as well wait a few minutes here. The conductor said the head waitress won't be able to meet with us until all the passengers have been served anyway."

Meghan didn't mind delaying their meeting with the woman who would have charge of their lives for the next six months, though she refused to acknowledge any hesitancy. Instead, she gave free rein to her curiosity and let her eyes take in her surroundings from the relative coolness of the shade. Her sense of adventure crowded out her anxiety, and she tried to see everything at once. "Someone on the train said there was a park across the street from the front of the hotel. Santa Fe Park? The company put it in when they built the hotel. He said there were trees there. It will be nice to have a place to sit in some shade every once in a while."

"I have a feeling even the shade here in the summer would bake a lizard." Natalie turned her face toward the hot breeze, lifting her bangs and closing her eyes.

Eventually passengers began trickling out of the hotel and boarding the westbound train. On the other side of the passenger train, a freight train sat roasting. From a car near the front of the freight train, a pair of men lethargically lowered a ramp, banging it off the hard-packed dirt. A man emerged from the dark, square opening, leading a horse. He handed the animal over to another worker and disappeared. In moments, a string of animals stood in the sunshine, and the workers removed the ramp and closed the doors. The poor animals must be positively wilting, stuck in that boxcar. She hoped they had a nice, shady place to go to, one with water and a breeze.

A man in a straw cowboy hat strolled by, capturing her attention. His shoulders stretched the fabric of a faded blue shirt, and well-worn jeans covered his long legs. Battered boots scuffed the concrete, and his steps were so slow and measured, she wondered if he'd ever hurried in his life. He barely glanced at her, touching his finger to his hat brim and dipping his chin. Something about his face intrigued her, but she couldn't quite put her finger on what it was. He continued on toward the hotel doors, and Meghan shook her head when she realized she had wandered out of the shade to stare after him.

She returned to Natalie's side, staying out of the way of the travelers boarding the train. One of the passengers, a woman with two small children, dropped a bag and spilled the contents across the hot concrete. Meghan handed her valise to Natalie and hurried over to help the poor mother as the engine whistled and the train puffed smoke, signaling its imminent departure.

"Thank you. Thank you," the woman said again and again as she grappled the baby, who started to cry, and the toddler who wanted to get too close to the train wheels.

"Hurry. Climb aboard." Meghan stuffed a toy dog, a string of wooden spools, and a crocheted blanket into the bag.

The conductor came trotting toward them and lifted the toddler. "Whoopsie-daisy! All aboard!" He handed the woman up into the train and scooped the child onto his arm, a cheery smile on his face. Inexorably, the wheels began to move. Swinging his set of steps aboard, the conductor hopped onto the platform with a wave.

Meghan stepped back a pace as the train picked up speed. Movement to her left caught her eye, and she noticed the string of horses being led down the wide sidewalk toward them. The train whistle pierced the air in a quick blast, and Meghan raised her hand to wave at the conductor who leaned out from the train saluting her.

His expression changed from cheery to alarmed, and he pointed behind her, his shout drowned out by another whistle blast. She turned and froze. One of the horses had broken free of its handler and bore down on her at a gallop. A rope trailed from its halter, and with a wild, panicked neigh, the animal leaped a stack of flour sacks in its way and raced toward her. She gathered her skirts to leap out of the way of the juggernaut, but she was too late to escape a collision. The horse brushed her shoulder, sending her spinning. The impact threw her toward the train. She staggered, let go of her skirts, and cast out her hands to brace her fall.

Lord, help me!

The prayer screamed through her head, but she couldn't make a sound. The cars whizzed by, gaining momentum as she flailed, teetering on the edge of balance. Her throat squeezed shut, and she knew she was falling toward the iron wheels.

At the last moment, strong hands yanked her back. She collided with a solid wall of chambray and muscle. Arms came around her, absorbing the violence of her headlong sprawl.

Caleb McBride had just finished folding the shipping papers and tucking them into his shirt when a shout and a loud neigh grabbed his attention. One of the horses he'd come to pick up had broken free from the string and now barreled up the sidewalk straight toward an empty-headed woman who didn't even have the sense to get out of the way of an oncoming horse. He tried to sprint her way, but the instant his left foot hit the ground, a shaft of pain and weakness shot from his heel to his hip, and the limb almost buckled beneath him. He gritted his teeth and forced himself forward, praying no one saw his hitching gait. Thankfully, at the last instant, the horse veered away from the woman, only grazing her. She staggered, her arms windmilling, but she was flailing the wrong direction, toward the moving train instead of away from it.

He reached her as she staggered only inches from the side of a car. His fingers closed on the fabric of her shirt, near her waist, and spun her away from the cars and into his arms. This time as the pain shot up his leg, it buckled beneath him and down they went, scrunching his shoulder into the sidewalk. She landed atop him, shoving the air from his lungs.

"Meghan, are you all right?" Another woman, silhouetted by the sun dazzling his eyes, bent over them.

So the woman in his arms was named Meghan. She didn't respond at once, and he feared that in saving her from the train, he might've hurt her. Then she stirred and struggled, sinking her elbow into his diaphragm.

"Oof!" The sound shot out of him. He looked up into the most striking pair of green eyes he'd ever seen. Green as new grass, and only inches from his face. Freckles peppered her nose and cheeks, and her little mouth gaped as if gasping for the air she'd knocked out of him. He vaguely remembered nodding to her on his way to the freight depot.

"I'm so sorry." She scrambled off him in a flurry of limbs and skirts. Her hat sat askew, dragging her fiery curls out of their pins. He caught a glimpse of shapely legs in black stockings and white lacy edging of a petticoat. With a flick, she tugged her skirts into place so they fell just above her pretty ankles.

Massaging his middle, he tried to ignore the pain radiating up his left leg. Carefully, he rolled to his right side and pushed himself to his feet. "Are you hurt?" Her near-miss sent weak ripples through him. If she'd been killed, it would've been his fault. Those horses were his responsibility, even if he hadn't been the one leading them through the train yard.

"I'm fine, I think, thanks to you." Her voice quivered, and her hand shook a bit as she righted her hat. "I thought I was a goner."

"You almost were."

"Whose horse was that?" The other woman spoke up, full of indignation. "Whoever it was should be held accountable, letting an animal like that run loose on the sidewalks." Her blue eyes snapped fire and a hint of color tinted her cheeks.

Caleb stooped to pick up his hat and rubbed his hand on the back of his neck. "It wasn't done on purpose, I assure you, miss. I apologize for the accident, and I'm glad no one was injured."

A bit of the heat went out of the blond woman's expression, and she took a shuddering breath. "Are you saying the horse was yours?"

"That's right. The train whistle must've spooked him into bolting." Something he'd have to make sure he trained out of the animal in the next few weeks. He took a couple of steps back, and the redhead's eyes widened.

"You've hurt yourself. Did you twist your ankle? You're limping." She reached for his arm, and he stepped away again, angry with himself.

"I'm fine. No harm done."

He glanced up the track and breathed a sigh of relief. Someone had managed to capture the escaped horse and now led it back toward the hotel. He couldn't afford to lose any horses, nor could he count on the goodwill of the people of Needles if the animal found its way onto the streets. Hot pain raced up his calf and behind his knee, but he set his jaw and whacked at some of the dust covering his pants and shirt. He leaned all his weight on his right foot and tried to ignore the messages from his left boot.

The girls gathered their scattered belongings and brushed themselves off. He studied them from under the brim of his hat, the blond with the arched brows and even features and the redhead with windblown hair and color now so high it nearly obliterated her freckles. Not as immediately pretty as the blond, but a face one would remember. Especially those eyes.

"I'm sorry, Mr. McBride, he bolted on me." The man leading the rest of the horses drew near. He took a greasy kerchief from his pocket and wiped his face. "I couldn't hold him."

"That's all right, Al. No harm done, as it turns out. They caught the runaway and are bringing him back now." He motioned up the line.

The fugitive animal arrived at the same time as Mrs. Gregory in full sail, her white uniform more blinding than the sunshine glaring off the hotel, appeared. She stomped the ground with nearly as much force as the gelding had, and she blew and sputtered more, too. A formidable woman, Mrs. Gregory. If she kept a list of people she disliked—and Caleb figured she probably did—his name would reside at the top. In capital letters. And maybe underlined. Her eyes glittered, and she looked loaded for bear. Dread settled in his chest.

"Are you Miss Thorson and Miss Daviot? I've been expecting you inside. What are you doing out here with this—this person?" She pulled herself up to her full height, which was tall enough to look him square in the eye, and she tilted her head to stare down her skinny nose. With a scornful snort she turned to the girls. "What on earth happened to you two? Harvey Girls do not appear disheveled, ever, and Harvey Girls do not loiter outside the hotel, especially not with the likes of him." Her mouth pinched like she'd just drained the vinegar barrel.

He stuck his hands into his back pockets. "And a good day to you, too, Mrs. Gregory. I hope you're feeling well? You look a mite liverish. Perhaps you should stop in to see Doc Bates. I'm sure he has something for biliousness." He smiled at her just to get her goat.

"Mr. McBride, take your filthy animals away. The hotel sidewalk is no place for horses." She made shooing motions toward the girls to get them moving and muttered a constant stream of indignant complaints as she headed toward the hotel. The girls picked up their bags. The blond hurried after her, but the redhead—Meghan—lingered for a moment.

"Thank you, sir. That was very brave of you to come to my rescue."

Her words twisted the ever-present knife in his gut. *Brave.* He swallowed and nodded.

"This way." Mrs. Gregory's command sliced the air. Meghan lifted her valise, holding her hat on and tripping along with the light steps of a schoolgirl.

She thought he was brave. A shame that she'd soon be told otherwise.

Chapter 2

Following in the head waitress's wake, Meghan barely had time to note the El Garces carved over the entryway or the floor-level fountain splashing gaily in the open-air courtyard. In the lobby, arrangements of wicker chairs and sofas clustered in cozy groups, and potted palms rose majestically, splashes of green against the white walls. Ceiling fans spun slowly, and she soaked in the relative coolness. The hotel's designers had known what they were doing. Thick concrete and high ceilings, ceramic tiles and splashing fountains all combined to thwart the oven outside.

"Don't straggle." The head waitress, identifiable as much by her commanding manner as by the all-white uniform they'd been told to expect, turned at the base of the staircase and stopped, crossing her arms and pinching her lips. A handsome woman with bold features, dark eyes, and hair streaked with gray, she reminded Meghan of her Aunt Penelope. All starch on the outside but soft as pudding on the inside. You just had to crack the outer shell to get to the real woman.

"I'm sorry. I was admiring the beautiful lobby." Meghan shifted her case to her other hand and tucked a strand of hair off her face. "How many guestrooms are there?" Perhaps the woman was just hard to get to know at first. Or really busy. Running the restaurant and lunch counter and overseeing all the wait staff couldn't be easy.

"Sixty. Please try to remember you are not a tourist." Icy frost blew through the woman's voice. "This way."

Meghan shot a look at Natalie, whose eyes widened. Her shoulders lifted slightly in a shrug, and she followed their new boss up the stairs. Meghan took one last glance at the newsstand and front desk and mounted the staircase, her footsteps sounding loud on the tile.

On the second floor, they traveled down a long hallway punctuated with doors. "These are rooms for the paying guests. The staff is housed at the end."

Meghan hustled to keep up, her bag hampering her. They turned a corner and entered a narrower hall. "Are there a lot of girls working here?"

"You two make twenty. The minimum I need to run a successful establishment. I asked them to send me at least six experienced servers and they sent me you two, green as tadpoles. Not only did they short me, but they didn't even take the time to train you properly. Now I'll have to take over the task." She let her glance flick over Meghan. "Look at your hair and dress. How am I supposed to turn you into a credit to the company? You"—she motioned to Natalie—"you at least show some promise. Have you ever worked in a restaurant before?"

"No, ma'am. This is my first job."

"Heaven help me. And what about you? I don't suppose you have any experience either?"

Meghan tamped down her ire and smiled. "No, but look on the bright side. We won't have any bad habits that you'll have to correct. We're like clean slates, all ready to be trained in the way you see best."

This didn't seem to impress the starchy woman.

"You two will share a room, the second on the right. You're expected to keep your room clean and tidy. Inspections are frequent and unannounced. Your uniforms are in the closet. Kansas City sent along your sizes. You are responsible for sending them to and retrieving them from the laundry downstairs." The tall woman checked the timepiece on her lapel as she stopped before a white door. "Be downstairs in uniform and ready to work in thirty minutes." She opened the door to their room, stepped back, and turned on her heel to head back the way they'd come.

"Excuse me." Meghan almost shouted. She was tired, disheveled, and suddenly fed up with being condescended to. She let her suitcase thump to the floor. The woman stopped, keeping her back to the girls.

"What?"

"Do you have a name?"

"You may call me Mrs. Gregory."

Meghan gave in to impulse. She jogged down the hall and circled around Mrs. Gregory to stand in front of her. "How do you do?" She stuck out her hand. "My name is Meghan Thorson, and it's a pleasure to meet you. I look forward to working with you for the next six months."

Mrs. Gregory sniffed so hard her nostrils sucked inward. "Miss Thorson, I suggest you turn your attentions to preparing yourself for work. No doubt it will take every single one of the now"—a quick check of her watch—"twenty-eight minutes you have left."

She left Meghan standing, hand outstretched, in the middle of the hallway. Meghan blew her bangs off her forehead and grimaced, letting her hand fall. So much for thawing out the old girl. She headed back to her room, scooping up her suitcase by the door.

"You shouldn't have twisted her tail like that." Natalie opened the closet door, took out a black uniform, and held it up. "At least the laundry is right here in the building. It shouldn't take much time to get uniforms back."

"I wonder where the laundry is here. In the basement? And can you imagine how hot it must be working there?" Meghan sat on the side of one of the beds, testing the springs. "I'm surprised they don't have laundry facilities at every hotel. I meant to ask during that whirlwind orientation why they only had two laundry centers. Seems odd to ship everything to Needles or to Kansas then ship them all back again."

"They must find it easier to keep everything consolidated. At least we won't have to worry about running out of clean dresses and having to wait for them to arrive on the next train." Natalie removed a snowy apron from a hanger and laid it on the other bed.

"This is a nice room. Look at all this space." Meghan ran her hand along the curved white metal footboard of her bed and scuffed her feet on the colorful rug. "I wonder where the bathroom is on this floor."

"I think you'd best stop wondering and start getting ready."

"Before Mrs. Gregory comes back and breathes fire all over me." Hauling herself up off the bed, she removed her hat pins and hat and shook out her curls. "Do you think she's that starchy with everyone, or did she just take a dislike to me?"

"You have to admit, the conditions in which she first found you were less than desirable, sprawled all over a strange man on the sidewalk out front. And you didn't do yourself any favors out in the hall pointing out her lack of manners in not introducing herself."

"I couldn't exactly help what happened outside. I'm only fortunate someone was there to help me, otherwise. . . ." She shuddered. "I know I shouldn't have been rude to her in the hall, but I couldn't stand it anymore. She looked like she wouldn't wipe her feet on me if I was a rug." Meghan dug in her bag for her hairbrush. She'd show Mrs. Gregory she could be the perfect Harvey Girl. Not that she had any idea just what that entailed, but she was a bright girl and she could learn.

"Look at this." Meghan peered at a framed piece of paper by the mirror as she jerked her brush through her hair. "Take a gander at this list."

— EMPLOYEES ARE REQUESTED NOT TO SCRATCH MATCHES, DRIVE NAILS OR TACKS, OR IN ANY OTHER WAY MAR THE WALLS OF THEIR ROOMS.

— NO RUBBISH OF ANY KIND MUST BE THROWN IN THE TOILETS.

- BATHTUBS MUST BE THOROUGHLY CLEANED BY EMPLOYEES AFTER USING.
- LOUD TALKING AND LAUGHING IN ROOMS AND HALLS SHOULD BE AVOIDED.
- EMPLOYEES MUST BE IN THEIR ROOMS BY 11:00 O'CLOCK P.M. UNLESS GIVEN SPECIAL PERMISSION BY MANAGER TO REMAIN LONGER.
- ROOMS MUST BE KEPT IN TIDY CONDITION AND WEARING APPAREL MUST BE KEPT IN ITS PROPER PLACE.
- CLOTHING OF ALL EMPLOYEES MUST BE NEAT AND CLEAN AT ALL TIMES.
- EXPECTORATING ON THE FLOORS IS POSITIVELY FORBIDDEN.
- THE PURPOSE OF THE ABOVE RULES IS TO BRING ABOUT A TIDY AND HOMELIKE CONDITION IN YOUR ROOMS AND WE REQUEST YOUR COOPERATION SO THAT THE DESIRED RESULTS WILL BE BROUGHT ABOUT.

FRED HARVEY

"I feel like I just joined the army. Are we supposed to salute Mrs. Gregory or the hotel manager when they come by?" Meghan wrinkled her nose.

"I doubt we have to salute, though a bit of deference and respect would surely be in order. We'll get into the swing of things soon enough. The rules will become second nature and we won't even have to think about them." Natalie continued dressing. "Fred Harvey might have passed away, but his son, Ford, is following all the guidelines set down by his father."

"I'm not complaining. I know the company has to have rules. I just didn't think they'd be posted in our bedroom." Meghan finished tidying her hair, checking for stray curls. "At least we've got running water in the basin here." She turned the tap and ran her hand under the cool water before dipping a pristine towel into the liquid. A sigh escaped her lips as she wiped her hot, soot-streaked face. A bath would be wonderful about now.

"The clock's ticking, Meghan." Natalie took the cloth from her hand and gave Meghan a friendly nudge toward the closet. "You've made enough of a first impression on Mrs. Gregory for one day. Don't add 'late' to the list."

Meghan heaved a playful sigh and quickly removed her travel-stained dress, took a sketchy basin-bath, and donned the black uniform. The snowy apron was so starched it almost crackled. She slipped her arms through the armholes and tied the bow in the small of her back. Twisting and turning before the mirror on the dresser, she checked to see that every button and fold was in its proper place.

"Do you suppose the laundry here does the ironing and starching for us?" Ironing was the bane of Meghan's existence, and she didn't look forward to trying to keep half a dozen uniforms pressed and crisp.

"We can only hope." With one last check in the mirror, Natalie turned around. "How do I look?"

Meghan studied her while hopping on one foot trying to get one of her new black shoes on. They were the latest style, with laces down the front that were purely ornamental. A tight, elastic gusset on the inside of the top allowed just enough movement so they could be slipped on. The trouble was, the elastic did such a good job she could hardly get her foot into the shoe.

"You look perfect. Like the quintessential Harvey Girl." She finally managed to get the boot on and straightened. "How about me?"

Natalie eyed her critically. "Neat and tidy. Let's get downstairs. If I'm not at least five minutes early, I feel late."

They found their way to the first floor, through the lobby, and past the tinkling, floor-level fountain that sent diamonds of droplets into the air. Meghan wanted to linger and watch the cool water for a moment, but Mrs. Gregory's clock ticked in the back of her mind. When they inquired as to where to find the head waitress, the man behind the front desk directed them toward the door marked LUNCHROOM.

Three horseshoe-shaped counters, each with twenty-five stools, filled the room. Meghan stopped in the doorway to admire the glass-fronted refrigeration case full of the day's menu items. "Can you believe they have a refrigerator right in the lunchroom?"

"We'll look at it later. Come on." Natalie took her elbow and urged her toward the far end of the lunchroom where several Harvey Girls stood at one of the counters. As they arrived, Mrs. Gregory emerged through a set of batwing doors, holding some files. Meghan glanced at the clock. Five minutes to spare.

The woman's dark eyes raked over them from head to toe, her nostrils thinned and pinched, and she turned away. Meghan let out a sigh. They must look all right, or the head waitress surely would've said something, audience or not listening on.

"Girls." Mrs. Gregory clapped her hands to get their attention. "This is Miss Daviot and Miss Thorson." She opened one of the file folders and consulted the pages inside. "Miss Daviot, you will be serving in the dining room, first as the drinks girl, and when I feel you've made satisfactory progress, you will be given charge of your own tables. Only the most well-mannered and accomplished waitresses are allowed to serve in my dining room. I have a feeling you will fit in well there."

The head waitress flipped open the other folder. "Miss Thorson." Her voice was as dry as the desert outside the lunchroom windows. "You appear to be more suited for the lunchroom. I've already encountered your ready tongue. See that you hold to the standard and keep your conversation with customers to a minimum. We are to serve them with a smile, get them in and out as quickly as possible, and not bore them with mindless chatter, understood?"

Heat charged into Meghan's face, and she bit the inside of her cheek. Hard. In that instant, she vowed to prove to Mrs. Gregory that she was the best Harvey Girl ever to don the uniform. Her service would be above reproach, her appearance impeccable at all times, and her customers would rave about the way she took care of them. Mrs. Gregory would have no choice but to recant her initial assessment and beg Meghan to work in the formal dining room.

"Yes, Mrs. Gregory. I understand perfectly." Keeping her voice modulated cost her quite a bit of effort, but she even managed to put on a pleasant smile.

"Good. Dining room girls, I want the linens changed and the tables set. Then there is the silver to polish and the stations to clean. Come, Miss Daviot. Miss Plunkett, you take charge of the lunchroom. You all know what to do. Miss Thorson, do as Miss Plunkett tells you until I can get back here to show you how to do things right."

More than half the girls, including Natalie, followed Mrs. Gregory through the double doors that led to the dining room, leaving a handful at the counter.

"Whew, what'd you do to Gregsie?" An extremely short girl of about twenty-five stuck out her hand. "I'm Jennifer, by the way. Miss Plunkett when Gregsie's around." She had laughing pale blue eyes and straight, light brown hair pulled back from her round face.

"Gregsie?"

"Mrs. Gregory, but you'd best not let her hear you calling her that. Trust me, that's one of the nicer nicknames she has around here."

Several of the waitresses giggled. One tall girl with a long, narrow nose and a dimple in her chin paused as she passed Meghan. She cast a look over her shoulder toward the dining room door and bent to whisper, "I heard one of the busboys call her 'Iron Drawers' the other day."

Jennifer snickered and then put on a stern expression. "She'd better never hear you repeating that one either or you'll find yourself on report."

The tall girl shrugged. "I'm on report half the time the way it is. My employee record must be about the size of the dictionary by now."

"This is Barbara. Miss Charteris. She takes care of the soda fountain just through those doors." Jennifer pointed to a pair of saloon-style half doors. "She started out in the dining room, got shifted to the lunchroom, and now she's relegated to the soda fountain. Which she needs to get back to, since it's always open." Jennifer tilted her head toward the doors.

Barbara snapped to attention, gave a smart salute, and disappeared, leaving the doors flopping in her wake.

"She's a good egg, but she doesn't pay close enough attention sometimes. And Mrs. Gregory isn't as bad as she seems at first. She runs a tight ship, she's good at her job, and she's got more prickles than a beaver-tail cactus, but she's loyal to her girls. Just do as you're told, follow the rules, and she'll be your staunchest ally. Buck the rules, and you'll be her favorite target."

Meghan renewed her vow to be the best Harvey Girl on the line. She'd have Mrs. Gregory eating out of her hand in no time.

Caleb nudged his mount to go a bit faster, conscious of the growing heat and ready to be home. The barn and corrals shimmered ahead. The string of horses he led plodded along in the heat, tired from their long, hot journey and ready to stop. He checked over his shoulder to see that the men he'd hired to bring the rest of the horses were still keeping up.

Buildings grew closer. He led the string of horses into the corral and dismounted. His left leg ached from his knee clear to the ends of his toes, but he refused to give in to the pain. He had no one to blame except for himself, running toward the train like he had. Still, if he hadn't, that girl might've fallen under the wheels and been killed or at least badly injured. A little pain wasn't too much to bear to save a life, right? Especially since he was used to the pain.

The girl—Meghan—he let his mind try out her name for the hundredth time since he'd left town. Meghan what? It had been a long time since he'd held a pretty girl in his arms. More than three years now. Ever since Patricia threw him out like yesterday's stall bedding.

The familiar ache, as familiar as the one in his leg, squeezed his chest. He needed to get his mind off the girl at the hotel. He'd learned his lesson, had it burned into his memory. Only a fool repeated his mistakes expecting a different outcome.

The hired men, Carlos and Diego, led their strings of horses into the corral. They swung out of the saddles, their boots making puffs of dust.

"Just unsaddle your mounts and leave the saddles on the top rail." He hooked a stirrup over the saddle horn and pulled on the latigo strap. Grasping the blanket and saddle together, he hoisted it onto the corral fence and looped the cinches up out of the dirt. He then turned to study the horses, untying the lead rope and feeding it through the halter rings to free each animal. "Turn 'em loose, but don't take off the halters."

Fifteen new horses joined the twenty already in the big corral. All browns or bays, not a pinto, gray, or buckskin in the lot. Just as his supplier promised, just as his customer ordered.

"*Señor*, what you going to do with so many horses out here?" One of the men shoved back his hat and scratched his head. "You don't got no pasture. How you goin' to feed them?"

"Barn's full of hay and grain. And there's plenty of water." Caleb jerked his thumb toward the muddy river a hundred yards past the corral fence. His first, backbreaking job when he took up residence on this hard-scrabble piece of roasted earth was to install an irrigation pipe and pump from the river to the corrals. House water came from a well sunk deep and a cistern, though the cistern was almost always bone dry with less than six inches of rain falling in a whole year out here. Nothing like the Vermont woods of his boyhood, that was for sure, or even the Kentucky horse farm where he'd worked upon escaping Vermont. Still, he didn't own this land, nor even rent it. His employer took care of all that, and Caleb had few complaints.

If only the stark landscape didn't look quite so much like the barren dryness he felt inside.

Shrugging aside these notions, he reached into his pocket for his wallet and pulled out some money for each of the men. "Thanks for helping me get them here from town. If you'll give me a minute, I'll drive you back."

"*Gracias.*"

Caleb made sure the water troughs were full and opened two bales of hay for the new arrivals. They would settle in with the herd that had been here for a fortnight already. Most of the horses stood dozing under the shade shelter he'd erected. Siesta time. Work was for morning and evening when the temperatures were more manageable. Funny how quickly he'd adapted to the rhythm of life here in the high desert.

When these basic chores were done, he headed toward the dilapidated building he called a garage. Inside, he flipped the tarp off his brand-new truck. The pale blue paint gleamed, and the highly varnished wood shone. A 1918 Chevy, fresh from the dealership in Barstow. His chest swelled, and he admitted satisfaction when Carlos and Diego sucked in their breaths and made approving noises. The six hundred dollars the truck had cost him had been worth every penny. The larger of the two men, Diego, ran his hand along the door and with a guilty start jerked back.

"She is beautiful, señor."

"Climb in."

Diego piled into the back while Carlos took the passenger seat.

They headed back to town at a zippy twenty-five miles an hour, creating a dust plume that hung in the air behind them in a brown-yellow haze.

"What you do with so many horses, señor?"

"They're army mounts. For the cavalry. The army is paying me to break them, and when they're ready, I ship them to Fort Riley up in Kansas. From there they head to Europe and the war."

Carlos tugged his weedy moustache. "A shame to send so many fine horses to war."

It was a shame. Caleb loved horses—loved working with them, caring for them, just being around such noble beasts. To think of animals he'd befriended and come to know heading into the perils of battle sat heavily on his shoulders. And yet, a well-trained mount could save a man's life. Could save many lives. Officers rode horses, couriers rode horses. Command and communication relied on swift, brave, intelligent mounts, well trained and reliable. Often horses could go where automobiles and cannons could not.

"You going to work alone? That's a lot of horses to manage by yourself."

"I have a hired man." The outline of Needles showed to the northwest. Hired man. At least as much of a hired man as he could afford full time.

Joshua Hualga waited for him on the front porch when Caleb returned to his ranch. A full-blooded Mojave Indian, Joshua, at eighteen, reminded Caleb of a forest white-tail from back home in Vermont—lean and graceful. His big, dark eyes were reminiscent of a deer, too, watchful and shy.

His father, Cairook Hualga, in contrast, reminded Caleb of a black bear, with thick, muscled arms and shoulders. His figure was made even more imposing by the fact that he had followed the ways of the Mojave and tattooed his chin. Black lines scored his jaw, chin, and cheeks like cactus needles, poking upward toward his eyes.

Cairook tilted his big head and scrutinized his son as if the boy were a stranger. "Are you sure this is what you want? He has no experience with horses. He prefers to be indoors reading rather than hunting or growing crops." Cairook rubbed his finger down his cheek and over his tattoo. "I don't know what kind of Mojave he hopes to be. He won't even get his tattoo."

Joshua said nothing, but his fingers tightened on the porch rail.

"If it doesn't work out, send him home." The big man picked up his walking stick from where it leaned against the porch rail and wheeled away. He did not look back at his son.

Joshua's narrow shoulders sagged, and he tucked his hands into his pants' pockets.

Caleb slowly made his way up the steps to the porch and sagged into one of the two straight-backed chairs, grateful to get the weight off his aching leg for a moment. He motioned to the other chair.

With a sigh, the boy joined him, easing his lanky frame into the rocker with a fluidity Caleb envied. "Why did you ask me to come here? There are plenty of boys on the reservation who would be better suited to working on your ranch. I don't know anything about horses."

"You're smart, and you can learn. That's why I wanted to hire you. That, and you want to get off that reservation so badly it's eating you alive. You're hungry for something that you can't find there, and maybe working for me is the first step to finding what it is that you need to fill you up."

Joshua's head came up, and his glance collided with Caleb's. Caleb knew that look of longing, for he'd felt it himself, many times. A desire to be more than he was, to break free of the bonds holding him back and fly as high as his dreams.

"How'd you come to be called Joshua? That's not a Mojave name."

"The boarding school gave white names to every student. They allowed us to pick our own from a list. I chose Joshua."

"For the biblical character? Caleb and Joshua worked pretty

well together in the Old Testament, if I remember correctly."

He shook his head. "For the Joshua tree. A Joshua tree stands alone in the desert. Like me. My tribe is like the brush that grows at the river's edge, so close their limbs get tangled, unable to grow upright unless they are supported by those around them. And they all look the same, blending one into the other. If one of those bushes grows alone, the wind blows it over and rips it out of the earth, sending it tumbling away. But the Joshua tree stands without help, alone and proud." The boy's spine straightened, and his youthful jawline tightened as he spoke.

Caleb caught himself reaching down to rub his lower leg and stopped his hand. He pondered the boy's analogy, admiring his way with words and identifying with him more than ever. Caleb, too, stood alone like a Joshua tree while the town of Needles grew up entwined and enmeshed like riverbank brush. "That can get pretty lonely, standing by yourself. Sometimes you don't realize how much you miss things until they're gone."

"I am fine alone. I've always been alone, even when I am in the middle of my family."

"You have a big family?"

"I have four younger brothers, all just like my father. Father is proud of them, proud of the way they are like him. I think he does not know what to do with me. We were strangers even before I was sent to the mission school, but since I came home, it is worse. I think he was as relieved when you asked if I could come work for you as I was."

Caleb crossed his legs, took off his hat, and hooked it over his boot toe. "Dads and sons don't always see eye to eye, but maybe if you give it some time, things will get better."

"Did you get along with your father? Did things get better?"

A hollow feeling pressed against Caleb's breastbone. "I haven't seen my father in almost ten years. He wasn't glad to see me then, and he was happy to see me leave."

"Then I don't think you are one to give me advice on how to deal with my father." Sober judgment coated Joshua's expression.

Caleb forced himself to his feet. "You're right. When it comes to dealing with parents, I don't have a leg to stand on."

Meghan flopped onto the bed and immediately bounced up to check her uniform. She was so tired she'd forgotten she mustn't muss the dress or apron. As she removed her apron, Natalie slipped into the room and closed the door, leaning back against the white panels and closing her eyes.

"I'm so tired I can't even think."

"Me too, and we didn't even serve any customers yet." Meghan unbuttoned her black dress and peeled it off, enjoying the relative coolness of the evening air coming through the window. "I had no idea we'd spend so much time polishing. If I never see another piece of silverware or a coffee urn again, it will be too soon."

Natalie straightened and began preparing for bed, albeit slowly. "But tomorrow we have to get up and do it all over again, and this time we'll be polishing and cleaning in between serving six different sit-down meals."

Meghan fought with her shoes. The elastic had all but embedded itself into her ankle, and her toes cried out to be free. "Ah, that feels so good." She peeled off her stockings and wriggled her toes, crimping them into the rug a few times before padding over to the cool tile.

"How many miles do you think we put on our feet today?" Natalie flipped a nightgown over her head and tugged it into place.

"About a million. Last thing before I came upstairs, Mrs. Gregory told me we have to have the menus memorized before tomorrow." Picking up the stiff pages from the counterpane, she perused them before giving them to Natalie. She struggled into a nightgown and dunked her washcloth into the basin to cool her face. "We can quiz each other."

Half an hour later, yawning and with her head full of unfamiliar words like Albondigas soup and Chicken Lucrecio, Meghan turned out the lights and crawled into bed. Tired as she was, the instant her head hit the pillow, her mind snapped awake.

Unfamiliar night sounds filtered through the window. A dog barked, and footsteps sounded in the hall. A moment later their door eased open. Meghan sat up, clutching the sheets to her chest. "Who is it?"

"Just me. Jennifer. It's my night to do a bed check. Sorry to disturb you. G'nite, and see you in the morning."

Bed check. Meghan eased back onto the pillow while Natalie mumbled and turned over in her bed, causing the springs to creak.

As her mind hopped and skipped from one impression to

another, she remembered her mother's wise words. "If ever you can't sleep, spend the time praying. Your heart and mind will calm, and you will put your burdens into the hands of the One who cares more for you than anyone else ever could."

The thought and worry always on her heart and mind these days was her brother, Lars. He must've reached France by now. The last word they'd had, before she left home, was a postcard mailed from New York. A postcard printed by the army with general words and places for him to fill in blanks. "The weather here is _____ and I am in good health. I arrived safely and they are feeding us well. I especially like the _____ the mess cooks fix for us." The army mailed the cards once the troop transport ship reached England. Though the blanks had been filled in by Lars himself, and the postcard was addressed in his own hand, it wasn't as if it really contained his words and thoughts. If only they would receive a letter from him.

Even now he might be engaged in battle against the Kaiser and the German army. Was he in one of those dreadful trenches? Did he have his gas mask with him? Would she ever see him again?

Realizing her hands had fisted at her sides and her stomach had begun to ache in a familiar way, she forced herself to relax and pray, asking for God's protection on Lars and all the American and Allied soldiers fighting in this Great War.

And for a fleeting instant, the face of the man who had rescued her today flitted across her mind. How soon before he signed up and headed off to war?

Chapter 3

N o, no, no. Every pat of butter must have fork marks. The diner must be assured that his food was handled appropriately. The butter must always be cold enough to hold crisp fork marks." Mrs. Gregory pursed her lips and showed Meghan how to put butter on a plate *The Harvey Way*. "Never use your fingers or a knife to put butter on a plate."

Nothing escaped the head waitress's scrutiny, and nothing Meghan did seemed to please her. After less than an hour of her tutelage, Meghan had no doubts as to why the busboys called Mrs. Gregory Iron Drawers. And *The Harvey Way* covered everything from how to sweep the floor to how to fill salt shakers. Meghan's head swam with all the directions, methods, and instructions coming her way.

"When you take the beverage orders, use the cup code. That way the girl coming behind you will know what the customer wants without you having to tell her. See?" Mrs. Gregory flipped the coffee cup over and rested it in the saucer. "An upturned cup in the saucer means the customer wants coffee. For milk, flip the cup and put it next to the saucer. Iced tea; rest the cup against the saucer." She went through the three positions for the three variations of hot tea: black, green, or orange pekoe.

Meghan bit her tongue and concentrated, trying to ignore the "in-way-over-her-head" feeling rising up her windpipe every time she relaxed her guard. She would not fail. She would not be sent home. She would not disappoint her papa again. Amen.

"Bread is baked here at the hotel and not sliced until the customer orders it. Every slice must be three-eighths of an inch thick, no more, no less."

Was she supposed to carry a ruler in her pocket to measure? What would happen if she accidentally served a customer a slice of bread that was a whole half an inch thick? Chaos? Rioting in the streets? Meghan stifled a giggle and kept her face composed.

Girls bustled around them behind the counters preparing for the first customers of the day. The hands on the wall clock climbed relentlessly toward the time when the train was due. Miss Ralston hurried up with a piece of paper and waited until Mrs. Gregory had finished slicing off a perfectly-proportioned piece of bread.

"Mrs. Gregory, here are the numbers." She handed the paper over, stepped back, shot Meghan a sympathetic glance, and hurried through the doors to the soda fountain.

The head waitress glanced at the page. "Hmm, Miss Thorson, tell the chef we're expecting fifty-one for the lunchroom and twenty-nine in the dining room."

Meghan hustled off to the kitchen where pots steamed and the smell of fresh bread drifted through the brick archway that separated the cavernous kitchen from the bakery. High transom-like windows let in sunshine and let hot air escape, and cooks in white shirts, aprons, and trench caps stirred, sliced, and sautéed. The chef, recognizable by his tall, white hat, expertly flipped a skillet of browning potato chunks. The smell of bacon and sausage cooking made her mouth water. Too nervous to eat this morning in the midst of all the chattering, confident Harvey Girls, she'd only nibbled a slice of toast and sipped a glass of milk.

She relayed the message from Mrs. Gregory, and the chef's friendly smile and nod emboldened her to ask, "Is that a lot of people or about average?"

"Zat is more zan before ze war. Now we have soldiers on nearly every train. And zey have big appetites." He turned and spoke to one of the cooks in rapid French before returning to his skillet.

Meghan returned to the lunchroom where activity had picked up in anticipation of serving breakfast to eighty passengers in under thirty minutes in order to keep to the train's schedule.

"Miss Thorson, come here. You have too much to learn to be gawping and standing idle."

She got a firm grip on her temper and side-stepped a girl carrying an armload of stacked plates. Mrs. Gregory tapped her foot.

"When you are not serving customers, you will be caring for your equipment and your station. Also, the coffee urns. These are the most visible symbol of Harvey hospitality." Pride swelled her voice. "They must be spotless at all times." She waved her hand at the immense silver urns anchoring the end of each of the long counters. "I will now show you the proper way to make the coffee."

Meghan wanted to protest that she'd been making coffee for a long time and how hard could it be, but she bit her tongue and followed in the head waitress's wake.

"No less than eight ounces of freshly ground—not too fine, mind you—coffee per gallon. The customers will ask what brand we use, so be sure to tell them we use only Chase & Sanborn, and we never reheat and serve old coffee. Every two hours you will empty each urn, rinse them with scalding water, and brew fresh coffee."

Blinking, Meghan knew her mouth had fallen open. "Every two hours? Isn't that wasteful? What do you do with the old coffee if you don't reheat it?"

Mrs. Gregory rolled her eyes. "We are not some border-town cantina or lowbrow slum restaurant. This is a Harvey establishment. Old coffee is thrown away. On the rare occasions when the chef needs cold coffee for a dessert, some of the brew is reserved, but that is the exception rather than the rule." The head waitress had more starch in her voice than in all the aprons in the room.

"Don't any of the Harvey hotels practice hooverizing?" In this time of voluntary rationing so every soldier on the Allied front could have the best possible diet, such waste was criminal. How did the hotel handle the Meatless Mondays or Wheatless Wednesdays? If Mrs. Gregory wouldn't even reheat coffee, Meghan doubted she would serve cornbread squares in place of dinner rolls or rye instead of white bread cut exactly three-eighths of an inch thick.

A drawstring-bag pucker tightened Mrs. Gregory's lips, and an icy snowdrift invaded her eyes. "Lest you think us unpatriotic, Miss Thorson, perhaps you should get your facts before you judge. The Harvey Company has a contract with the government to serve soldiers on their way to Europe. The military has granted us the concession, and they have approved our menus and practices. The food we serve and the methods we employ are fully in keeping with our agreement with the War Department and have the approval of Herbert Hoover himself as the head of the US Food Administration. We—the company and the staff at this hotel—are very patriotic and fully behind the war effort."

Meghan wiped the incredulous expression off her face. Mrs. Gregory took a deep breath, the color fading from her cheeks. "My own son has recently enlisted and left for Europe only a week ago." The cords in her narrow neck stood out as she raised her chin. "I'm very proud of him, and as the mother of a soldier, I can assure you, my patriotism is without equal." She turned, but not before Meghan caught the glimmer of tears.

Well, the old duck did have a heart. Meghan's conscience chided her. No wonder she was a bit prickly with her son heading off to war that very week. A feeling of kinship swept over Meghan. They both had loved ones fighting for the cause.

A bell sounded near the lobby door. "The train's been sighted. Places, girls!" All emotion vanished from Mrs. Gregory's face and voice, and she once again became a martinet, ruling the establishment with her steely will.

Though her head spun from the speed at which she was expected to move, her first customers were so friendly and gracious, Meghan discovered partway through serving her first meal as a Harvey Girl that she was having the time of her life. She remembered the majority of the menu and even managed to navigate the mysterious cup code with only a couple of mistakes.

Perhaps part of her lightheartedness came from the customers themselves. Every last passenger this morning was dressed in the olive-brown uniform of the US Army. Straight from training camp in central California and headed to Europe. Fresh-faced, young, exuberant, reminding her of her brother.

"Say, I sure wish the train wasn't leaving so soon. Never expected the scenery to be so nice here in the desert." A sunburned recruit with white-blond hair held out his coffee cup. "Wouldn't mind staying around for a while."

Meghan poured his coffee, holding the handle of the pot in her right hand and using a white towel in her left to support the spout, just as Mrs. Gregory had shown her. "I bet you say that to all the girls."

Jenny passed behind her with two steaming plates. "He said it to me, not three minutes ago."

The sunburn deepened, and Meghan laughed. "Not that it isn't nice to hear." As she moved on, his buddies elbowed and kidded him.

One dark-eyed boy grabbed her attention, not through anything he said, but because he was so somber and quiet in the midst of this boisterous crowd. He cupped his coffee mug, staring into space and not touching his food.

"Is there anything I can get you, sir? Can I warm up your coffee?"

He blinked, as if just returning from a faraway land. "Pardon?"

"Would you like more coffee?"

"Um, sure." He held out his cup.

"Where are you from?"

"Monterrey."

She did a quick gallop around her knowledge of California geography. "That's on the coast, right?"

"Yep. Grew up within sight of the sea. My whole family is there." His voice vibrated with homesickness, and her throat constricted.

"I bet they miss you already, and they're looking forward to the day when you come home. Do you have a big family?"

He dug in his shirt pocket and pulled out a photograph. "I'm the oldest of ten kids."

"That *is* a big family." She admired the somber faces, picking him out and scanning the family all the way from the father down to the baby on the mother's lap. "I only have one sibling, a brother who is already over there."

"I've never been away from home before. I don't know how they're going to manage without me. Pa has a bad back and can't work too much, so I've been running the store."

Meghan studied the picture a moment longer before returning it to him. "I imagine your younger brothers will help out, and you can send pay home, right?"

"Miss Thorson, you are neglecting your duties." Mrs. Gregory's hand gripped Meghan's shoulder, slowly turning her around and guiding her toward waiting customers. Though she wanted to shrug off that commanding clamp, Meghan allowed herself to be drawn away. She glanced back at the homesick soldier and gave what she hoped would be an encouraging smile.

Meghan poured enough coffee to float a transport ship, smiling and chatting briefly with each man but ever aware of Mrs. Gregory's stern gaze following her around the horseshoe-shaped counter.

In what seemed an incredibly short amount of time, the room cleared and the noise died down. With barely a pause to draw a deep breath, the Harvey Girls went about the task of cleaning their stations in preparation for the next train. Meghan leaned against the counter and wiped her brow, eyeing her station.

"You're standing idle again, Miss Thorson. Start wiping down the counters and chairs. And Miss Thorson." Mrs. Gregory's skin stretched over her cheekbones as she pursed her lips into the now-familiar pucker. "While we do endeavor to be friendly and cheerful with the customers, chatting up young men while you are supposed to be working will not be tolerated. Your job is to present a friendly face and superb service, not a shoulder to cry on, an ear to gossip into, or a flirtatious manner to titillate or lead on."

"But Mrs. Gregory, I wasn't—"

"And you are never to argue with the head waitress. Is that understood?"

Meghan's cheeks burned. Though none of the workers around

her had so much as paused, she knew every ear in the room had heard the dressing-down.

"Yes, ma'am. I understand."

"Good, now get to work. The next customers will be arriving soon."

Caleb made his way through the maze of greenish-brown woolen uniforms filing into the lunchroom at midday. Why had he come? Sure, he had an appointment in town this afternoon, but he could've steered clear of the El Garces. He hadn't needed to come in early, and he certainly didn't need to have his lunch at the hotel.

And yet, here he was.

It was that girl. The redhead he'd rescued yesterday. All night she had haunted his dreams, her brilliant green eyes, her saucy walk, and most of all the beautiful sound of her voice as she called him brave. Over and over in his dreams he'd rescued her at the last moment, savoring the sense of accomplishment, her gratitude, and the feel of her in his arms.

Shaking his head, he chided himself for the millionth time. Most likely she didn't even remember him, or worse, she'd talked to someone and gotten the whole story. By now she knew this town wouldn't wipe their muddy feet on him.

And yet, here he was.

He'd just peek into the dining room and see if she was there. Glancing down, he checked that his clothes were presentable. White shirt, cloth vest, dark brown pants. His boots were worn, but he'd polished them the best he could. No dust or dirt. He'd even scrubbed under his fingernails, all the while telling himself he was sprucing up for his appointment, not on the off chance that he might run into a certain Harvey Girl.

Mr. Stock, immaculate in his dark suit, stood in the dining room doorway, smiling at the customers filing inside. The manager stiffened for a moment, his smile slipping when he caught sight of Caleb, but he quickly recovered, returning to the consummate hospitality professional. "Will you be dining with us today, Mr. McBride?"

"I thought I might."

"Dining room or lunchroom?"

Caleb looked into the paneled dining room with its snowy tablecloths and quiet austerity. Men dressed in business suits, ladies in traveling attire. In contrast, across the lobby, the soldiers filing into the lunchroom jostled and joked, talking loudly. He'd be more comfortable in the dining room away from all the military men, but where was the girl? The blond woman who had been with Meghan yesterday crossed the dining room, weaving between the tables with a tray of china cups. Caleb stood awkwardly, undecided.

At that moment, someone behind him laughed loudly, and he turned toward the sound. He glimpsed Meghan's face through the throng in the lunchroom doorway, and a strange jerky feeling landed in his chest. "Lunchroom."

"An excellent choice."

Caleb joined the line filing into the lunchroom and, once

inside, scanned the room to locate Meghan before choosing a spot at her counter. Soldiers filled most of the chairs. Half a dozen girls in black dresses and white aprons bustled, conversations buzzed, and the sounds of cutlery and glassware chimed.

Meghan carried two silver coffeepots. She went to one of the tall urns near the wall and filled them. His eye was drawn to the perfect white bow nestled in the small of her back and the way her hair lay in smooth waves under a white, lacy headband. Nothing like the disheveled creature he'd held in his arms only the day before.

Then she turned around, the vivid green of her eyes evident, even at ten paces. He hadn't over-imagined the color. If anything, they were more emerald than he remembered.

"What can I get you to drink?"

He dragged his gaze away from Meghan and noticed the short waitress in front of him for the first time.

"Coffee." The word came out before he realized it, and he almost took it back. He loathed the taste of coffee.

She turned his cup over and placed it in the saucer. "Cream and sugar are right here. Would you like a menu, or would you prefer me to tell you what the chef's prepared today?"

"Um, a menu, please."

He pretended to peruse the stiff card. Meghan started at the far end of the counter pouring coffee and smiling and chatting with the soldiers. Their faces lit up, and they joked and teased. A pretty flush crept up her cheeks at the joshing of one fellow, and a whole new feeling hit Caleb's gut, something so foreign and unexpected, he couldn't identify it at first.

Before he could make sense of that bit of absurdity, she stood before him.

"Hello. If it isn't my rescuer. I was hoping I'd see you again soon." She poured the fragrant brew into his cup. He never minded the smell of coffee, it was the taste he couldn't stand.

"I wanted to thank you properly for saving me from harm yesterday."

Her eyes shone, and color filled in the space between her freckles.

"You thanked me at the time." Clearly no one had gotten to her yet with their low opinion of him, or she wouldn't be greeting him with a smile. He didn't know whether to be relieved or uncomfortable. If she didn't know now, it was only a matter of time until she did. Would she hop on the town's bandwagon, or would she decide for herself what kind of man he was? How quickly would she take back the notion that she thought him brave?

"Actually"—she poured another cup of coffee for the next customer—"I can't thank you properly until I know your name. I'm Meghan Thorson. And you are?"

"Caleb McBride."

"Caleb. That's a good strong name. It means bold, right?"

He sipped the hot coffee, trying not to screw up his face at the taste. How foolish could a man get? Ordering a drink he didn't even like, just because a pretty girl was pouring it. He must have holes in his head. He reached for the sugar bowl.

"That's right."

"And are you? Bold, I mean?"

"Miss Thorson, there are customers waiting." Mrs. Gregory

spoke over Caleb's shoulder. "We've already discussed this once. I shouldn't have to tell you again."

"Yes, Mrs. Gregory." Meghan glanced one last time Caleb's way and continued up the counter.

"Mr. McBride, I would prefer if you didn't detain my girls. They have work to do."

Frost feathered the back of his neck at her icy tone.

"Gentlemen," she addressed the men in uniform on either side of him, "if there is anything we can do for you, please, let us know. Nothing is too big or too small for our men in uniform. Just ask. The Harvey Company is behind American *soldiers* one hundred percent." Leveling a flat stare at Caleb and treading heavily on the word *soldiers*, she made it clear she didn't include him in the admiration of The Harvey Company. She swept on to the next group of recruits, and he forced his jaw to relax.

The man on Caleb's right elbowed him. "You signed up yet?" His voice carried painfully far, and several men swiveled their heads his way.

He should've eaten in the dining room. Scratch that, he shouldn't have come to the hotel at all.

"No." Caleb kept his eyes on the menu.

"You're a likely looking lad. Why aren't you in uniform? You ain't a German sympathizer now, are you?" Though he said it in jest, his loud tone drew even more attention. Men lowered their coffee cups, knives, and forks, staring.

The muscles in Caleb's upper back and neck tightened, and his mouth went dry. Meghan's eyebrows rose, and her lips parted. Of all the eyes in the room, he was especially aware of hers.

"No. I'm no friend of the Kaiser's."

"Well, why ain't you upped yet?"

"That's my business." He dug in his pocket for a coin, laid it with a snap on the counter, and stood. His appetite had fled.

Doctor Malcolm Bates pushed his spectacles up onto his forehead and pinched the bridge of his nose. This latest missive from his younger brother had him worried. A military surgeon stationed at Fort Riley, Captain Paul Bates wasn't one to cry wolf. Nor was Doc one to run around yelling that the sky was falling. But there was a definite thread of worry in the missive, a faint bell clanging in the background that didn't bode well. He picked up the letter and resumed reading.

> *Mac, I've never seen anything like it. A small group of men showed up at the infirmary complaining of fever, sore throat, and headache. At first I assumed it was a mild illness traveling through the camp. But I soon came to the conclusion—or rather had it forced upon me—that I'm dealing with something altogether different. Soldiers are succumbing to this sickness in shocking numbers. Strong young men in the morning, and by nightfall, they're dead. I can only pray it runs its course quickly.*
>
> *Many strange things are at work here. The contagion*

passes swiftly from one man to the next. Having the soldiers crammed into the barracks as they are contributes to the communication of the sickness, but this particular malady seems more virulent than anything I've met up with. Worse than a cold or the measles or standard influenza. On top of that, the men who should be best suited to fight off a bout of sickness are the first to fall prey. Strong, healthy, young. This thing shouldn't be attacking with such vigor.

The speed with which the sickness strikes is astounding. And the violence. These men are literally drowning. Fluid builds up in the lungs so fast the body can't siphon it away. The feet and hands start to go black as circulation diminishes, the fever rages, pain in the joints and muscles, and a cough that tears apart the pulmonary tissue. The patients who reach the stage of expectorating blood have, without exception, died.

Lest you think I am exaggerating, I went from eighteen cases the first morning to more than one hundred by that same evening. And more are crowding in every hour.

I'm sorry, I didn't mean to go on like this, but I will admit, this sickness is disturbing. We saw some cases of influenza last year that were particularly strong, but this strain defies description. It feels good to be able to talk things over with you, to voice my fears. You have always been a good friend to me, despite the twenty years separating us. You've mentored my medical career every step of the way, and I find myself longing for your counsel.

Your little practice out there in the desert is looking more and more appealing. After this war is over, I hope to join you there.

Until that day, I remain faithfully yours,
Paul.

Doc folded the letter, glancing at the photograph on his desk. He and Paul smiling into the camera on Paul's graduation day. And how proud he'd been when Paul had chosen to follow in his big brother's footsteps and pursue a medical career. Paul was the only person on this planet who called him Mac, short for Malcolm. He'd just been plain old Doc for so long to the people of Needles, he'd taken to thinking of himself by that name.

Shrugging into his white coat, he stuffed the letter into a pocket and scanned his appointments for the afternoon. Or should he say appointment, since he had only one penciled in.

Caleb McBride. 2 p.m.

One of his favorite patients. And one of his most stubborn.

The bell on the front door chimed.

One of his most prompt, as well.

He stepped into the hallway. The first floor of his home housed his office, his examination room, his sick ward, and his waiting room with the kitchen out back. His private apartments took up the second floor. Nothing like living close to one's work.

Caleb removed his hat and hung it on the rack beside the door.

"Afternoon, Doc."

"Come on in."

As was his habit, he allowed the patient to enter the examination room ahead of him to give himself some time to look things over.

Caleb didn't perch on the examination table. Instead, he chose one of the chairs along the wall that Doc used for anxious parents who brought in a sick child. Caleb spun the chair around, straddled it, and crossed his arms along the back. Resting his chin on his arms, he looked Doc over.

"Haven't seen you out at the river lately."

"I've had to forgo my fishing pleasure lately. A touch of tonsillitis made its way through the elementary school. Not to mention the chicken pox which landed on quite a few of the youngsters. A common spring malady, though this was later than usual, but now they're all on the mend." He settled into his customary chair and tipped it back against the wall, hooking his heels on the rungs. "Things should settle down this summer, and you'll find me on your riverbank in the mornings again."

They talked of the fish they'd pulled out of the muddy waters of the Colorado River, the ones that got away, and the ones they were sure still lurked under the ripples.

"That record-breaking pikeminnow is only a single cast away." Doc rubbed his chin.

"You're a true addict." Caleb grinned and straightened, wrapping his fingers around the curved back of the chair. "One thing I always appreciate about you, Doc, is that you never seem to be in a hurry, always have time to chew the fat before talking anything medical."

He shrugged. "That's because I'd like to think we were more than just doctor and patient. I'd like to think we were friends who had more in common than just medical diagnoses and treatments, needs, and services."

And also because treating the patient was about more than prescribing medicine or sewing up wounds. He gleaned more from these little chats than most of his patients realized, the astute Caleb McBride included.

"Truth is, you're about the only friend I've got in this town. Nice to see a friendly face every once in a while. Might as well get to the medical part though. I can't take up your whole afternoon." The young man pushed himself off the chair and replaced it along the wall.

"This just a regular check-up? Or is something else bothering you."

"Nothing serious; I just need a new pair of boots." He steadied himself with one hand against the exam table and stuck his foot out. A gap had opened along the inside of the left toe as the upper came apart from the sole, and the sole itself had worn paper thin. The right wasn't in much better shape. "They don't fit as well as they used to either, so I figured I was better off getting a new pair than trying to fix these."

"Those look fairly hard used for a man who is supposed to limit his physical activities." Doc raised his eyebrow.

Caleb shrugged. "Work won't do itself."

"Peel them off and we'll have a look."

Doc fussed with some papers on the small desk in the corner. Caleb sat on the exam table and pulled off his left boot—with considerable effort and a grimace—and rolled up his pant leg.

"How's the pain these days?" More sorting of papers, pretending he didn't know how difficult it was for Caleb to be open about what he considered a shameful flaw.

Another shrug as he stripped off his sock. "You want them both bare?"

"Please."

He slid his other boot off easily, took off the sock, and stuck it into the boot top.

Doc kept his face neutral, though the sight always jarred him. Caleb's right leg was strong, muscular, and robust, everything a young man's leg should be. The left was enough to make one want to wince and look away—though he would never do that to any patient, especially Caleb.

Wizened, atrophied, and shrunken, his left leg bore more resemblance to the leg of a ninety-year-old than a man in the prime of life. The foot, especially, drew attention—smaller, with an odd buckle in the middle. Infantile paralysis—polio—was a cruel disease.

Caleb stared hard at the wall over Doc's shoulder, gripping the edges of the exam table as if he feared it would throw him off at any second.

Gently, Doc took the withered foot into his hands. Cool flesh. To be expected. Polio-afflicted limbs were often cool to the touch. He wrapped his fingers around Caleb's healthy right foot. Warm, almost hot.

"I need you to be honest with me if I'm going to treat you effectively. How is the pain?"

Caleb shrugged again, but Doc waited for a real answer.

"It bothers me now and again. I can tell when I've done too much."

"Which is pretty much every day? How about when you're resting?"

"Some cramps, especially at night." He lifted his foot out of Doc's hand. "I know what you're going to say, but forget it."

"I'm going to say it anyway. If you'd wear the brace, it would help. You need the support along the back of your leg and your heel."

"I'm not walking around like a freak. People take one look at leg braces and assume you have the intelligence of a turnip. Their eyes slide over you, and they start doling out the pity, or the contempt." Caleb muttered the words, his shoulders hunched, arms straight, palms jammed into the tabletop. "I just need a new pair of boots."

Doc sighed. "You're a stubborn man."

"I prefer to think of it as strong-minded."

"I bet you do." He chuckled. "We can't just send the measurements from the last pair. Your leg has changed some. That's why this pair of boots doesn't fit as well. I'll need to make a new mold. Wait here while I mix up the plaster."

Returning to the exam room with a tray of supplies, Doc noted that Caleb had replaced his right sock and boot.

Using cotton strips dipped in a tray of wet plaster of Paris mixture, he wrapped the limb in several layers. "Is it too warm?"

Caleb shook his head. "How long will it take?"

"Don't you remember last time? It will take about forty-five minutes to set up hard enough so I can cut it off."

"I meant how long until the new boots come?"

"A month, give or take. It's not like walking into Claypool's and plucking shoes off a shelf."

"I suppose."

He wrapped the last white strip, smoothing it with his fingertips. "There. Now we wait a bit. You want some coffee? Oh, wait, I forgot. You don't like coffee. Water?"

"I'm fine. Just came from the hotel."

"That's unusual. One of those Harvey Girls catch your eye? Maybe that redhead you rescued?"

His eyes widened, and a dull flush rose from his collar. "You heard about that?"

"You forget, Needles is a small, isolated community, and I am one of its oldest and most-respected residents. I hear things. So, you didn't answer my question. Are you sparking one of the waitresses? As a rule you steer clear of the El Garces."

"Which is a rule I should've remembered before I had lunch there. Lotsa soldier boys down there today." Though he kept his tone offhand, Doc knew it had to bother him.

When Caleb had first come to town, Doc had signed his draft notice certifying him as 4F, physically unfit for military duty. As the only person who knew about Caleb's malady, the two had formed a bond that extended beyond doctor and patient or casual friend. Caleb trusted Doc never to reveal his deepest secret, though often Doc had longed to do just that, to fight back against the prejudice and wrong judgments hurled at Caleb by some of the folks in this town by telling them the truth. Mrs. Gregory had taken a particular dislike to Caleb, putting out the word around town that Caleb was too cowardly to fight in the war, but not above profiting off it at the same time by breaking horses for the cavalry. Doc ached to set her and the rest of the town straight.

But Caleb would hate him for that. He'd rather suffer in silence and protect his pride than reveal the truth about his leg.

"Do you know the Hualga family?" Caleb changed the subject.

Doc went to the sink in the corner to wash his hands. "I do some work over on the reservation from time to time, so I've met the family. Why?"

"The oldest boy, Joshua, is working for me now."

"I don't know him too well. He's been away at school for the past several years. He's working with the horses? He didn't strike me as the horseman type." He began tidying up his equipment.

"From what I can tell, he'd rather be reading books than cleaning up after horses. But I think he'd rather work for me than stay home. He doesn't get along with his pa." Caleb rubbed the back of his neck. "I know what that's like."

Doc quit fussing with his instruments and sat down. Befriending and doctoring Caleb called for perception and patience. He revealed things about himself only slowly. Admitting he hadn't gotten along with his father was a big step of trust.

"Fathers and sons don't always see eye-to-eye."

A rueful smile brushed the corner of Caleb's mouth. "My father couldn't stand the notion of having a crippled son." He went silent for a moment. A shudder went through him, and his eyes took on a faraway, painful look. "I was only five when the polio hit. Living in Vermont. A whole slew of kids went down with it. Worst pain I've ever felt." He jerked his thumb at his casted foot. "What's going on in there now isn't a shade to waking up in knots, feeling like your muscles were being ripped off your bones, but not able to move. My brain screamed at my leg to run away from all that pain, but it was like my leg couldn't hear it. Even now, the communication isn't too good, though it's better than it was."

He took a deep breath, his brows lowering, still introspective. "My folks sent me to a hospital for polio kids somewhere near Albany, New York. I was there for two years. They came to see me once in all that two years, and my pa barely looked at me. When the hospital had done all they could for me, they shipped me home. My pa took one look at my leg brace and crippled foot and never spoke another word to me. Within a week I was in another hospital, this one for freaks and crazy people. People nobody wanted. My ma used to come and visit a couple times a year, but never my pa. He was too ashamed of me."

That explained so much. No wonder he refused to wear a brace or tell anyone about his leg.

He seemed to have realized how much of himself he'd revealed, and the shutters closed. His face molded into the familiar mask of remoteness he used on the citizens of Needles, and he crossed his arms, leaning his back against the wall.

"How about we play some checkers while that finishes setting up?" Doc rose. "I think last time you beat me. Time for some revenge."

As he headed to the office to get the game board and pieces, Doc filed away what he'd learned. As surely as Caleb wore a plaster cast on his leg, he also wore a cast on his battered heart. What would it take to peel back and chip away that brittle covering and get to the man, the emotions, and the heart underneath?

Chapter 4

Meghan pulled off her shoes and stockings, hiked her skirts to her knees, and dipped her toes into the soothing basin of cool water. "Fourteen hours."

"What?" Natalie's muffled voice came from the pillows. She'd come in, removed her uniform, and sprawled face-down on the coverlet in her shift.

"That's how long it's been since I sat down. The alarm went off at five. It is now seven o'clock in the evening. I've poured a million cups of coffee, my face hurts from smiling, and my feet have gone on strike." She put on her best "Mrs. Gregory" tone. " 'A Harvey Girl must never be seen sitting down while in uniform.' We were so rushed with that special train, I even ate my lunch standing up in the kitchen."

Natalie rolled over with a groan. Her hair straggled from its pins where she'd dragged her lace headband off. "I had no idea being a

Harvey Girl would be so much work. You'd think after two weeks working seven days a week, I'd have gotten used to it by now. I can't even move."

Glancing at the clock on the dresser, Meghan scowled and wiggled her toes. "Move is just what we'll have to do if we're going to make it to the Red Cross meeting."

Another groan. "I forgot about the meeting. Go without me."

"Oh no, I'm not facing Mrs. Gregory all by myself. You know she doesn't like me. After all her picking and poking this last fortnight, I'm beginning to wonder if all of the apostles and prophets rolled together could please her. I doubt even a biblical saint could live up to her exacting standards. What's a poor Irish-Norwegian lass like myself supposed to do?" Meghan lifted one foot and rotated her ankle as all the commands, orders, corrections, and opinions she'd received from Mrs. Gregory washed through her memory.

Her vow to be the best Harvey Girl the company had ever seen had taken a beating over the past two weeks. At the moment she was tempted to settle for just being good enough to be ignored by the head waitress.

Hold on there, girl. When did you surrender your courage? You're no coward, ready to duck and run for cover. You're a Celtic-Viking lass, and you'll fight to the bitter end.

She straightened her stiff shoulders. "I'll tell you what I'm going to do. I'm going to go to that meeting tonight and dazzle the picky head waitress. I'm going to show the dragon-lady that I'm the best little Red Cross worker and pledge-gatherer she's ever seen, and then perhaps the dragon-lady will come to appreciate my talents and abilities and might even deign to speak nicely to me every so often. I ain't licked yet."

The bedsprings creaked as Natalie pushed herself upright and braced herself on her palms. "You say that every day. That you're going to be the best Harvey Girl the company has ever seen. But if tonight goes like the past fortnight, you'll get down to the meeting, Mrs. Gregory will say something you object to, and you'll spout off something that will get you further into trouble."

Meghan giggled, shrugging and wrinkling her nose. "How is it that you know me so well, when we've only been friends for less than a month?"

A head-splitting yawn preempted any immediate attempt at speech. Natalie flopped back onto the bed. "It must be my astute powers of observation. That, or you really stink at hiding your emotions. Promise me you won't ever try to hustle a game of poker, all right? You'd be fleeced like a sheep in a heartbeat."

Promptly at eight o'clock, dressed in an ivory muslin gown she hoped wouldn't be too warm and with exhaustion still pulling at her limbs, Meghan followed Natalie into the large, screened veranda at the end of the hotel's first floor. Ceiling fans circulated the air, but even at 8 p.m. the mid-May heat of the day lingered. Tables had been pushed to the sides of the room and rows of chairs stood in their place. Most of the Harvey Girls were already there. Several women clustered in small groups, as well as a handful of men in shirtsleeves.

Mrs. Gregory stood with a pair of older ladies at the head of the table. All three wore Red Cross armbands and nearly identical expressions of officialdom.

Natalie made for the closest empty chair and subsided into it as if her bones had turned to jelly. Meghan dropped down beside her, her feet throbbing from being thrust back into her shoes. She leaned over to whisper. "I sure hope this doesn't go on very long. I'm liable to put my head right on the table and go to sleep."

"I won't be able to wake you, because I'll be passed out right beside you," Natalie whispered back. Though she smiled, dark circles hovered under her eyes, and her skin looked thin and translucent. She looked every bit as tired as Meghan felt. Maybe even more. As the days had gone by, she had become more dear to Meghan, but she'd also grown more remote, more self-contained. When Meghan asked her about it, she shrugged and said it was nothing. Maybe she was just a touch homesick, but it was nothing to worry about, she was working through it.

Meghan squeezed Natalie's elbow and tried to coax a smile. "I'm sure it will get better. We'll get used to the work and the heat, and we won't be so tired."

"I hope so." She fingered her necklace, a gold chain she wore beneath her uniform during the day since Harvey Girls were forbidden from wearing jewelry at work.

Meghan scanned the room, seeing familiar faces. Things had been so busy she'd had to make friends on the fly. Hopefully, she'd be able to deepen some of those friendships over the coming months, but for now, she was glad she had Natalie. This place would be intolerable without her new best friend.

Mrs. Gregory called the meeting to order. "Ladies and gentlemen, thank you all for coming."

"Like we had a choice." Meghan rubbed her hands on her lips and spoke *sotto voce*.

"Behave yourself," Natalie murmured, stifling a yawn.

"Tonight we're launching a new campaign to raise funds and gather materials to help the war effort. While we appreciate all this community has done to help up to now, the needs of our soldiers are fast outgrowing the efforts we've made in the past. We've got to do more." A fervent light gleamed in her eyes.

"I cannot impress upon you strongly enough how important our efforts are. Every pound of scrap metal, every bushel basket of peach pits, every truckload of rubber ensures the safety and well-being of our soldiers and brings the end of this terrible war closer."

She held up a poster of a Red Cross worker cradling a battle-torn soldier in her arms. Emblazoned across the top were the words IF I FAIL, HE DIES. The Red Cross nurse on the battlefield held one arm out, imploring a Red Cross volunteer sitting at a desk for help. A ripple went through the crowd, shoulders straightening, backs stiffening, resolve almost audible.

Meghan blinked and stared at the poster, all levity gone. The boy in that picture was a perfect rendition of her brother. The face, the coloring, the build, everything. He could've posed for that painting. Her throat closed, and her mind raced.

"What is it?" Natalie nudged her. "You're not sleeping with your eyes open, are you?"

Meghan shook her head, unable to look anywhere but at that soldier. The combination of serving all those fresh-faced, brave young men in the lunchroom and seeing the perfect image of her brother on that poster. . .

"It is with great pleasure and honor that I introduce our speaker this evening. Mr. Leonard Gibson, a Red Cross volunteer who has seen firsthand the atrocities the Kaiser has committed, and an impassioned speaker who is currently crossing this country speaking at Red Cross events to raise awareness of the needs of our boys over there. Organizing volunteers and calling upon citizens to rise up and do something for the cause." Her eyes glowed, and color suffused her cheeks.

Meghan had to admire her fervor, and she couldn't help but be drawn in as the room burst into applause. Bowing slightly, Mrs. Gregory turned the podium over to a balding man with a florid, jowly face. Mr. Gibson bounced on his toes, gripped the edges of the stand, and launched into his speech.

"I have come to bring you news from the front. I have come to carry messages of great need and suffering from our brave soldiers. And with your help, I will return to the battlefield with evidence of your love and support, with supplies and hope and all your prayers and best wishes for our boys.

"The war goes hard for us. The need is great. We need ambulances, medical supplies, food, clothing. And most of all we need funds. Funds to buy these things here and ship them to Europe, funds to purchase supplies there, funds to get our Red Cross nurses and doctors and volunteers to where they are most needed."

The entire room seemed to hold its breath, and Meghan found herself leaning forward, her hands clutched in her lap. She saw herself wearing the white armband emblazoned with the red cross, standing shoulder to shoulder with her fellow Americans, a vast army of volunteers contributing to the war effort, contributing to saving the lives of the valiant young men who sacrificed family, home, and even their very lives in order to preserve freedom, not only for America but for the Allied countries. If serving soldiers in the lunchroom could be a worthy calling to help the cause, how much more would additional volunteering and service be?

The speaker drew vivid pictures of the courageous men battling pitiful conditions. He told of how the Red Cross was in the best position to help those in need, but not without the help of volunteers. Meghan lived every word, stirred up inside and ready to answer the call. The longer Mr. Gibson talked, the more impassioned he became, drawing his listeners along with him until electricity fairly crackled in the air around them.

"I ask, nay, I demand! I demand that the citizens of Needles rise up and come to our aid. Anyone who would do less than his or her best, would sacrifice less than these brave men, is a coward to be shunned and shamed. Won't you join us in the fight? Won't you stand with us against the evil forces of the Kaiser? Or will you be one to turn a blind eye, to ignore our pleas, to leave our brave young men to face the enemy alone?"

He smacked the pulpit with all the fervor of a revival preacher, his face glowing with sweat and emotion.

Every last person in the room surged to their feet, cheering and clapping. Some women wiped tears, and Meghan's heart threatened to burst out of her chest. Even Natalie seemed to have regained some of her vigor, for her eyes shone, and she dabbed her eyes with a lacy hanky.

Mrs. Gregory stepped up to the podium, shaking Mr. Gibson's hand. They stood there together a full minute as the applause continued. Finally, she made damping motions, encouraging everyone to take their seats.

"Thank you, Mr. Gibson, for that rousing account. I am sure you will find the citizens of Needles and the employees of The Harvey Company to be most patriotic. By the time you return, we will have proven this through our efforts. Now, before we conclude our meeting tonight, I want to take this time to assign each of you who is willing—and who wouldn't be willing after such a stirring call to arms?—to a particular task. I have several here that I've come up with, and Mr. Gibson will be available to talk with you if you would like to hear more ways we can help. For now, I will list a few." She consulted a piece of paper.

"There are several things we're collecting. Used kitchen grease. Peach pits. Rubber. Scrap metal. Yarn." The paper fluttered as she spread her arms wide. "There are dozens of drives we might put on. In addition, we'll be collecting funds door-to-door, including encouraging folks to buy more war bonds, and we'll have several knitting bees to make socks. I believe Trudy Rivers has a new knitting machine we can use."

Mr. Gibson stepped forward again. "I challenge you each to sign the pledge sheets. Put your name down and how much you think you can raise for the war effort. Be sure to include in your sum the amount you yourself will be contributing. Every bit helps."

Conversations buzzed, the excitement still high in the room.

All around Meghan, folks chattered, passing the sign-up lists and jotting their names down. But none of the activities seemed big enough or grand enough to match the zeal in Meghan's heart. Each time she glanced at that poster, now hanging from the front of the podium, each time she thought of those stories Mr. Gibson had told and imagined the bravery with which those soldiers were fighting, she wanted to do something substantial and tangible to help them.

She left Natalie dithering between signing up to roll bandages or to collect peach pits to be used in the making of gas masks and sought out Mr. Gibson. She had to wait for her turn as he was surrounded by eager faces.

"What they really need there on the front are more ambulances. A single ambulance can be the saving of dozens of lives. If only the cost wasn't so steep. One thousand dollars to purchase and ship an ambulance from the US to France. Most groups of this size, communities of this size, aren't up to committing that kind of money." He tucked his thumbs behind his suspenders and bounced on his toes. "Still, if we pool together a lot of little efforts, I'm sure it will make a difference."

"A thousand dollars?" One girl's jaw dropped. "We'd have to collect dimes from now until forever to come up with that kind of money. Especially as we'll be asking folks for bandaging materials, yarn, grease, iron, rubber, and about anything else that isn't nailed down. We've already been through rationing and buying war bonds. I don't think the folks of Needles could raise that kind of money."

Meghan stepped forward. "I'll raise the thousand dollars."

Conversations slowed. Mr. Gibson's eyebrows arched, and he

plunked down off his toes, landing hard on his heels.

"Young lady, I admire your spunk, but perhaps you should attempt a more modest monetary goal."

Nothing less would do. One thousand dollars, one ambulance. "I can do it." The hot coals of zeal burned bright in her chest. No sum was too big, no obstacle too immense. She could and would get an ambulance to France. She would prove her courage and her value. And no one, not Mrs. Gregory or her father, or anyone would be able to deny what she had accomplished.

She stepped up to the pledge sheet and boldly wrote her name with a flourish. Beside it, she wrote the sum: One Thousand.

"A lofty goal, Miss Thorson." Mrs. Gregory's voice pricked like a pin. "I hope you have a plan for raising such a significant amount of money in only a few months. The Red Cross takes these lists very seriously. They plan ahead based upon the pledges made by citizens. I'd hate for them to fall short because you bit off more than you could chew."

Meghan's glance flicked to the paper and a splash of uncertainty damped a bit of her enthusiasm. Then the crowd parted a bit and her gaze fell on the poster: IF I FAIL, HE DIES.

And she mustn't fail. Not for his sake, nor for her own.

Now if only she had a plan.

Chapter 5

A week later Meghan felt like she was the only one not contributing to the war effort. Every idea she had failed to stand up under much scrutiny or was already being done by someone else. She considered the calendar on the bedroom wall.

"Mr. Gibson said he will return October 15th, and between now and then, I've got to come up with a way to raise one thousand dollars." She tapped her front teeth with her fingernail, racking her brain.

Natalie finished pinning up her hair. "I wish you hadn't made such a pledge. If you'd shown more sense, not let yourself get caught up in the fever in that room, you wouldn't be worrying so much now. You're spending every waking minute trying to come up with a way to raise the money, and it's affecting your work, your appetite, even your sleep. You tossed and turned for hours last night."

The thousand dollars had consumed her. To fail would be not

only to humiliate herself in front of Mrs. Gregory, but to let down her brother and men like him. Men such as she served every day on their way to war. How could she do that to them? Not to mention what Papa would say about what he would call another one of her harebrained schemes.

She couldn't fail. She'd have to come up with a way, and that was that.

"Are you ready?"

After three weeks of steady work, Meghan and Natalie had finally earned a half day off. With the arrival of two more new girls, Mrs. Gregory had enough staff to allow them their one afternoon off each week, and Meghan could hardly wait to get out of the hotel and explore the town.

Only she wished their half day was in the morning when it was still marginally cool, but they were low in the pecking order and their days off were assigned accordingly. She took a deep breath that seemed to bake her lungs in her chest. The afternoon sun roasted everything in sight. Only the palm trees seemed indifferent to the swelter.

They passed through the front doors of the hotel and crossed into Santa Fe Park. Though it had been created ten years before when the new hotel had been erected, the trees looked small, stunted, and brittle. Nothing like the lush, greenness of Minnesota. Her eyes longed to see a blue spruce or red maple. The ground crunched under their shoes, parched and hard as terracotta tiles.

"Where should we go?"

"Jenny said Claypool's is the best store."

They meandered slowly. As they walked along the wide street, railroad track after railroad track stretched by on their left, shimmering in the heat. A hot wind blew against their faces, and Meghan scanned the eastern landscape.

"There's the river. Jenny said sometimes the girls take a trip out there to swim. Wouldn't that feel nice, to sink into the water? There's not a soul out here on the street right now."

"And there's the sign for Claypool's." Natalie fanned herself with her handkerchief. "Nobody is silly enough to be walking around in this heat. We should've stayed at the hotel and taken a nap."

"I don't care how hot it is. I'm tired of the hotel. It feels good to get outside for a change. Back home, unless it was a blizzard, I never stayed indoors."

"I could use a blizzard right now." Natalie dabbed at her throat and temples, her brows coming together. "It's unbearable out here."

"I tell you what, as a reward for coming out with me, we'll stop and get some ice cream at the drugstore on the way home."

"I'm going to hold you to that, though we could've gotten ice cream at the soda fountain in the hotel."

Meghan frowned a little, but let Natalie's comment slide. The heat made everyone a touch irritable, even the normally even-keeled Natalie.

They stepped into Claypool's, and once out of the sunshine, the temperature dropped to almost tolerable.

"Afternoon." The clerk barely looked up from his newspaper.

The store stocked everything from groceries to clothing items on two floors. Ceiling fans stirred sluggish air, and the place looked dead. Meghan began to wonder if Natalie wasn't right, that they should've stayed at the hotel. Still, they were here. They might as well look around. She just might find some inspiration for her Red Cross pledge idea.

Nothing caught her eye. Housewares she skipped by quickly, in no mood to look at coffeepots or gravy boats. She saw too many of those every day. The book department slowed her down some as she ran her fingers along the spines. Not much time to read right now and less when she figured out what her Red Cross project would be and got it into full swing.

"Help you with anything?" The clerk scratched his ribs and yawned. "You from the hotel?"

"Yes. We're Harvey Girls."

"Figured. Seen enough of them. They having a social up there this Friday? Been awhile since they had one."

"I believe Mrs. Gregory is planning something, not for this Friday but for next. A Dime-A-Dance to raise money for the local Red Cross chapter."

"Good. Always like those Harvey socials. I'll bring the wife. She'll enjoy it."

Natalie stopped to study a bin of yarn balls, and Meghan found herself in the fabric and notions section of the store. Bolts of cotton, muslin, denim, and twill, patterned, striped, plaid, and plain. She missed her sewing machine at home. Working the treadle, feeding pieces of cloth through, turning bits into a finished garment or quilt.

Her hand stilled on a bolt of bright red cloth. A single thread of an idea wisped through her mind. She grasped it and tugged gently.

Sewing. Maybe she could use her love of sewing.

Suddenly, full-blown, the idea surged into her head.

"I've got it!"

Natalie dropped a skein of yarn, and the sales clerk jerked.

"I've got it." She grabbed Natalie's hands and swung them. "Why didn't I think of it before? I'm going to make a quilt. A signature quilt. I'll sell space on the blocks for folks to have their signatures embroidered, and I'll sell advertising space to the businesses in town, and when it's done, I'll raffle it off." She hugged Natalie, who stood like a wax doll, blinking her long lashes.

Stirring herself, Natalie's brow wrinkled. "A quilt? Are you sure? That's an awfully big project to take on. Not just the sewing but the embroidering and the selling of names? And how are you going to afford the fabric and such? Or find a sewing machine? You'll be so tired."

The idea had taken such a hold in Meghan's mind, she didn't want to hear anything dampening. For the first time in a week, she felt like she could breathe freely.

"As my grandma is fond of saying, 'No one ever died of tired.' I'll figure it out." She turned to the clerk. "Do you have a piece of paper I could use? I need to do some figuring."

The man produced a scrap of brown store paper and a stubby pencil, and Meghan went to work.

"The women in my mama's auxiliary at home in Mantorville made a quilt like this last year. I don't know why I didn't think of it before. A white quilt with red crosses and red names embroidered in the corners of the squares. They had four names per square, and fifty-six squares. Plus some room on the end of each row for a business name or a big donor. . ." The pencil scratched as she slashed out a sketch of the quilt as a whole, a single quilt block, and some rough estimates of cloth, batting, and thread. "I would need at least two hundred twenty-four names to fill the blocks, and with seven staggered rows of eight squares each, that leaves seven half-blocks on alternating ends to be filled with company names."

"Meghan, please, think about this before you jump in boots and all." Natalie tugged on Meghan's sleeve. "I'm sure it isn't too late for you to amend your pledge to something more manageable. You could knit socks with me. Just stop and think, please?"

She looked up from her scribbling, her mind racing so fast she had to concentrate on what Natalie said. "I've done nothing but think about this for the past week. I made the pledge, and it is up to me to see it through. I've been quilting since I was a little girl. Just imagine. In a few months, I'll have a whole thousand dollars to turn over to Mr. Gibson, and he can buy an ambulance to help our wounded soldiers. I don't care how hard I have to work. The end result will be worth it."

"What if you don't raise enough money?"

"I will. I have to." She turned back to her paper. "If I get two dollars for every signature, plus maybe ten dollars to have a business name on the quilt. . ." More scratching. "Then I can raffle the quilt or auction it off. Didn't Mrs. Gregory say something about having an auction on the night Mr. Gibson comes back?" A glow burned in her chest. This would work. She could do it. She just needed to get started.

"Where are you going to get the money for the fabric and such?" Natalie crossed her arms and tapped her foot.

Meghan narrowed her eyes and her thoughts raced. The idea was so big, so perfect, she couldn't wait to get started, and it bothered her that Natalie wasn't as excited as she about it. Instead of joining in her enthusiasm, Natalie insisted on pointing out all the roadblocks. Meghan turned to the clerk. "Do you own this fine establishment?"

He chuckled and scratched his ribs. "No, ma'am. You want to talk to William Claypool."

"And where would I find him?"

"Back there in the office." He pointed them to the rear of the store.

Twenty minutes later, Meghan clutched a scrip for fabric and thread as well as a ten-dollar donation to get Claypool's name embroidered in one of the half-blocks on the quilt. She put a superior little skip into her step as she showed Natalie the paper and the cash.

"He was most kind."

"You got him to donate the fabric and some money? How?" Natalie's eyes narrowed. Her hand went to her hip, and a school-marmish pucker drew in her mouth.

"You act like I robbed the man. I simply told him what I wanted; explained how, as a leading citizen of Needles, I was sure he would want to be at the forefront of any civic cause; and he did the rest."

She would not mention her nervous stumbling, how she'd invoked the name of the Red Cross several times, and—her conscience gave a little shiver—pandered just a wee bit to the man's pride. Flattery often got you what plain speaking couldn't.

"Miss Thorson." Mr. Claypool stuck his head out of the office doorway. "Thank you for your patronage. I look forward to seeing the end result. Mr. Weeks, be sure you give them just what they ask for."

The clerk snapped to attention like he'd been poked in the ribs. "Yes, sir."

He unrolled bolts of cloth onto the cutting table and with an enormous pair of shears, snipped off lengths of white and red fabric. Natalie found skeins of embroidery thread to match, and Meghan selected a suitable length of fiber batting.

"I'll have these delivered to the hotel for you." Mr. Weeks tucked his pencil behind his ear after totting up the total.

"Thank you." Meghan hesitated at the door. No time like the present to get started. "By the way, would you like to make a two-dollar donation and have your name on the quilt? I'm sure, as someone so familiar in the community, you would want be an example for your friends and neighbors." She smiled. This was exactly the phrase she'd used on Mr. Claypool. "I imagine folks around here would notice if a name as prominent as yours didn't appear on the quilt."

His hand was already diving into his pocket. "Best put my name and my wife's on there too. She'd be put out if she got left off."

Meghan and Natalie headed to the drugstore, and Meghan couldn't help but put her chin in the air a bit. "Fourteen dollars *and* free materials."

Natalie rolled her eyes. "Only nine hundred eighty-six dollars and one whole quilt to piece, embroider, and auction off left to go."

Caleb handed Joshua the metal bucket and length of pipe. The bucket had a rusted out hole in it anyway and couldn't be any less useful. It would do for what he had in mind.

"When I give you the signal, you go to whacking on it."

"Why? You've got that horse eating out of your hand. He's perfectly trained and bridle-wise. We've done nothing but school horses for the past month, and each one is as gentle as a lamb. Why upset them?" Joshua set his jaw, an expression Caleb was all too familiar with. Nothing seemed to happen on this place without an argument from his hired man. No, not quite a man, or he'd quit arguing all the time and do what his boss said. He was a hard worker, Caleb would grant him that, it was just that he expected to be informed of the reason behind every chore before he'd stir a step.

"You're a smart lad. I'll leave you to work it out." He headed toward his mount. Grit filtered through the seam in his boot, working its way through his sock and abrading his skin. Those new boots couldn't come soon enough. Sunshine baked everything around him, whitening the sky and making him squint, even under the broad brim of his hat.

The bay stood quietly in the morning sunshine, one hind leg tucked up, resting. A level-headed, hardworking, honest mount, typical of the animals sent to him by the US Cavalry's horse buyer for the Southwest. Major Alexander had a good eye for horses and a firsthand knowledge of what was needed in a military mount.

Caleb gathered the reins and jumped, landing on his stomach across the saddle and scrambling upright. Once mounted, he slipped his right foot easily into the stirrup, but he had to guide his left leg into position. He couldn't mount any other way, not with his bum foot. The maneuver might not be pretty, but it was effective. Settling aboard, he couldn't help but miss the deep seat on his favorite saddle. This flat, cavalry saddle was what the officers at Fort Riley and overseas would be using, so he trained with it, but he didn't like it as well. Being forced to put more weight on his left leg than he otherwise would caused the muscles to radiate weakness, but he gritted his teeth, balanced himself, and gripped with his knees.

Shaking up the reins, he put the horse into a slow walk, then trot, then canter, circling the big corral. When the horse had fallen into a rhythm, he lifted his hand to signal Joshua. As the horse approached the boy, Joshua did justice to his job and banged the bucket with vigor almost under the animal's nose.

The horse jerked his head up and bolted, skidding sideways and seeking to escape the cacophony. He added a few bucks, just for good measure. Caleb hung on to the swerving animal, keeping a tight rein and finally, on the far side of the corral, bringing him back under control. He let the horse stand for a moment, trembling and sweating. With soft words and a few pats on the neck, Caleb soothed his mount.

"Easy, boy. You're all right." Squeezing his knees, he asked the horse to walk out.

With much head-tossing and sidestepping, he obeyed, but when they got near Joshua and the racket began again, he fought the bit and skidded backward.

"Whoa." Caleb brought him to a halt, calmed him, and tried again. This time, though the horse hastened his pace, he kept going in the circle. By the fifth time, the animal continued on without changing course, though he kept an eye on Joshua.

Finally, Caleb dismounted and motioned the boy to come over. "Here, unsaddle him and walk him out a bit to cool him down, and then give him a drink."

Joshua set the bucket and pipe on the ground near the gate. He rubbed his hands on the back of his jeans and took the reins. "I figured it out."

"Did you?"

"You're sending these horses into battle where there will be lots of loud, sudden noises. You're getting them used to it so they don't bolt into trouble."

"I knew you were a smart boy. And having you here makes it so much easier. I was stacking up buckets and cans and knocking them over as I rode by, but this is a lot more effective."

Joshua shrugged. "I should've seen it right away. But banging on a bucket is a long ways from cannon fire. How're you going to get them ready for that?"

Caleb opened the gate so Joshua could lead the horse out. "I guess we could always blow something up and see how they react."

Joshua stopped. "You can't—" He grinned ruefully when he realized Caleb was teasing.

"All right, we can't blow up anything, but we'll do the best we can. The bucket, a shotgun, a nice big smoky fire. We'll put them through their paces as best we can, then when we turn them over to the military, they can take it from there. If we've already conditioned them not to jump at loud noises or get spooked over a little fire and smoke, they'll be well on their way to making cavalry mounts."

The boy nodded and led the horse away.

Caleb headed toward the water trough, dragging his hat off and dunking his head into the cool water. Straightening quickly, he flung droplets into an arc over his head. Rivulets ran down his face and neck, soaking his shirt but already beginning to evaporate. He swiped his forearm across his brow and resettled his hat. Time for some rest.

Because Joshua had his back turned fifty yards away, Caleb went ahead and gave in to the ache in his ankle and limped over to the shade of the front porch. Dropping down into one of the chairs, he dug his fingertips into his left calf above the boot and kneaded. On days like today, when the ache persisted no matter if he was resting or working, wearing his brace seemed more and more attractive.

And yet, he knew he wouldn't. Not even when he was alone. If he didn't use his leg, it would atrophy worse. And if anyone saw him in the brace, he'd be the object of pity, and that was something he refused to stomach.

The new boots would help. The note from Doc Bates said they would arrive in a month or so, about the time for him to take a string of horses in to meet the train.

Thinking of Doc Bates made his insides squirm. He'd never

meant to reveal anything about his past, especially not his father, but something about Doc's patience and acceptance made Caleb want to spill everything. Up to and including all about Patricia.

His mind balked. Not Patricia. Never Patricia. He never wanted that name to pass his lips again. He certainly didn't want to blab about it to Doc.

Which reminded him, he'd best stop letting his mind wander to Meghan, too. He had more than enough evidence that his future held no place for a woman in it, and he was foolish to even daydream about a girl like Meghan. If she ever found out he was crippled, she'd run as far and as fast as Patricia had. So he had to make sure she didn't find out, and the surest way to do that was to stay away from her.

This Friday, when he went to town, he'd go to the station and deliver the horses, and head home. The hotel, the lunchroom, and Meghan Thorson were strictly off limits.

"You're sure he won't mind us cutting through his property?" Meghan held her hat on her head as the hotel car bounced and jounced along the rutted road. Girls laughed and jostled, talked and sang all around her, but all Meghan's thoughts were on Caleb McBride. The minute the excursion to the river had been voiced, she knew she would go along. Cajoling Natalie to join her had been the most difficult part.

"He won't care. We probably won't even see him. We didn't last time. Anyway, Doc comes out here to fish all the time, and he said Caleb wouldn't care if we picnicked by the river." Jenny turned in her seat and waved to the automobile behind them. Sunlight flashed off the windscreen and paintwork, as well as the twin rails of the railroad tracks parallel to the road.

"I wonder what came over Mrs. Gregory to up and give the whole lot of us the afternoon off."

Natalie, a picnic basket balanced on her knees, dodged Jenny's elbow. "She said the three-thirty had engine trouble and wouldn't be coming through today, so we might as well have the time off, though she did promise at least half of us would have to help with the breakfast prep when we got back."

Jenny shrugged. "Who cares? A whole afternoon to paddle in the river, lay about in the shade, and be lazy. Look, there's the turnoff."

They bumped over the railroad tracks and followed a narrow drive toward the smudge of green bushes that marked the riverbank.

A plain, single-storied house came into view, drab and gray, with a rusty tin roof. A wide porch shaded the front of the structure, and miles of corral posts and rails wove in and around the house. Open-sided shade shelters stood at various angles, and horses dozed, lazily swishing their tails, heads down, standing still. Trying not to be obvious, Meghan took in as much as she could as the car bumped through the farmyard.

She tapped Jenny on the shoulder. "Shouldn't we stop and at least let him know we're here?"

"There's someone." Jenny pointed toward a low outbuilding. Meghan craned her neck, but the figure emerging from the building wasn't Caleb. Blue-black hair and a slouching, lean look. Too young to be Caleb. She quelled her disappointment.

The driver, one of the porters from the hotel, honked the horn. Jenny waved wildly, half rising from her seat. The young man waved back, and the car bounced on.

The road dipped down into a cut with sandy walls rising on either side. Brushy trees and scrub bushes clung to the earth walls, obscuring their view of the house and corrals a few hundred yards away. A sandy spit of beach opened before them, and everyone piled out of the cars. Girls in high spirits continued to talk and tease as they unloaded blankets and baskets and belongings. Meghan took out her handkerchief to wipe the dust and grit from her face while she surveyed the beach. The river slapped against the bank in lazy, breeze-induced waves. Her spirits lifted at the sight of the water, and she couldn't resist walking right down to the edge and trailing her fingers in the lukewarm liquid. The picnic area was in a small cove carved out of the sand, like sitting in a bowl. From here, they couldn't see the house or very far up or downstream.

"I'm going wading." Jenny plopped down on the sand and tugged at her shoelaces. Her stockings followed, and she lifted her hem and strode into the water. "Ah, heavenly. I've been wanting to do this for weeks."

Several of the girls followed, but Meghan, mindful of her fair skin, headed back to the safety of the shade.

Natalie joined her on a blanket, drawing her legs up and wrapping her arms around her knees. She covered a yawn. "I could stretch out right here and sleep the afternoon away. That's what I was going to do before you talked me into coming out here."

Slight guilt skipped through Meghan's heart, but she bumped shoulders with Natalie. "It's cooler by the river than upstairs in our room. At least there's a breeze."

Natalie nodded, stretched out on her side, and pillowed her head on her arm. "Wake me up when it's time to go."

The girls laughed and splashed. Another carload, this time of railroad men, joined the party, swelling the numbers to nearly twenty. Flirting and boisterous jesting became the rule of the day.

Meghan rose and tugged Jenny away from a brawny switchman. "What are they doing here? What would Mrs. Gregory say? We're forbidden to mix with the railroaders."

Jenny shrugged. "Who cares? Mrs. Gregory isn't here. She said we could come to the river. If other people show up at the same time, we can't be blamed, can we? Don't worry so much."

When the men began splashing the girls, accompanied by shouts and screams, Meghan wandered upstream and around the jutting bank to get away from the noise. Natalie must be exhausted to slumber in spite of the activity.

A hundred yards upstream, she found a patch of shade under a twisted juniper tree that hung over the water. Lifting her hem, she divested herself of shoes and stockings and poked her toes into the water. Her eyes closed, and a deep sigh relaxed her. Meghan loved being around people, but after awhile, she needed to be alone to let her soul fill up again. She sniffed the warm desert air, inhaling scents of water, mud, and tangy juniper. Sand trickled through her fingers as she breathed a prayer of thanks for this time alone.

The ground thudded, and her eyes popped open. Coming toward her on her left, a horse and rider flew along the shallow edge of the river, sending up sheets of water. She yanked her feet back as the rider pulled the horse up a few yards away.

Though his hat shaded his face, she knew him instantly.

"Mr. McBride." She tugged the hem of her skirt down as far as it would go, though it didn't cover her bare feet and ankles. Deciding to stand, she pushed herself up and brushed the sand from her dress.

He nudged his horse out of the water and slid to the ground, his eyes wide. "What are you doing out here? Are you lost?"

She wet her lips and tried a laugh, but feared it didn't sound natural. He was more handsome than she remembered. His worn shirt stretched across his shoulders, and he'd rolled up the sleeves to reveal muscular forearms. He had the long legs and lean waist of a natural horseman, and his face would turn any girl's head for another look.

"I'm not lost. There are a few of us from the hotel and rail yard having a picnic just around the bend." She motioned toward the south. "You don't mind, do you? I asked Jenny if we shouldn't stop at the house and ask permission, but she said you wouldn't care." Her hands twisted in front of her, and she was very conscious of her bare feet.

He looped his arm over the saddle and leaned into the horse, putting all his weight on one foot. "I don't mind. You just surprised me, that's all. I wasn't expecting anyone along this stretch." He patted the horse's rusty-brown neck. "I was just taking the edge off this fellow. He had a long, tedious afternoon in the corral learning to respond to voice commands, and I thought he needed some of the cobwebs blown out with a good run along the river."

She edged forward and brushed the animal's velvety nose. He whiffed her fingertips and submitted to a few pats before tossing his head and sidestepping away. "He's a beauty, Mr. McBride."

"Smart and capable. He'll be a good mount. And call me Caleb." A smile quirked his lips. "How come you're up here by yourself and not with the rest of the picnickers?"

"It was getting pretty loud. I just wanted some time away from all the people and noise."

A shadow passed over his face, and he backed up a step. "I don't mean to intrude. I'll leave you alone then."

Her hand shot out and touched his arm, warm, masculine, with a dusting of blond-brown hair. "Please. I'd like you to stay." Heat at her boldness crept into her cheeks, but she looked him in the eyes.

He tilted his head, studying her for a moment, then, as if making up his mind, he tied the reins to a juniper branch and lowered himself to the sand.

Meghan sat beside him, a few feet of sand between. "Have you always lived in Needles?"

He shook his head, plucking a stem of long, dry grass from a clump under the juniper and breaking it into small pieces. Tossing them into the water, one by one, he watched them bob and drift. "No, I've only lived here a few months. I hail from Vermont originally. I live here because of the horses. The army rented the place because it was a good location along the railway."

"What do you do with the horses?"

"Work them, condition them, train them." Another inch of grass stalk voyaged southward. "Then I ship them east so the army can feed them to the war machine." His face hardened. "This stupid, endless, murderous war."

"You don't approve of the war?" Her eyes widened. Was he a German sympathizer?

"Should anyone really approve of war?" His glance flicked toward her and then back to the river. The horse lowered his head to drink, making the bit jingle.

"Well, no, but when it becomes necessary, it is our duty as citizens to stand up and fight the oppression of our allies. We cannot let the Kaiser overrun sovereign nations on a whim. He must be stopped, and it is the duty of every American citizen to do what they can to help reach that goal." Her shoulders straightened, and her back stiffened.

He laughed. "You sound like a recruitment poster."

Heat flooded her face, and a pebble of pride lodged in her throat. "And you, sir, sound like. . .like. . ." She faded to a stop.

"Now, don't take offense. I didn't mean anything by it. Of course I think everyone should do their part to help America win the war. I save my paper, grease, and peach pits, just like everyone else."

Steering away from the topic of war, she asked, "Do you miss Vermont?"

"I miss the green, and sometimes when it's hot enough to melt rocks out here, I miss the snow."

"Not your family?"

Again his face hardened, and she knew she'd touched another nerve. "I have no family to speak of."

"Not anyone?" She couldn't comprehend what that must feel like. What would her life be like without having her parents and her brother; her aunts, uncles, cousins, even her grandparents back in the old countries?

"Nobody who claims me, nobody I lay claim to." He shrugged and threw the rest of the grass into the water.

The isolation in his voice tugged at her. "That must be lonely."

He shrugged again. "Loneliness isn't the worst hurt a man can endure." Pushing himself upright, he stumbled and grabbed onto a low-hanging branch to steady himself. Stepping out of the shade, he judged the angle of the sun. "You'd best get back to the others. I imagine they'll have eaten all the food by now. Anyway, I doubt your lady-boss would approve of you wandering off by yourself and keeping company with the likes of me."

Meghan gathered her shoes and stockings. This whole conversation had been so unsatisfactory somehow, and she wasn't ready to let it go. Everything about this man intrigued her—his face and form, his mind, and above all, the bewildering sense of strength and vulnerability that tangled around him.

"Will I see you again?"

"I don't go to town much. In case you hadn't noticed, Needles doesn't take too kindly to strangers. It's like an island in the desert here. If you work for the hotel or the railroad, you can come from anywhere and be accepted, but if you come for any other reason, you're measured by a different stick."

The thought of not seeing him left an empty place in her heart. He was a puzzle she needed to figure out, and somewhere inside him was a wound she felt compelled to heal.

"There's a social coming up on Friday to raise war funds. A dance at the hotel. I'd love it if you would come. The whole town is going to be there. Perhaps, if you came, the people of Needles would get to know you better and begin to accept you."

He chuckled and shook his head, loosening his horse's reins from the tree. "A dance? At the hotel? I don't think so. But thanks for the invitation. I'd best be getting back to the house before Joshua thinks I drowned in the river."

Swinging the horse around so the animal stood between them, he gave a one-legged hop and swung into the saddle. Touching his hat brim, he sent the horse flying along the water's edge once more in the direction from which he had come.

Meghan stood there watching him ride out of sight, wondering what it was about him that so intrigued her.

Chapter 6

I t's going to feel good to be dressed up for once and not in that uniform, don't you think?" Meghan laid her primrose gown out on the bed and studied it. Organza, with barely off-the-shoulder sleeves of ruffled lace, the dress had been her graduation gift from her parents.

Natalie nodded without looking up, twirling a curl around her finger and reading a letter she'd received that day.

Meghan tried again. "You're going to look lovely. I wish I could wear pink, but alas, as a redhead, that is one color that is definitely off limits. My hair turns bright orange, and I look like I got sunburned. Redheads have to be so careful about the colors they wear. You, on the other hand, look stylish no matter what." She sighed and picked up her own letter from home. "Mama wants to know if I can come home for a visit anytime soon or if I have to wait the whole six months. She says the mill is doing fine. The crops are growing well, and Papa is practically living at the mill. Lars sent another letter. I wish he'd write to *me*. I sent him my address. Still, I suppose when you're a soldier, it's all you can do to get one letter written from time to time, and he knows Mama will send along any news. He's probably somewhere in France; that's all we know. So much of his letter was redacted, it's impossible to tell just where he is for sure."

"Hmm."

Meghan set her letter aside and went to the mirror to brush her hair. "A whole evening of dancing. Isn't that wonderful? I haven't danced since last fall, and that was a barn dance put on by the local farmers' association. Tonight won't be anything like that. Did you see the decorations? All those banners and bunting. Flags everywhere. I hardly recognized the loggia. I'll tell you something, Mrs. Gregory might be a tartar when it comes to following the company rules, but she sure knows how to get things done. She's more organized than an accountant and more vigilant than a Victorian governess. How many dances do you think there will be? And how many partners? Too bad that train full of soldiers pulled out. If they were here, I bet we'd be danced off our feet most of the night. Though it would seem wrong to take dimes from the very soldiers we're trying to raise money for, wouldn't it?"

No response.

Meghan turned from fussing with her hair. "Natalie?"

Tears streamed down Natalie's cheeks, and she let the pages of her letter fall to her lap. Her hands came up to cover her face. Silent sobs shook her shoulders.

Meghan dropped the hairbrush and knelt by the chair. "What

is it? Are you all right?"

She shook her head, still trembling. A small, keening sound escaped her throat, full of pain and fear.

"Did you get bad news from home? You've been so quiet since you got that letter, and here I am babbling on like a silly nitwit." She rubbed small circles on Natalie's back, chastising herself for not paying better attention.

After a moment, the worst of the storm passed, and Natalie's muscles eased. Slowly, she lowered her hands, revealing tear-stained skin and drowning eyes. "I know I shouldn't, but I have to tell someone." Her voice rasped, sob-roughened. "Can you keep a secret? I mean, never-tell-a-soul-not-even-if-your-life-depended-on-it keep a secret?"

Sitting back on her heels, Meghan studied her. "What is it? Are you in trouble? Is something wrong at home? You can tell me, and you know I'd never repeat it."

Natalie took a shuddering breath and gripped the letter in her lap. "I have someone at home who is very ill. Her medical bills are so large I had to leave home to find work. I tried to find a job near her, but nothing I was qualified for paid enough to make much difference. Then I saw the advertisement for becoming a Harvey Girl. I applied, and I volunteered to come to Needles because of the bonus pay."

Meghan chewed her lower lip and took Natalie's hands, squeezing them. She'd taken the Harvey job more as a lark, an adventure, a desire to see more of the world than Mantorville, Minnesota, and to do something bigger and more challenging than helping out in the family business and waiting for someone to come along to marry her. And here was Natalie, far from home where she was needed, trying to earn enough money to help with a relative's medical care. And she'd never said a word, never complained, carrying the burden all alone.

"I'm sorry you've got an ill relative, but why is it a secret? Lots of the girls here send money home to help out. There's no shame in that. Is this relative's condition worse?"

Natalie swallowed and freed one of her hands to wipe her cheeks. She pressed her lips together, as if battling with herself. Finally, she whispered, "The sick woman is my mother-in-law."

"It's an honorable thing for you to help your mother— What? Mother-*in-law*?" Meghan lost her balance and toppled onto her backside. She braced herself on her palms, sprawled in an unladylike heap. "Mother-in-law as in. . . ?" She gulped. "But that would mean. . . You're a widow?" A frown tugged at her forehead as she grappled with this notion.

"No, I'm not a widow. At least I pray I'm not." Her eyes closed, and a wave of pain contorted her features. "My husband is a soldier. By now he's in Europe."

"You're married?" Her voice squeaked.

"Shhh! Not so loud." Natalie made a damping motion. "Do you want the whole hotel to hear you?"

"I'm sorry." Meghan lowered her voice and straightened her limbs until she could wrap her arms around her updrawn knees. "It just caught me so off-guard. Married. No wonder you want to keep it a secret. Have you been married long? How did your husband feel about you leaving your family to take this job?"

"Derek has no idea I've left home. Things happened so fast. We were already engaged when America entered the war, and we decided to marry before he enlisted." A shiver rippled through her slight frame. "He wanted me to have his pension if anything happened to him. He left for training, and while he was gone, his mother had a stroke. I had left my job as a store clerk when we got married, and they hired someone else in my place. In any case I knew that salary would never cover hospital and doctor bills. When I saw the Harvey ad, I jumped at it. Derek got leave to come home and visit his mother for a few days before he shipped out, and we, his parents and I, decided we wouldn't tell him I was leaving for California. He had enough to worry about. He returned to his unit the day before I met you in Chicago to come here."

"Oh, Natalie." Meghan pressed her fingertips to her lips.

"I know. I'm breaking all kinds of rules. If Mrs. Gregory found out, she'd have me on the first eastbound train. But she can't know. I can't lose this job. My salary and Derek's army pay are supporting all of us. My father-in-law is elderly, and it's all he can do to take care of his wife. He can't work. I have to stay here, at least until Derek comes home again." Her blue eyes swam with tears and worry. "You won't tell, will you?"

"Of course not. I'm only sorry you didn't tell me sooner. Here I've been blathering about silly things like dances and dresses and such, and you've been worrying about your mother-in-law and your—it seems so strange to say it—your husband. No wonder you look so pale and drawn all the time. And you've the appetite of a finch, down to skin and bones."

"Sometimes I think I'll go mad with worry, but I'm so thankful for this job. It keeps me busy; I can't worry too much while I'm working, and I'm making far more money than I could at home, and I send almost all of it back there. I only wish I didn't have to lie to Mrs. Gregory or to Derek. If he knew, he'd be crazy with worry. He's always been protective of me, since we were kids. One of the last things he said to me before he left was how glad he was that I was safe with his parents. That he rested easier knowing we were together and taking care of each other."

"How do you keep it secret from your husband?"

"I write letters to him and send them home to Springfield. His father sends them on for me. When one of Derek's letters arrives there for me, they pass it along here. We can only hope no one from home writes to him, at least until after I've made enough to cover the medical bills and Genevieve is doing better." Natalie glanced at the clock. "We'd better hurry and dress. I wish I didn't have to go to this social. The last thing I feel like doing tonight is dancing with strangers."

"Maybe we can work something out so you don't have to. There's always the refreshment table, though after a day of serving food, you probably don't want to do that either."

"Actually, if it meant I could get out of dancing, I'd serve punch until sunup."

A half hour later, they walked out onto the loggia. This wide, covered seating area on the second floor was reserved for hotel guests and provided an excellent place to view the rugged desert hills surrounding the town. Festive lanterns illuminated the open area reserved for dancing, and a long table held a punch bowl and a variety of cookies and cakes prepared by the bakery that day. A small cluster of musicians optimistically calling themselves the Needles City Orchestra tuned up, and Harvey Girls fluttered around like brightly colored flowers with nary a black dress or starched apron to be seen. More guests drifted up the stairs, local men and women in their Sunday best. Meghan spied Mr. Weeks from the department store and waggled her fingers his direction. He had a smiling woman on his arm whom Meghan took to be his wife.

Mrs. Gregory sailed across the floor in a dark blue dress with black beading along the bodice and down the front of the skirt, clapping her hands for attention. She'd powdered her face and wore a bit of lip rouge, which made her look a bit softer, especially under the light of the paper lanterns.

"Ladies and gentlemen, thank you all for coming. I'd like to give you a few instructions as to how this social will work. First, note the donation box on the end of the refreshment table. All proceeds go to support the Red Cross, and we ask you to be generous. As many of you know, this is a dime-a-dance social. So all the ladies, if you will pick up dance cards from Miss Ralston"—she waved to Jenny standing by the conductor—"and gentlemen, you are free to either pay each lady for a dance or you can settle up at the end of the evening. We want you all to have a good time and to dance a lot. Remember, every dime you donate is a blow against the Kaiser." She fisted her hand and swung it upward in a little arc as if bopping the German leader in the nose.

Meghan, her mind still ruminating on Natalie's surprising disclosure, waited her turn to pick up a dance card. All the while, she scanned the room. Boys of sixteen or seventeen huddled together, eyeing the girls. Middle-aged men in suits, most with their wives on their arms, talked in small bunches. Conspicuous by their absence were young men. Every man between eighteen and thirty-five, it seemed, was gone from the town of Needles.

Except one.

Though he'd said he wouldn't come, she spent a few moments imagining what it would be like if he had. Would he ask her to dance? What would he look like all dressed up? And why, out of all the young men in town, hadn't he enlisted? She supposed his work for the army was important, but someone older could train horses, couldn't they? Someone who wasn't able to enlist? She'd wanted to ask him when they sat on the riverbank, but something wouldn't let her voice the words. As if she was afraid of the answer. His jibes about the war had set up a faint echo of doubt in the back of her mind, but she quelled it whenever it whispered.

She remembered the strong feel of his arms around her when he'd rescued her, his face only inches from her own, the scents of sunshine and soap and hard-working male surrounding her. At the lunch counter, in the midst of all those soldiers, he'd looked closed off, almost wounded. She had a feeling there was so much more to Caleb McBride than anyone here knew, and she longed to discover more about him. Many times a day, and even more often at night as she lay in bed waiting for sleep to claim her, her thoughts strayed to the horseman, and though she watched the door of the lunchroom for him every day, hoping he would come in, true to his word, he stayed away.

"May I have the pleasure?" A young man with a cowlick stood at her elbow.

"Of course." She smiled at him, offered him her dance card, and read the name when he returned it to her. "Of course, Lawrence. I'd be delighted." She allowed him to swing her into a waltz, joining the twirling figures already dancing.

Her dance partner was so nervous, he stared at his feet and counted the steps under his breath. Perhaps a bit of conversation would help him relax. "Are you a student at the high school?"

He looked up, stumbled, and righted himself. "Um, no. Not anymore. I graduated last month. Just turned eighteen." His narrow chest swelled a bit, and he dared another glance at her face. "Just enlisted, too. Gonna go kill me some Germans."

A lump formed in Meghan's throat at the eager light in the boy's eyes. He was so young, on the cusp of manhood, eager to go to war. How soon before battle jaded his fresh, smiling eyes or snuffed out his life altogether.

She smiled her warmest smile at him. "I'm proud of you. Everyone must do their duty. We'll all be here praying for your safe return."

Natalie stayed by the refreshment table, serving punch and cakes. When Meghan stopped by after the third dance, Natalie smiled and winked. "Mrs. Gregory approved my overseeing the refreshments." A bit of color had come back into her pale cheeks, and her eyes looked less tense. Perhaps sharing her secret with someone really had eased some of her burden.

Meghan danced and chatted and got to know the people of Needles. They were friendly and accepting of the Harvey Girls. Most of the men worked in some way for the railroad, and they considered the waitresses part of the Santa Fe Railroad family. She enjoyed herself and added quite a few dimes to the donation box. She even added a few names to her quilt list, thanks to Mr. Weeks spreading the word. But the night lacked a certain luster.

Then at half past eight, Caleb McBride emerged at the head of the stairs. Impossible to miss his entrance, because a murmur went through the crowd and Mrs. Gregory sucked in a sharp breath. Meghan, dancing with the man who owned the drugstore, tripped a bit and had to right herself, leaning on her partner's guiding arm.

Caleb looked fine all dressed up. Better than fine. He took her breath right away.

Caleb resisted the urge to turn around and go back down the steps. He was all kinds of a fool. In spite of repeated warnings to himself to steer clear of the hotel, this dance, and Meghan Thorson, here he was, dressed like a strutting turkey and acting like a besotted beagle pup.

He scanned the crowd, aware of the eyes turned his way but trying to ignore them as he sought out the one person he'd come to see. There she was, dancing with the druggist. What was his name? Cooper? Hooper? Didn't matter. Caleb never went into the drugstore anyway. Come to think of it, he hardly went anywhere in Needles anymore. Feed store, Claypool's for groceries once a month, Doc Bates's, and to church where he sat in the back, kept to himself, and ducked out the minute the music for the final hymn started.

And now here he was at the El Garces. Second time this month. He was definitely loco.

The song ended, and Meghan slipped from her partner's arms and allowed him to lead her off the dance floor. The druggist's touch on her elbow made Caleb's gut churn, and he forced himself not to go over and yank the man's hand away from her. Surprised at the strength of his reaction, he reminded himself he had no claim at all on Meghan, and moreover, he didn't want to have one. But if that was the case, why was he here? Why was he doing this to himself? He was like a starving, penniless man standing outside a bakery window, salivating over what he couldn't taste. Coming here was a mistake. He could still get out of here. It wasn't too late.

Then she looked right at him, and her smile smote him in the chest like the kick of a mule. She excused herself from her partner and walked toward him. He hadn't counted on talking to her, hadn't thought beyond just getting to see her. He'd figured by now Mrs. Gregory would've spilled out all her dislike of him to Meghan, and Meghan would disdain him like the rest of the town. Just getting a glimpse of her would've been enough. But here she was, coming at him all friendly, like he was a welcome guest.

That yellow dress was sure something. Pretty as a spring sunrise. And her smile. He couldn't look away. She acted like he was the only one in the room and she couldn't wait to talk to him. Unlike every other person here. He hadn't missed the pinched lips, the whispers, the pulling aside of skirts as he passed.

Her green eyes sparkled in the glow of the paper lanterns and lightbulbs strung along the balconies as she stopped before him and held out her hand. "Caleb, I'm so glad you came." Her smile warmed him, and he couldn't help but notice how burnished her coppery hair looked and how a rosy tint graced her cheeks.

"Evening. After your reminder down at the river that everyone should do his part, I figured I should come and lend my support to the cause." His voice rasped like he'd swallowed a fistful of horseshoe nails. When their fingers touched, warmth zipped up his arm, and he had to remind himself to let go.

"I'd been hoping to see you in the lunchroom, but I suppose you're busy with your horses. How is the training going?"

"Fine." She'd been watching for him at the hotel. That thought shot him through with golden arrows, and he cautioned himself, though it seemed to do precious little good. Her friendly reception was like water to his parched insides.

She flicked open a lacy, yellow fan and stirred the air, but she wasn't using it as a flirting tool like some girls did. No lowering her chin or batting her eyes. Instead, she looked right at him, her lips parted, eyes such a deep green he wanted to sink into them and forget to come back to reality. "I hope the work won't keep you away indefinitely. With so many strangers and travelers coming through, it's nice to see a familiar face once in a while."

He dragged his mind away from how creamy-smooth her skin looked and how several delicate russet curls wisped at the nape of her neck. "I'll be sure to stop by next time I'm in town."

Now where had that come from? Hadn't he just told himself he wasn't going to—?

"The orchestra is about ready for another song." She consulted her dance card.

And he could dance about as well as a peg-legged duck on ice. How was he going to get out of this? Why hadn't he thought how awkward it would be coming to a dance and not being able to take a turn around the floor?

Because he'd been too busy thinking about how lonely his life was and about how pleasant it was when a pretty girl noticed him. Not just noticed him, but was nice to him. Treated him with respect instead of like something she needed to scrape off her shoe.

She glanced at him expectantly, and he noted the three men waiting nearby, eager to claim her for a dance.

"I'm not much for dancing. If I pay the dime, will you sit out this dance with me?"

A small furrow appeared between her brows, and questions invaded her eyes, but she nodded. "Of course. Would you like some punch?"

He cupped her elbow, savoring the whisper-softness of her skin, and led her to the refreshment table. The three men hoping for a dance faded away, and he made sure his face bore not a trace of smugness.

"You remember Natalie?" Meghan accepted a cup of lemonade.

"I do. A pleasure, ma'am." He reached up to touch the brim of his hat before he remembered he'd left it downstairs at the hatcheck.

Back home they'd call it the coat check, but the need for coats was so rare here, he didn't even own one anymore.

Natalie handed him a crystal punch cup. His fingers were way too big to fit them into the tiny handle, so he wrapped his fist around the whole cup instead. "Lots of folks here tonight." A sip. Tart coolness slid down his throat.

Music started up and couples swung out onto the floor. A few dowdy matrons sat on benches along the balcony rails, and a few older men clustered at the far end of the loggia, smoking cigars. He was the only man over twenty and under forty in sight. The old biddies glared at him, especially Mrs. Gregory.

Caleb tried to cut her some slack. After all, she was a widow woman who had just sent her only son off to war. She had to be scared and probably mad at circumstances and life. For all he knew, she was maybe even mad at God. Lotta good that would do. Caleb had been known to get mad at God himself from time to time. Didn't change anything, except to make himself miserable.

With a grimace he drained his cup and gave it back to Natalie.

Meghan sipped her punch, watching the dancers and only occasionally glancing up at him. What was wrong with him? He'd thought of not much else than being with her over the past month, and now, when he had the opportunity, he couldn't think of a thing to say.

She set her cup on the table. "It's so warm up here. Would you like to go down to the lobby? I know it isn't much cooler, but the sound of the fountain always refreshes me. I think I've earned a break."

The tightness in his chest relaxed as they made their way down the stairs and away from all the prying eyes. Concentrating on concealing his limp and thankful she wasn't in a hurry, he even grew bold enough to put his hand on the small of her back—the same place her apron bow usually rested—to guide her through the deserted foyer to the edge of the fountain. Moonlight tinted everything bluish-white and cast deeper shadows under the balconies and loggia. Over their heads, the music drifted down like rain.

Water splashed from the marble tower in the middle of the pool and rippled the surface of the water. He skirted potted palms and ferns scattered around the edges of the open space and guided her past a row of empty wicker rocking chairs. White pillars stood at attention around them like silent sentinels. The only electric light came from wall sconces along the perimeter of the atrium, creating an almost magical mix of lamplight and starlight.

"It's so peaceful here in the evenings. Though most nights I'm too tired to enjoy it. And Mrs. Gregory doesn't really like to see us lounging in the public areas. She says the guests don't pay good money to run into the hired help in the lobby."

"She runs a pretty tight ship, doesn't she?"

Meghan shrugged. "I suppose so, though from what I under-stand, that's what the company requires. Everything here has a proper procedure, and it's Mrs. Gregory's job to see that we follow it. She has high expectations, and at first I thought they were impossible, but you know what? Now that I've been here for a few weeks, I find myself able to meet those expectations and standards without too much effort. And I love the work, especially serving the soldiers. They're so brave and manly in their uniforms."

He pressed his lips together and let his hand fall away from her back. Every conversation always seemed to wind its way back to the war. His gut tightened, and he shoved his hands into his trouser pockets.

She knelt and scooped up a handful of water, letting the droplets trickle through her fingers. "And they're always so nice and full of fun. It's heartbreaking to think that some of them won't be coming home. That's why we must do all we can, like tonight's appeal for funds, to see that our soldiers have the best of everything. That's why I'm working on a project, a rather ambitious project, to raise one thousand dollars to purchase an ambulance to send to Europe to help our boys. I know it's a lot to take on, but after hearing the speech that Mr. Gibson from the Red Cross gave, and knowing how badly our soldiers need help, I couldn't do any less." She was so eager and innocent. How soon before she realized that life couldn't be conquered just because you wanted to conquer it? Someone needed to educate her before she got hurt.

"A thousand dollars? Where are you going to get that kind of money? I'd be surprised if tonight's dance netted you more than twenty-five after you take out the money for the refreshments and such." No one in their right mind would try to raise that kind of money, not here in Needles where most folks made less than a thousand dollars in a whole year.

"Oh, I expect to see it accomplished. The cause is too great for me to fail, and anyway, I gave my word." She linked her arm through his and did a happy little hop. "Mrs. Gregory is going to be so surprised. And Mr. Gibson. He came to the organizational meeting to get us all started on service projects, and he'll be back in a few months to see how we've done. Everyone chose a project and how much they thought they could raise."

"And you put yourself down for a thousand dollars. What are you going to sell to raise that? The Statue of Liberty?" He jerked his thumb at a war poster someone had fastened to one of the columns. Lady Liberty stood with outstretched hands, imploring America to send her sons to protect her and her Allies. The words came out harsher than he had meant, and she let her hand fall away from his arm.

Those incredible eyes blinked, and her arched brows drew together in puzzlement. "No, nothing like that. I'm making a quilt. A Red Cross signature quilt, and I'll sell space for folks to have their name embroidered on it."

"That's crazy. Who would want to pay to have their name put on a blanket?" The notion baffled him.

Her spine stiffened, and her chin came up. "Patriotic Americans, that's who. People who realize what an honor it is to sacrifice a little of our comfort here so that those men fighting for our freedoms, who have sacrificed much more than we ever could, can have proper medical treatment, food, and clothing. I'm not trying to squeeze Needles to death. I have a plan to go door-to-door in the neighborhoods, visit all the local businesses, and I got permission to have a donation jar on the front desk. That way travelers who are so inclined can donate and print their name on one of the slips I'll leave there. Dozens of people come through here every day, people with enough money to travel. Surely some will contribute. Not all the money has to come from the citizens of Needles. I've thought it all out. I'm not stupid, you know." Her voice vibrated with fervor, and her green eyes glowed with the conviction of her cause. He couldn't help but notice her beauty as she stood before him all zealous and eager in the starlight.

"Someone ought to take your photograph like that. Or paint you for a recruitment poster. You'd sell a million war bonds and have soldiers enlisting in droves."

Relaxing, she gave him a soft tap on the arm. "Don't be silly. Not with this red hair and freckles. I'm no great American beauty, not like Natalie." A touch of something wistful crept into her voice. As if she knew without a doubt the truth of her words and longed to be different.

His voice went gruff on him. "Natalie's all right, but she's not to every man's taste. Some men like fiery redheads who believe in things so strongly they can almost stir a dedicated cynic to action."

She raised luminous eyes to him, and he found himself stepping closer, drawn to her fire and innocent, untouched air. Her sweet lips parted, and a slight breeze fluttered the lace on the neckline of her dress. His fingers found hers, entwining, slowly drawing her closer. Time seemed to stand still as he drowned in her eyes, in her goodness, drawn to her fire and courage. He had a feeling this girl held the power to heal some of the broken places in his heart, the starved, atrophied, dead places he'd locked away.

Her breath came in shallow gasps, as if she, too, were caught in a maelstrom of unfamiliar feelings. It was all so sudden, and she was so sweet and passionate and fresh. He wanted to crush her to him, to stave off the loneliness that stalked him.

It had been so long since he'd allowed himself to feel anything but anger and shame. Even longer since he'd let himself care how someone else thought of him. Warning bells clanged in his head as his mouth went dry. She wore a beguiling perfume that wrapped around him, muffling the doubts. The last time he'd let his defenses down, had allowed someone into his heart, she'd used that power to crush him. And here he was on the verge of making the same mistake again.

He drew her nearer. His lips hovered over hers, a mere breath away. She wasn't resisting, but then again, she was so innocent, she probably didn't know of the raging hunger sweeping over him, the need to kiss her and see if she tasted as sweet as she looked. The warning bells got louder. He had to stop before he got hurt, or before he was so deeply ensnared he couldn't escape.

"What on earth are you doing?" Mrs. Gregory's scalded-cat screech jerked them apart. "Miss Thorson." Like an avenging angel, the head waitress strode across the courtyard, hands fisted at her sides.

Meghan backed away from him a couple of steps. "Mrs. Gregory, I—we—"

"Your behavior is scandalous. Bad enough for you to be caught dallying with a man right in the hotel, but this man!" She raised her bony forefinger to pierce the air before Caleb's nose. "I won't stand for it. If you want to keep your job, Miss Thorson, you'll get yourself upstairs to that dance this instant." Cold, terrible wrath poured from her eyes.

"We weren't doing anything wrong. Is it wrong to get a little air? We're here in plain sight. We were talking about raising money for the Red Cross. Mr. McBride is very interested in helping out the war effort in any way he can, I'm sure. Why else would he come to the dance?"

Her defensive tone hurt Caleb. Why should she have to explain herself to a woman who deserved no explanation? He winced when she invoked the name of the Red Cross, which she seemed to hold sacred.

Mrs. Gregory snorted. "Why indeed? He's shown not the slightest interest in the war or our efforts until now. In fact, until you arrived in Needles, he never came to the hotel, not even to eat. He's like a stray dog slinking around. A yellow-bellied cur at that. And if you know what's good for you, you'll stop encouraging him. It's disgraceful, and I won't have it. Get yourself upstairs now. And when this dance is finished, you and I are going to have a frank discussion about your behavior and your choice of companions."

Caleb stepped between her and Meghan. "Mrs. Gregory, nothing happened. If you want to be angry, be angry with me, not Meghan."

"Don't tell me what to do. I am constantly reminding Meghan not to be too familiar with the young male customers. I should've known it from the first day she arrived. This is the second time I've found the two of you in a rather compromising situation. The first could've been explained away as an accident, but there is nothing accidental about this." She flicked her hand at them. "You, Miss Thorson, are supposed to be upstairs earning money for the Red Cross. Not only are you in violation of the conduct rules for a

Harvey Girl, you are stealing from the war effort by your absence at the dance."

Meghan's reddened face paled, and her eyes widened.

"I paid for a dance, Mrs. Gregory," Caleb cut in.

"That may be, however, three dances have come and gone since you two scuttled off."

Taking a deep breath to keep from saying something he would regret, something that might make the situation worse for Meghan, Caleb stepped back. "Mrs. Gregory, I apologize for your distress, though there is no need to take your ire at me out on Meghan. She isn't at fault here." He dug in his pocket and withdrew a dollar. "Here you go, Meghan. Put that in the kitty. It will more than cover the time you spent with me."

He had to press the folded bill into her palm. "Go on upstairs. And thank you for telling me about your project. I'm sure it will be a success."

A *harrumph* from Mrs. Gregory. "We don't need money from the likes of you, Mr. McBride. The Red Cross in Needles will not take a coward's cash. You won't assuage your conscience in this manner, or for so paltry a sum. I may not be able to ban you from this hotel, but I can make sure you stay away from my girls. I won't have their reputations sullied, not by your amorous advances nor by being associated with a yellow coward like you."

Meghan stood frozen, her expression shifting from guilt to confusion. Soon the confusion would give way to disgust, the same disgust dripping from Mrs. Gregory's every word once Meghan had a talk with the head waitress. A sense of fatalism gripped him.

Why even bother to fight back, to declare he wasn't evading military service? She'd only ask why he didn't enlist, and he'd rather be boiled in oil than ever let Mrs. Gregory know of his leg. He'd been a first-class fool to come here, to think that anything had or would change. In the eyes of this town, he was and always would be a coward.

Meghan climbed the stairs to the party and dropped the well-creased dollar into the collection box. Natalie drew her behind the refreshment table, her pale blue eyes full of questions.

"Where did you get off to? Mrs. Gregory is searching for you, and she looks fierce."

"I know. She found me." Meghan couldn't keep the tremor out of her voice. She'd just come within a small cat's whisker of kissing Caleb McBride.

"What happened? Where were you?"

"Downstairs in the courtyard by the fountain."

Natalie searched Meghan's face and jumped to the correct conclusion. "And you weren't alone, were you? You went down there with Mr. McBride. Meghan, what were you thinking?"

"I wasn't thinking. But nothing happened. We just walked a little and talked. It's not illegal to talk to someone, is it?"

Mrs. Gregory emerged at the top of the stairs. Her piercing eyes found Meghan, but she was prevented from marching over as someone stopped her to talk. The current waltz ended, and the band began to pack their instruments. A smattering of applause rippled from the guests, and several of the musicians bowed and nodded. The dancers seemed loath to leave, however, and they lingered in little groups, visited the punch table one last time, and strolled under the colorful lights.

Filling yet another punch cup, Natalie handed it across the table. She kept her voice low. "It isn't illegal to talk to someone, but it is risky, especially the likes of Mr. McBride. After you left, Mr. Weeks and his wife mentioned to me that Mr. McBride isn't well thought of here in town. Some folks say he's a coward who won't enlist. They say he's making a mint off the war by selling horses to the army. What kind of a man would try to make a profit off a war he's too afraid to fight in? Everyone's shocked to see him here at all. He usually stays away from town, and he never accepts hospitality, not that it sounds like anyone's offering him any these days. Folks say he's a recluse."

The need to defend him coursed through Meghan. "He's not like that. Surely he has an exemption to the draft, since he's in agriculture? He works for the army."

Natalie shook her head. "Mr. Weeks says since he doesn't grow crops or raise animals for food, he shouldn't be exempt. And lots of men enlist anyway, even if they could claim an exemption."

"Girls."

Meghan jumped as Mrs. Gregory's hand came down on her shoulder. "I can see, Miss Daviot, that you are filling Miss Thorson in on a few facts. You would do well to heed her warnings, Miss Thorson. Mr. McBride is not a suitable companion for any young lady, much less a Harvey Girl. You mustn't allow your head to be turned. Caleb McBride is a coward and an opportunist. He allows others to fight for his freedom while at the same time pocketing a profit at their expense. Surely you don't want to be linked with such a man?"

Meghan's cheeks grew hot as she realized that several partygoers had stopped talking to listen in. Heads nodded and tilted toward one another, and a couple of hands went up to shield whispers.

"Of course you wouldn't," Mrs. Gregory answered for her. "You may not appreciate it just now, but I truly do have your best interests at heart."

Chapter 7

Meghan called at the front desk for her mail and Natalie's.

"Here you are, Miss." The desk clerk's gray moustache twitched. "Something to enjoy on your afternoon off?"

She scanned the envelopes. One from Mama, and a small, square envelope addressed to her in a hand she didn't know. For Natalie, a nice thick one from Indiana.

"Thank you, Mr. Johns." Flashing him a quick smile, she headed out the main doors to the park in front of the hotel where Natalie was already spreading a blanket under one of the trees. A picnic basket rested beside the trunk, and Meghan anticipated a quiet afternoon of reading and not thinking about work. The thin shade cast by the trees in Santa Fe Park did little to lower the heat, but at least today there was a breeze. Short of going downstairs to sit in the walk-in refrigerator—something Mrs. Gregory forbid the girls to do, more's the pity—the park was the coolest place they could find to spend their afternoon off.

Natalie eased down onto the blanket and looked up when Meghan arrived. "Anything?"

"Here you go." She tossed the letter. "It's a fat one, too."

Settling herself, Meghan slit open the letter from Mama, eager for news from home. She could almost hear Mama's Irish lilt as a blanket of homesickness settled around her shoulders.

> *Your papa is forever polishing that motorcar. He takes any*
> *excuse to get it out onto the road. The Ladies' Aid purchased*
> *a knitting machine to assist in making stockings and hats for*
> *our soldiers. It works fairly well, I suppose, but I prefer my old*
> *knitting needles.*

Word of the Ladies' Aid reminded Meghan that she needed to get busy on her quilt. Over the last three weeks, she'd managed the cutting and begun the piecing, but she still needed folks to donate to get their names on the quilt. A lot of folks.

She finished Mama's letter and unfolded the brief note she'd included from Lars. She glanced at the date. Written almost six weeks ago.

Hey, Megsie, The familiar term made her throat tighten. Nobody but Lars called her Megsie.

> *Ma tells me you've moved out west and taken a job in a*
> *hotel. You're a Harvey Girl? Don't they have a lot of rules?*
> *How are you holding up? Remember when you took it upon*

*yourself to campaign for class president, even though the
teacher said you couldn't since you were a girl? Bless me if you
didn't convince her to change the rules and then went out
and won that election. You never were one for following the
crowd. I figured you'd have taken over the Ladies' Aid or the
Red Cross by now. I can't imagine you handing out menus and
filling coffee cups. You're too much of a crusader. I'm surprised
General Pershing hasn't knocked on your door and asked you
to run the Expeditionary Forces for him. I've been telling my
buddies here that if they'd just put you in charge of the War
Department, we'd all be home by Mother's Day.*

She chuckled. Her brother had teased her ever since that day
in the seventh grade when she'd challenged convention and gotten
a whole class to change their minds about who could run for class
president. Her folks had both said she would get herself in trouble
with her crusading someday, but Lars was always proud of her for
dreaming big and taking up causes others tried to ignore. What
would he say about her signature quilt?

He closed with the plea to keep sending letters.

*They're what keep me going these days, Megsie. Don't
let on to the folks, because they don't need the worry, but
conditions here are horrible. We're stuck in these trenches day
after day, up to our knees in mud most of the time, and always
and forever dreading the order to go "over the top" and into
the path of enemy fire. I keep my gas mask with me all the*

time, and my rifle, but we all know that when it's your time,
you won't have time to grab either one. Twice now I've been
nearly buried alive when a mortar shell hit our trench. I've
lost so many friends. Some days it's all I can do to hang on.
Pray for me, Megsie. And write often.

Love, Lars.

She glanced up, blinking hard. Her poor brother. Mortar shells
and mustard gas and mud. How she wished she could do more to
help him and all the boys over there. Pouring coffee and sewing
quilts seemed so feeble in the light of what they faced every day.

Natalie was lost in her own letter, so Meghan picked up her other
piece of mail. Turning the card over, she frowned. No return address
and no stamp. Hand delivered? Slowly, she stuck her fingernail
under the flap and ran it along the edge.

A single sheet of plain white paper. Her gaze dropped to the
signature, and her heart started bumping. She swallowed and raced
through the lines.

Miss Thorson,

I apologize for any difficulty I might've caused you last
Friday evening. Now that you know the regard in which I am
held in this town, I am sure you want no further dealings with
me. I wish you all the best with your project. You even inspired
me, and I'm beyond inspiration these days.

Sincerely,
Caleb McBride.

She read the lines again, remembering his face in the moonlight, the stoic mask that fell over his features when Mrs. Gregory found them. And all the questions flooded back. Why hadn't he enlisted? Was he really just out to make a profit off this war? Comparing Lars's letter with all she'd heard said about Caleb set up quaking doubts. Perhaps Mrs. Gregory was right. And the head waitress wasn't the only one who held such beliefs. The temperature of the party had gone down several notches when Caleb arrived at the dance.

And yet, Meghan couldn't deny the pull of attraction she felt toward Caleb. Something about him drew her, and it wasn't just his handsome features. There was something inside him, something wounded and sheltered and guarded that she longed to uncover, bring to the light, and heal.

She shook her head for being so fanciful. Lars would tease her about her penchant for helping lame dogs cross the road and taking up lost causes.

Natalie folded her letter and used her cuff to swipe at her eyes.

"Is everything all right at home?"

"Yes, thank the Lord. My mother-in-law is doing better. She's starting to talk again, though slowly, and she's learning to do more with her left hand. The doctor is sending his nurse every day still to bathe her and change the linens, but the money I send home is covering that expense with a little left over for them to buy food. The church is also helping out, bringing meals and supplies."

"Any word from Derek?"

She nodded, and whether it was from the heat or something Derek had put into his letter, her cheeks pinked. "He's fine. Misses us all. He says he can't wait to come home and take a walk with me down by the creek. When we were first courting, we'd stand on the bridge and drop leaves into the water and make a wish, then hurry to the other side of the bridge to see which one came out first. A silly game, but so fun." Her eyes took on a dreamy, faraway look. "If we were together now on that bridge, neither of us would have to make a wish, because our most important wish would've already come true."

Meghan tamped down the surprising envy that oozed out of some hidden place inside. What would it be like to have someone's fondest wish be just to be with you? Unbidden, Caleb's face rose to her mind. *Stop being silly. He would never feel that way about you, and you shouldn't feel that way about him.*

Footsteps on the gravel path caught her attention. Jenny Ralston, skirts gripped in one hand and the other gripping her lace headband, ran toward them.

"Did you hear?" She flopped down onto the grass beside Meghan and Natalie, panting.

"Did we hear what, and you'd better not let Mrs. Gregory catch you sprawling on the grass in your uniform." Meghan nudged her shoulder. "You should've heard the bawling out she gave Sarah Jane yesterday for having a coffee stain that was no bigger than a pin head on her apron. Imagine what she'd be like if she found a grass stain."

"She won't have time to notice, not with the news she just got."

"It must be something to have you running in this heat." Natalie tucked her letter back into its envelope and leaned back against a tree trunk, letting her eyes fall shut. A trickle of worry coasted down

ERICA VETSCH

Meghan's spine. Natalie looked paler and more drawn every day. She was still tired at night, and she didn't eat enough.

"Natalie, what say we go back inside and sneak down to the cold store and cool off? It's hot enough, I'm thinking of going wading in the fountain."

"I'm not getting caught doing either. I need this job too much." Natalie spoke without opening her eyes, her voice just above a murmur.

Though she'd only been playing, a prickle of guilt feathered across Meghan's conscience. "I know, Nat, and I won't do anything to jeopardize either of our jobs."

Jenny grabbed Meghan's arm. "Are you even listening to me? This is the biggest news to hit Needles since the railroad came to town. Mrs. Gregory just got word that a *celebrity train* will be coming through on a Red Cross appeal trip. And guess who will be on it?"

"Woodrow Wilson." Meghan couldn't resist teasing Jenny, though the words "celebrity train" sent her mind spinning and her heart racing.

"Better." Jenny's eyes grew round.

"Better than the president?"

"That's right. The celebrity train will carry none other than Charlie Chaplin and Mary Pickford!" Jenny stacked her hands under her cheek, tilted her head, and batted her eyes. "Can you imagine? Charlie Chaplin and Mary Pickford, right here in little old Needles. And they're dining at the hotel. Mrs. Gregory is about fit to be tied. She's been such a grump since her son enlisted—not that she was exactly cozy before he left, but at least she was bearable—but when she got this news, she actually smiled. A real smile all the way up to her eyes and everything. I hardly recognized the old girl."

Movie stars coming to the hotel. Meghan bit her lower lip. Her mother loved the cinema, and together, she and Meghan had cajoled Papa into taking them over to Rochester whenever a new Mary Pickford film came to the theater. And Charlie Chaplin? Maybe President Wilson and the Kaiser were more famous than Charlie Chaplin, but only maybe.

"When?"

"One week." Jenny stood and smoothed her apron, checking for spots. "That's why I came out here. Mrs. Gregory sent me to fetch you. No more time off until after the movie star train has come and gone. She says we're really going to concentrate on the polishing."

Meghan groaned. "We already do concentrate on the polishing. If I rub those coffee urns any harder, they're going to wear right through."

Jenny held out her hand and pulled Meghan to her feet. "C'mon. She'll be out here in search of us in a minute."

Meghan and Natalie hurried to their room to change, Meghan with alacrity, Natalie lethargic.

"If I wasn't so excited, I'd gripe about missing our afternoon off." Meghan threw her letters onto the dresser and reached for her uniform, but thought better of leaving Caleb's note out in plain sight and tucked it into her top bureau drawer. She lifted her dress off the hanger and shook it out, studying it for flaws. "I hadn't counted on having to wear this again today."

Natalie moved slowly, putting away her letters. "I'd counted on a nap this afternoon. I'm so tired. This heat just saps the life out of me."

"Sounds like no one will get any afternoon naps this week."

The lunchroom, blessedly free of customers at the moment, was in a complete uproar. Harvey Girls bustled and chattered and laughed, and Meghan paused in the doorway. She hadn't realized it, but she really loved her job here at the hotel. They were a team, a well-trained and organized team, serving shoulder-to-shoulder to serve customers and represent the company.

"Girls." Mrs. Gregory clapped her hands, her signal for all work to cease and everyone to pay attention. Meghan had begun to hear those claps in her dreams. Skirts rustled and cutlery clanked as they hurried to gather around the head waitress.

"Girls, I'm sure you've all heard the news. Now, before you get all scatterbrained and giddy, let me assure you, I will not tolerate laxity, shirking, or silliness. You are professionals, and you will behave accordingly. Tonight, after the last train pulls out, we will start with the crown molding in both the dining room and the lunchroom and work our way down, cleaning every inch of every surface."

Meghan joined in the groan that rippled through the group. As if they didn't clean and polish nearly every waking minute already.

"I know." Mrs. Gregory made damping motions with her hands. "However, there will be a reward at the end. I will be watching each of you this coming week. The Harvey Girl who works the hardest, does the best job serving customers, keeping her station clean, and acts as the best possible representative of the company, will be given the honor of serving our distinguished guests when they arrive. Every girl, even the lunchroom staff, will be considered when I make my decision."

Meghan's mind fizzed and popped. A glimmer of hope that perhaps, if she worked hard enough, she could actually meet Mary Pickford and Charlie Chaplin, rose in her chest. And perhaps in the doing, she'd get off Mrs. Gregory's naughty list. They hadn't gotten off to a great start together, and since being found strolling in the moonlight with Caleb McBride, Meghan had the feeling Mrs. Gregory had been looking for any reason to fire Meghan and send her packing.

This was her chance. And she wasn't going to waste it. Her confidence in her abilities as a waitress had grown since that first day, and though Mrs. Gregory still found reasons to criticize, Meghan knew she was good at her job. Perhaps good enough to be moved to the dining room. Perhaps good enough to serve Mr. Chaplin and Miss Pickford.

Tiredness fell away, and she dove into the work. She had seven days until the train arrived. Seven days to prepare and prove herself.

The housekeeping staff, the kitchen crew, the busboys, and the groundskeepers joined in the task. Mr. Stock and Mrs. Gregory conferred often, compared notes, and critiqued. Meghan plastered a smile on her face, spoke only pleasant words, and worked until she could barely move.

One of her assigned chores was to remove the glass globes from the light fixtures and hand them down to Natalie who took each one while also holding onto the ladder for Meghan.

"Don't you dare drop one of these. That would be the end. Can you imagine the tizzy Mrs. Gregory would be in if one of the light bulbs was left bare?" She passed a frosted shade down while studying the whorls and twists of brass that made up the fixture itself. "There, that's the last. Now I just need the polish and a rag, and I'll have these lights shining like the King's scepter in no time."

The ladder wobbled, and Meghan clutched the top. "Whoa. Natalie?"

Natalie had abandoned her post of ladder-steadier and leaned against the lunch counter, pressing her hand to her forehead. Hurrying down as fast as prudence dictated, Meghan joined her friend.

"What is it? Are you ill?"

Keeping her eyes closed, Natalie took deep breaths. Her pulse jumped in her throat, and a faint sheen of perspiration clustered at her hairline. At last she opened her eyes and swallowed. "Sorry."

"What happened? Do you need to sit down?" Meghan tried to guide her to a lunch counter stool.

"I'm fine." Natalie resisted gently. "It was just a dizzy spell. The heat and working so hard got to me, and I imagine craning my neck gave me a spot of vertigo."

Her face was still the color of fresh milk, and her hand trembled as she smoothed her hair.

"Are you sure? Maybe you should take a break."

"No. I'm better now." She lifted the box of globes. "I'll just get these to soaking in hot water, and I'll be back."

"Let me take them." Meghan reached for the box, but Natalie swung it away.

"Nonsense. I'm fine. You have polishing to do." She disappeared into the dish room, setting the doors flopping in her wake.

Frowning, Meghan picked up the bottle of brass polish and the cleaning rag and ascended the ladder. The high ceilings of the hotel, helpful in keeping things cool, meant she had quite a climb, especially with no one holding the ladder. And in order to reach the highest points of the light fixture, she would have to stand on the next to last rung.

With a few wobbles, she finally got settled. The pungent smell of the polish wrinkled her nose, but she ignored it and began on the many nooks and crannies. Her arms, raised above her head as they were, began to ache, and a knot formed between her shoulder blades, but she refused to slow down. This very morning, Mrs. Gregory had praised the way she'd dusted and polished the ceiling fans. Meghan had every intention of garnering praise once more for her work on the lights. Sweat beaded on her forehead and trickled from her temples.

Shifting her balance carefully, she tilted the bottle of polish again onto a clean spot on the rag. Below her, Jenny and Sarah Jane attacked the swivel chairs bolted to the floor. Their scrub brushes swished, and not a particle of dust or dirt remained in their wake, not even around the bolt heads. The boots and shoes of hundreds of customers had kicked the stool supports and rested on the rails, but Mrs. Gregory insisted that the seating areas must be as perfect as when they were first installed.

Meghan hummed the popular tune "There's A Long, Long Trail A Winding." As she scrubbed, the humming became singing.

Nights are growing very lonely,
Days are very long;
I'm a-growing weary only
List'ning for your song.
Old remembrances are thronging
Thru my memory.
Till it seems the world is full of dreams
Just to call you back to me.

By the time she reached the chorus, she realized she wasn't singing alone any longer. Jenny and Sarah Jane had joined in, as well as Natalie, now holding the ladder once more.

There's a long, long trail a-winding
Into the land of my dreams,
Where the nightingales are singing
And a white moon beams:
There's a long, long night of waiting
Until my dreams all come true;
Till the day when I'll be going down
That long, long trail with you.

Natalie brushed a tear from her cheek and her lips trembled in a smile. Meghan's heart swelled to think of how happy Natalie would be when Derek came home from the war, safe and sound.

All night long I hear you calling,
Calling sweet and low;

Seem to hear your footsteps falling,

Ev'rywhere I go.

Tho' the road between us stretches

Many a weary mile.

I forget that you're not with me yet,

When I think I see you smile.

They finished with the chorus once more, and when they'd done so, applause from the kitchen and lobby doorways had them laughing. The hotel and kitchen staff grinned and waved, lots of white hats and aprons in evidence. One laundress clapped around a huge armload of bed sheets, her cheeks red and her hair straggling out of her mobcap. A couple of the busboys whistled and stomped before Mr. Stock, smothering a smile, sent them on their way back to work.

Meghan finished wiping the last brass curlicue and crevice and made her way down the ladder. The singing had somehow brought them all together, made them forget how tired they were, and lightened the burdens, if only for a moment. Natalie squeezed Meghan's arm.

"Thank you."

"For what?" Meghan capped the polish and wrapped the rag around the bottle.

"For just being you. I think we all benefitted from the singing. It was fun."

"Miss Thorson."

The prunes-and-persimmons tones of Mrs. Gregory's voice pierced the camaraderie.

"Yes, ma'am?"

"You have the brass polish. The counter rails are not going to polish themselves. I expect them to be finished today."

All the fun went out of the room, and once more heads bent and scrub brushes scratched.

"Yes, ma'am." Though she wanted to stalk over to the head waitress and poke her cheek to see if she was even human, or at the least roll her eyes and sigh, Meghan refrained. If she wanted to be chosen, she couldn't afford to give in to impulses. The restraint nearly killed her.

Think of Mary Pickford. Think of Charlie Chaplin. Think of anything except grabbing Jenny's scrub bucket and anointing Mrs. Gregory with its contents.

Gathering her skirts and apron so she wouldn't be kneeling on them, she began at the far corner. Three horseshoe-shaped lunch counters, each one possessing a continuous brass footrail for customers to rest their shoes on. Over a hundred feet of brass rail and brackets to polish. She raised her head like a gopher above the countertop to check the clock over the kitchen door. Only an hour until the next train arrived. She'd have to break off the polishing and make sure the light fixtures were reassembled. No way would she get the rails done today, not with two more trains expected and all her regular work to do as well.

Mrs. Gregory's foot tapped on the tiles. "Miss Thorson, is there a problem?"

Meghan returned to rubbing, jettisoning the idea of being finished before lights-out tonight. "No, ma'am. I'll get it done."

"See that you do."

By the eve of the celebrity train arrival, Meghan's muscles ached and her patience had worn paper thin. Mrs. Gregory drove everyone hard, but it seemed to her—and Natalie when consulted—that she was especially hard on Meghan.

Barely holding on to her determination not to complain, Meghan worked longer hours, did more tasks, and served more customers than any other Harvey Girl in the hotel. She rose extra early each morning to press her uniform and all her aprons in case she needed to make a hasty change during the day. She even pressed Natalie's, giving her roommate a little more time to sleep. Though it didn't seem to do much good. Natalie looked paler and tighter-drawn every day.

When the last train pulled out that night and the finishing touches had been put on every work station, Mrs. Gregory called all the girls together.

Meghan met Jenny's eyes and smiled, blowing a wisp of hair off her forehead. They'd done it. Not a thing remained on the list on the head waitress's ubiquitous clipboard. Both the lunchroom and dining room smelled of soap and polish, and every surface, from the woodwork to the marble to the brass and silver shone as if it had just come out of the box. Jenny shrugged and bit her lower lip. They'd all worked hard. Now it was up to Mrs. Gregory to choose who would have the honor of serving their special guests.

"You've all done amazing work this week. You are to be commended. I know some of what I asked you to do seemed unreasonable and overly picky, but you've all responded well. I couldn't be happier with the results."

Meghan gripped her hands together until they ached. Surely, after all her work, she would be chosen. No one had stayed later than she, arrived earlier, done more.

"Now to the awarding of the positions." Mrs. Gregory consulted the clipboard she had clasped before her. "Serving the drinks is Miss Ralston."

A quiver went through Meghan. Jenny beamed, her smile lighting up her face. Barbara threw her arm around her much shorter roommate and squeezed her shoulders, a broad grin making her glasses slide on her nose.

"And the waitress for the main table will be. . ."

Meghan held her breath.

"Miss Daviot."

Disappointment crashed through Meghan's chest, and her heart took an elevator to her heels. Natalie? Girls congratulated Natalie while Meghan stood rooted to the spot. Shaking herself, she smiled and hugged her roommate and friend. She was happy for her. She was! But it would be silly to deny being sad for herself.

Mrs. Gregory read the list of girls who would also be working in the dining room. "You six, plus Miss Ralston and Miss Daviot, are the best of the best. There will be nearly one hundred guests on the Red Cross train, and sixty-five of those will be eating in the formal dining room. The overflow will be dining in the lunchroom. You should all get your rest tonight. I expect everything to go smoothly tomorrow and for each girl to do her job as she has been trained."

She sent a pointed look at several of the girls who hadn't been chosen, and that piercing gaze rested longest on Meghan.

Meghan's chin came up. So, she hadn't been chosen. Fine. She'd show Mrs. Gregory she'd made a mistake. Meghan's customers would be the best served, most contented, most taken care of customers the El Garces Lunchroom had ever seen. Natalie and Jenny might be serving cinema royalty, but Meghan's customers would be treated better than royalty. She smiled politely to Mrs. Gregory, as if the decision to leave her off the dining room serving roster met with Meghan's complete approval.

Once back in their room, Natalie tried to apologize. "I wish it was you, Meghan. You deserved it. You worked the hardest, and everyone knows it."

Meghan hung up her dress and slipped into her housecoat. She shrugged and began unpinning her hair. "We all worked hard, and Mrs. Gregory had the final choosing. It's all right."

"But it isn't fair."

"If there's one thing this war and Mrs. Gregory are teaching me, it's that life isn't fair."

"You're taking this better than I thought you would."

"Am I? I'm disappointed, but it isn't the end of the world. I keep reminding myself that others have it far worse than I do." Meghan smiled at her reflection in the dresser mirror. Mocking green eyes stared back at her, rueful, a bit embarrassed. Though she tried to brush it off as no big deal, she knew better, and inside, her heart was bruised. She'd made no bones about how much she wanted to be chosen to serve the movie stars. And she hadn't made it. Hadn't made Mrs. Gregory's cut. Now everyone knew that in spite of her best efforts, she hadn't been good enough. And Mrs. Gregory's choice had little to do with Meghan's work over the past week. From the first, the head waitress had been biased against her, and all because of Caleb McBride. Caleb, who had taken Mrs. Gregory at her word and steered clear of the hotel since the night of the dance. Three weeks, and Meghan hadn't seen so much as a glimpse of him.

And yet he'd occupied her thoughts. How often she'd thought of him while scrubbing and polishing this week. His memory had the power to make her forget the celebrity train. The look on his face when Mrs. Gregory had accused him of being a draft-dodging coward seared her mind, and she knew she should forget about him, but when she was falling asleep, in that blessed twilight between wakefulness and slumber, another memory dominated her thoughts. Caleb McBride, his face so close to hers she imagined she could see her reflection in his eyes, his lips hovering over hers a breath away.

She set her hairbrush down and turned away from the now dreamy-eyed girl in the mirror. *Get a hold of yourself, you ninny. He's brought you nothing but trouble, and he's shirking his military duty. Quit mooning about him and pull yourself together.* "I'm happy for you, Natalie. I really am. You're going to do a wonderful job, and just imagine what you'll have to tell Derek when he comes home."

Natalie sank into the rocker and put her face in her hands, her shoulders shaking. "I only hope he can forgive me for lying to him."

Chapter 8

Caleb climbed out of his truck in front of the Feed and Seed and used his sleeve to wipe the dust off the hood ornament. With the roads so sandy and gritty out here, keeping the automobile clean was impossible, but he couldn't resist buffing the silver radiator cap shaped like a running horse. He'd poured over a catalog for a week trying to make up his mind whether to get the ornament or not, finally deciding to purchase it after squaring it with his conscience to give the equivalent amount in the offering plate the next week.

Joshua joined him, hands jammed in his pockets. "You want to load the feed first?"

"Sure are a lot of people in town." Wagons and motorcars lined the street, and peering through the window of the feed store, he spied quite a crowd at the counter. Not wanting to face all those disapproving eyes, he turned and studied the substantial bulk of the El Garces three blocks up the street. Hard to miss, since it was by far the largest building in Needles. That and the fact that his thoughts had strayed there again and again all week, in spite of the finality he'd tried to include in his note to Meghan. "We'll head over to Doc's first and then come back to the feed store." He started across the street.

"Wonder what everyone's doing in town on a Friday. Most folks wait till Saturday." Joshua sidestepped a group of teenage boys who laughed and shoved each other. He didn't move fast enough, and one of them knocked into him.

"Dirty Indian. Go back to the reservation."

Joshua tensed, his hands fisting. His face turned to stone except for his eyes which glowed hot. The town boys formed a half-circle with Joshua at the center.

Caleb stepped up onto the sidewalk once more. "Maybe you boys should move along."

"Maybe you should mind your own business, coward. You're too scared to fight the Huns, you'd best not mess with the likes of us." A cocky youngster threw out his chest, raised his fists, and danced, throwing a few playful jabs that just missed Caleb's chin. His compatriots laughed, egging him on.

"Go ahead. Smack his mug, Pierce. Show him what this town thinks of cowards."

"We should tar and feather him. Him and his dirty Indian friend."

"Enough." Caleb kept his voice even, but he sidled closer to Joshua so he could keep all of the young thugs in view. "You've had your fun, now move along. We don't want any trouble."

"Trouble? We haven't even started yet." The leader, Pierce, reared back to spit, his mouth twisting and his lips puckering. At the same time, he tried one more jab, this time aiming for Joshua.

Like a snake striking, Caleb grabbed the boy's fist and twisted his arm up and behind his back. "I said that's enough. Now, you and your friends back off and leave us be. I'm sure you have better things to do with your time, and I have better things to do than teach you all a lesson in manners."

The boys, eyes wide, backed up a step. Giving Pierce a push, Caleb sent him toward his friends. "Now get."

The boys slunk away, but regrouped half a block up the street and turned back to jeer. The smallest boy made a rude gesture before they took flight, running toward the hotel.

"Jerks. Punk wood for brains." Joshua stared after them, his muscles taut.

"Forget about it. Let's go over to Doc's."

Caleb started up the street, aware that several folks had witnessed the confrontation and were eying him unfavorably. You'd think he would be used to it by now, but it still stung. And with each new war report from the front, animosity and fear grew. Every time the list of casualties for the county was printed, his neighbors' eyes got harder, their lips thinner, their tolerance shorter. What had started out as dislike had begun to feel a lot like outright hatred.

They reached Doc's and Joshua stopped at the bottom of the porch steps. "Why do we have to come here? I'm not sick, and you aren't sick. Are you?"

"No, I'm not sick. I just have to see the doc for a minute."

"I'll wait out here. Don't know why I had to come to town today anyway."

"Stop your griping. You've met Doc before. He doesn't care if you're Indian, Chinese, or ancient Babylonian. It's too hot to hang around out here."

Caleb knew pricking Joshua's pride was the quickest way to get him to do what Caleb wanted. Often it was the only way.

Doc greeted him with a smile, looking over his half-moon glasses and setting aside the magazine he'd been reading. "I hoped you'd come to town today. Saved me a trip out to your place. Your order arrived yesterday."

His glance went past Caleb. "You brought reinforcements today, eh?"

Joshua stood by the door shifting his weight, his hand on the knob.

"Doc, you remember Joshua Hualga. He's working for me this summer."

"Ah, of course. I hardly recognize you. You've grown some since I last saw you." He came forward and held out his hand. "Come in, come in."

Joshua released the doorknob and eased his hand forward. "Sir."

"Caleb, why don't you head into the examination room, and Joshua, let me get you some cake. One of the neighbor ladies dropped it off, and there's no way I can eat it all by myself. And we'll get you some milk. You look as if you could use some to put some meat on those bones."

Caleb smiled at the wary look on Joshua's face and jerked his head to tell the boy to go with Doc. No sense fighting it. Doc was kind of like a flash flood. Barreling downstream and not much you could do to stop it.

Wiping his hands on a towel, Doc joined Caleb in the exam room. He opened a corner cupboard and withdrew a box. "Here, try these on."

Caleb sat on the ladder-back chair next to the doc's desk and tugged off his tattered boot. "Sure hope they fit. This pair has had it."

"That boy, Joshua, he's kind of prickly. Doesn't look much like his father, does he? Cairook's a big, broad man. Joshua could pass for a streetlamp."

Grunting, Caleb nodded. "He's skinny, but he's a hard worker. Surprised his back isn't bowed with the size of the chip he's carrying on his shoulder."

"Oh, really? Remind you of anyone?" Doc cocked a gray eyebrow, and his moustache twitched.

"Yeah, yeah." Caleb shrugged and rolled his eyes, unable to stop a smile at Doc's ribbing. He opened the box and withdrew the butter-soft leather boots. Rusty-brown, calf-high, they had the look of cavalry-issue footgear.

"Put on the right one first. Then we'll deal with the left. The manufacturer sent me some insoles so we can customize them further." Doc reached into the box and pulled out some leather of varying thicknesses while Caleb slid his right foot into the new boot and stamped it on. Perfect.

"Feels good. Hope we don't need to do too much to the other

one. Joshua can eat you out of house and home faster than a swarm of locust."

"He can have all the cake he wants. I'm not much of a fan of fruitcake, and Mrs. Bennington brought a whopper. Payment for a bottle of cough syrup."

"Guess you do a lot of barter these days, eh?" Searching the inside of the left boot, Caleb felt the rigid staves along the sides of the upper as well as the thick back wall. His stomach muscles tightened, and his palms slicked with sweat. *Please let these work, Lord.*

His arrow prayer surprised him a bit. Lately, he'd been working up quite a bout of frustration against God, and prayer wasn't on the top of his to-do list. Oh, he went through the motions, attending church, praying before meals and before bedtime, but he knew his heart wasn't in it. He and God had a few things to work out between them, but not until he was ready.

Working his mangled leg into the boot hurt, but he refused to stop until he'd pushed his toes all the way to the bottom. Snug, firm, and molded to every buckle and bend of his foot. He stood, keeping his weight on his right foot, gradually shifting so his left took more.

"How's it feel?"

He took a few steps. The upper gripped the back of his calf, supporting it and giving him some added stability. "Nice." Better than his last pair had been, even brand-new.

"Does it pinch anywhere?" Doc went through several checks, and when he was satisfied, he sat back, smiling. "It's not as good as a brace would be, but better than nothing."

"Thanks, Doc. These will be just fine. How much do I owe you?"

"The bill's in my office. Why don't you join Joshua in the kitchen and have some cake while I fetch it?"

Caleb found Joshua at the table reading. The boy looked up with a start, his hand around his milk glass and the other holding open the pages of a book.

"Any cake left?"

Doc entered, holding an envelope. Joshua quickly closed the book and pushed it away a few inches, leaning back with a bored expression. But Caleb knew better. Joshua, in the six weeks or so that he'd been living with Caleb, had blown through every book Caleb had in the house and had read several of them over again.

Doc hadn't missed it either. "Are you interested in medicine?" He picked up the book and turned it to look at the spine.

Joshua shrugged. "Interested in a lot of things. Not that it will do me much good."

"And why not?"

The boy rubbed his skin. "Don't you see this?"

"A fine example of healthy, human epidermis."

"It's Indian skin, and nobody can see past it. Doesn't matter if I'm interested in medicine and science. Doesn't matter that I was tops in my class at the mission school. Any college would take one look at me and send me packing. No way I'd get into a medical school."

The yearning in Joshua's voice caught Caleb's attention. It was the first time he could recall Joshua mentioning any specific desire he had beyond getting out from under the authority of his father and away from the reservation.

Doc poured himself some milk from the glass bottle. "Not with an attitude like that, I assure you."

"This attitude comes from years of experience, Doc. Ask Caleb. I can't even walk down the street here without running into some bucket-head who wants to remind me how low in the pecking order I am in this town."

"What you do is up to you, not someone else. If you want to be a doctor, you're the only one standing in your way. Don't use the color of your skin as your excuse not to try."

"Tell that to the marines." But the yearning in his voice and the spark of hope in his eyes belied his words. "I wouldn't even know where to start."

Doc pushed the book toward him. "Start here. Read it, study it, and when you're done, come get another one. If after a summer of learning medical terminology, anatomy and physiology, therapeutics, and diagnoses you still want a career in medicine, we'll see what to do next."

Joshua took the book, cradling it against his lean stomach, a determined tilt to his chin.

"Hey, Doc." Caleb took a slice of fruitcake. "Why're so many people in town today?"

"Don't you know? There's a movie star train due to pull into the station"—Doc slid his watch from his vest pocket—"in just under an hour."

"Movie star? Like who?"

"Charlie Chaplin and Mary Pickford, if the posters at the El Garces and over at Claypool's are to be believed. They're gathering money for the Red Cross from San Francisco to New York. Lots of bigwigs on the train and folks flocking to each stop. I thought I might go myself." He flicked a glance at Caleb. "I thought that might be why you'd come to town today. Surprised you didn't know about it. Folks have talked of little else for the past week."

"I haven't been to town for a while."

"Since the hotel dance? Didn't I see you there, and in the company of a certain titian-haired maiden?"

Caleb refused to be pushed off-center, but it was a fight. Doc saw way too much. Joshua looked up from his book, his dark eyebrows climbing. Caleb remained still.

Doc drained his glass and wiped his moustache. "Tell you what, how about we all head over there? I've a hankering to see me a genuine, for-real, in-the-flesh movie star." He put a funny drawl in his voice and winked at Joshua. "Don't you want to see one, Joshua?"

So Caleb found himself on the platform at the El Garces with several hundred of Needles's finest, watching for the eastbound train. Red, white, and blue bunting hung from every porch rail, and streamers floated in the lazy breeze. Caleb remained on the edge of the crowd, glad that everyone's attention was directed elsewhere. Maybe he and Joshua could get a peek at the movie stars and get out of the throng unnoticed.

Behind him, the doors to the lunchroom stood open, and from his position, he had a good view of the interior. Half a dozen Harvey Girls bustled behind the counters, disappearing through the kitchen doorways, setting the doors to flopping. Sidling a few feet closer and craning his neck, he spied Meghan filling a coffeepot. Nearly every stool was full, and she didn't see him, being focused on her customers.

His heart started the familiar crazy bumping it always did when she was near, and he tugged his hat down lower on his brow, turning away and leaning against the wall, taking the weight off his left foot and feigning boredom. Joshua joined him. Doc had disappeared into the crowd.

"What do you think they're like?" Joshua held the medical book tight to his chest behind his crossed arms.

"Just like us, I guess. Probably better dressed though."

"I've never been to a movie before. Seen the posters out front of the theater, but never been inside. Have you?"

"Couple of times."

"What's it like?"

Caleb shrugged. "Depends on who they have playing the piano. There's a piano down front and someone plays music to go along with the film. First time I went, the piano was so out of tune it sounded like a bloated cow, and the player must've been deaf, because he just kept banging away. Next time was much better. Music was good and sounded like it fit the picture."

A ripple went through the crowd and someone yelled, "Here she comes!"

Hissing, clanking, rocking, the eastbound chugged down the track, belching smoke and steam. Bunting hung from every roof edge and rail, mirroring the decking-out the hotel had received. As the train slowed to a stop so that the last car was opposite the main hotel doors, the crowd surged forward.

A small, dark-haired man emerged onto the railed platform smiling broadly and waving to the crowd. A cheer went up.

"Is that him?" Joshua had to shout to be heard.

"I guess so. I thought he'd be taller."

Charlie Chaplin himself. The little man turned back to the door and held out his hand. A woman emerged, her shoulders draped in a fox stole. Furs in this heat? She must've felt it too, for she let the fur slip from her shoulders and tossed it playfully back through the door into the car. The crowd cheered and clapped.

"Guess that's Mary Pickford."

"She's pretty."

Caleb shrugged. Pretty enough, he supposed, but nowhere near as beautiful as a certain waitress had been with the moonlight on her skin and the fire of her cause in her eyes.

The crowd swelled as the patrons of the lunchroom and dining room came out onto the sidewalk.

"Might be a good time to get some chow." Joshua straightened. "I don't care much for speeches from people I don't know."

Caleb checked around the corner. Not a customer remained in the lunchroom. One of the passengers must've had the same idea as Joshua about beating the crowd, because he climbed down from the train about midway up the line, skirted the throng, and walked to the lunchroom doors.

He was greeted by Mr. Stock, the guy in charge of the hotel. They held a quiet conversation as if Mr. Stock knew the man. Stock practically tugged his forelock and bowed as they spoke. The hotel manager's eyebrows rose at something the passenger said, and he gestured to the dining room, but when the man said something and shook his head, Stock nodded and stepped back so the man could go into the lunchroom.

"Let's get in and get out before the speechifying is done and the whole town moves in." Joshua nudged Caleb's arm.

This is a mistake. Why is it you vow never to come back to this place, and yet, you're always here?

At the doorway to the lunchroom, Mr. Stock stopped them. "Mr. McBride, you may go in, but I have to insist the boy stay outside."

Joshua gave a low figures-everywhere-I-go-people-treat-me-the-same-way grunt and hunched his shoulders.

Caleb went cold inside in spite of the heat. "Excuse me? Why would you want him to stay outside? He won't welsh on the meal. I'm paying his tab."

Mr. Stock's nose twitched like a rat's. "I'm sorry, sir. Hotel policy. Especially in light of the distinguished guests we have dining with us today."

"What hotel policy?" He knew what Mr. Stock was driving at, but he wanted to hear the man say it.

The skinny manager's Adam's apple lurched, and he dug a handkerchief from his pocket to mop his brow.

"Really, Mr. McBride, now is not the time or the place. Can't you see we have important guests today? I would rather not discuss hotel admittance policies at this time."

"I bet you don't, but I need to hear it, just so we're clear. I wouldn't want there to be any misunderstandings."

Lowering his voice along with his eyebrows, Mr. Stock leaned close to Caleb. "It is against the policies of the El Garces to allow Indians into the public areas."

"Since when?" Caleb raised his voice, not caring who heard. "The whole interior is decorated from top to bottom in Indian designs. You invite members of the Mohave tribe to stand out on the sidewalk all dressed up in their Indian finery and hawk their wares to the tourists and travelers, but you won't let them inside to eat at the lunch counter?"

The man who had left the train and entered the lunchroom ahead of them showed up at Mr. Stock's shoulder while the hotelier made damping motions with his hand and looked back toward the crowd and the train.

"Is there a problem here?" The man, though not big, had a commanding presence that certainly brought Stock up short.

"No, sir, not at all."

"Actually, there is a bit of a problem." Caleb put his hands on his hips.

"Forget it. It won't make any difference. I'm used to it." Joshua tugged on Caleb's elbow. "I'll wait outside for you."

"No way. If they won't serve you, they don't serve me."

The stranger's eyes widened. "What's this? Are you refusing admittance to these gentlemen?"

Stock looked like he wished one of the palm trees would crash right down on top of him and knock him out. He swiped at his brow with the sweat-soaked hanky again. "I just thought, with the prestigious guests—"

"Every guest at a Harvey House is a prestigious guest." The man nodded toward Caleb and Joshua. "My name is Ford. I'd be honored if you'd be my guests for lunch today. I hope you don't mind eating at the lunch counter. I'd rather bypass the hoopla of the dining room."

Caleb made sure he showed no triumph as they walked past the wilted Mr. Stock, but he would have been lying if he said he didn't feel at least a little bit of satisfaction.

They took their seats, one on each side of the man called Ford. Whether it was his first name or his last name, Caleb didn't know, but whoever he was, he had some clout.

The kitchen doors flopped, and Meghan came to a stop before them. "Hello, and welcome to the Harvey House lunchroom at the El Garces." Her smile lit on each of them, but when it got to Caleb's it wobbled just a fraction. "What can I bring you to drink? We've got freshly brewed coffee, or, if you'd like something cooler, there's iced tea, or I could squeeze you some orange juice."

She looked cool and fresh and every bit as beautiful as he remembered, but questions lurked in her green eyes, and he sensed her withdrawal from him. Mrs. Gregory's warnings must've penetrated even Meghan's idealistic heart.

But you'd never know it by the service she gave him. Everything was perfect, from the shine on the silverware to the easy way she set the plates before him. And it wasn't just him. When the speeches outside finished, diners crowded into the lunchroom until not a seat remained empty. The noise level rose, and the batwing doors into the kitchen were in constant motion with uniformed girls coming and going.

Meghan fairly flew, carrying, pouring, serving, chatting. And she never needed to write down an order. With a smile and a nod, she listened, answered questions, made recommendations, and hustled without ever seeming hurried.

Ford examined each item of his place setting as if he were preparing to buy it instead of just eat off it, and his eyes searched every part of the lunchroom like Pinkerton. Lifting his coffee cup, he inhaled the steam rising from the dark liquid and took a sip, savoring the brew. Caleb watched him but made no comment. The train brought folks from all over the country through Needles, and there were bound to be a few odd socks in the mix from time to time. If this fellow wanted to parse and examine every morsel and mouthful, that was his business. At least he'd smoothed things over with Mr. Stock. Joshua ate as if he'd never heard of fruitcake, much less eaten three pieces an hour ago at Doc's.

At the end of the meal, the Ford fellow sat back, patted his lips with his napkin, and neatly folded it beside his plate. "Miss, I must commend you on your service. I've never received better. Are you perchance filling in here at the lunch counter? I would think someone of your caliber would be in the dining room serving the distinguished guests."

Meghan paused, a smile curving her mouth. "No, sir, this is my customary position. And as far as I'm concerned, every guest of the Fred Harvey Company is a distinguished guest. But I do thank you for your compliment."

Ford followed her movements, a satisfied look in his eye.

Joshua couldn't keep still, watching everybody and everything, curious as a cat. Meghan treated him as well as everyone else, smiling, serving quickly, and when it came time for dessert, she chose the largest piece of chocolate cake from the refrigerator cabinet and placed it before Joshua.

"A growing boy deserves a nice big piece. They're all supposed to be cut exactly the same, but somehow this one came out a little larger." Her nose wrinkled, and Caleb found himself staring at her freckles.

"Can I get you anything else, Mr. McBride?"

He swallowed and shook his head. "No, thank you, Meghan." Her use of his last name pricked him. When they'd been together at the dance, she'd called him Caleb.

"Very well. Have a nice day, and thank you for dining at the El Garces." Her skirt belled out as she turned toward the coffee urns near the kitchen door.

He swallowed and tore his eyes away from the gentle sway of her hips and the narrow span of her waist.

"Do you know her?" Ford wiped his mouth with his napkin and crossed his knife and fork on his plate.

"We've met." He pressed his lips together at the memory of their first cataclysmic encounter, and his heart quickened at the thought of how close he'd come to kissing her in the moonlight during the dance.

"What's her name?"

He cleared his throat and his head. "Meghan. Meghan Thorson. She's been here. . .must be a couple of months now."

Ford stroked his moustache, his intelligent eyes following her every move. "Interesting."

A stab of what Caleb had to admit was jealousy pierced his gut. This geezer was old enough to be Meghan's father and here he was watching her like a hawk eyeing a mouse.

"Do you know the head waitress?" Ford dug in his pocket for his watch, flipped open the cover and compared the timepiece with the clock on the far wall.

"Mrs. Gregory. We've met." He rubbed his cheekbone. "I imagine she wouldn't be too pleased to see me and Joshua in here. She can be a bit sticky. Do you know her?"

"I've not had the pleasure, yet. She's new since my last trip through Needles. Promoted from housekeeping, from what I understand."

"Where is it you're from?"

"Kansas City. But I'm through here quite often, though with the war on, my travels have been more eastward than westward recently. What about you? That isn't a Southwest accent I'm hearing."

"Vermont, actually, though I haven't lived there in some years. Lived in Kentucky for a while, and moved here for a job with the army."

His eyebrows rose. "You're a soldier? My son, Frederick, is an aviator."

Why'd he mention the army? It only brought uncomfortable questions he didn't want to answer, but there was something about this man that made him feel more at ease than he'd felt in weeks. "I'm not a soldier. I train horses for the cavalry. Bring 'em in by train from the west coast, season them a bit, and ship them to Fort Riley to finish their training."

"Well done. We need men like you. You're doing good work, though I suspect you don't get quite the glowing accolades as those with more high profile jobs. The current circus-on-the-rails that I'm traveling with, they're doing good work, too, raising funds and such, but it does get to be quite the extravaganza. I prefer less ostentatious means of helping the cause."

Caleb's chest swelled. If only other folks thought like this man, his time in Needles wouldn't be so difficult.

Ford tucked his watch away. "Now, I must see Mr. Stock before it's time for the train to pull out. I enjoyed dining with you, and I suspect, after this, any time you want to bring the boy in with you to eat, there won't be any trouble."

With a brisk handshake, he rounded the lunch counter and disappeared toward the lobby. Caleb drained his water glass while Joshua polished off the last crumbs of his cake. Meghan appeared to clear their spaces, and when she picked up Ford's plate, a bill fluttered to the counter. She blinked.

"Ten dollars?" She searched the lunchroom. "He must've dropped this by mistake, or perhaps he thought he was putting a dollar bill under his plate, though that would be far too big a tip in any case. Do you see him? Which way did he go?"

"He headed toward the lobby. Said he had to see Stock before the train left." Caleb stood and dug in his pocket. "That was a fine meal, Meghan, and well served. Thank you." He left as big a tip as he dared, though it couldn't compare to ten dollars.

Her eyes collided with his, and he read all those questions and doubts she must be harboring about him. A pretty flush tinted her cheeks, and his heart bumped hard against his ribs. How he wished she'd heard what Ford had said about his job being vital to the war effort, even if it wasn't worthy of a medal or a headline.

"I need to find that gentleman and return his money to him."

"We'll help you look. He's bound to be around here somewhere. I'd like to thank him again for a little service he did me and Joshua." He stood and waited for Meghan to round the end of the lunch counter. "He's probably at the front desk."

Caleb identified Ford's voice before he actually saw him. Meghan, continuing on her way toward the dining room, stopped when Caleb touched her arm. Caleb raised himself up on his good leg to scan over the people.

"There he is." They crossed the tile floor near the fountain. Caleb almost paused in the spot where he'd nearly kissed Meghan before pressing on with a stern warning to himself to forget such foolishness. They wove through passengers now exiting the lunchroom and dining room and working their way toward the train. The man they sought stood near one of the pillars conversing with the hotel manager and the head waitress.

"Maybe we'd best hang back until they're done. Mrs. Gregory sees us together, she's liable to pitch a fit."

"Mr. Stock, I trust there will be no more unpleasantness with our guests. The El Garces will not refuse service to any paying customer. Is that understood?"

"Yes, Mr. Harvey."

Meghan gave a small gasp, and her fingertips came up to cover her lips. "Mr. Harvey?" She whispered, seemingly half to him and half to herself. Her green eyes widened.

Caleb put his lips close to her ear. "He said his name was Ford."

She clutched his arm. "Ford Harvey. Son of Fred Harvey, the founder of the company. I served Ford Harvey?"

"And Mrs. Gregory," Ford Harvey continued. "I have to wonder why the young woman who served my meal is being wasted in the lunchroom. She was as attentive to detail, as personable and professional a Harvey Girl as I have ever seen and certainly deserves to be moved up to the dining room. I hate to think of one of the girls missing out on the larger tips offered in the dining room if she deserves to be there."

"But, Mr. Harvey, she's only been here a short while, and there have been. . .some issues."

"Would you care to explain these issues?"

Meghan's eyes closed. Caleb wanted to draw her away, but he wanted to hear what Mrs. Gregory had to say as well. They certainly weren't having a private conversation, not out here in the crowded lobby where anyone could hear.

"She's been seen several times in the company of a rather undesirable man in the Needles community, and she's impertinent."

A small groan escaped Meghan, and she clutched Caleb's arm. "Let's get out of here."

"Right."

Their movement must've caught Mr. Ford Harvey's eye. "Excuse me. Miss Thorson, Mr. McBride."

They turned, and Caleb wondered if his face looked as guilty as Meghan's. "Sir?"

Mrs. Gregory's mouth pinched, and her eyes glittered. Mr. Stock looked like he wanted to sink beneath the floor and never return. Copious amounts of sweat leaked from his forehead, and his handkerchief swiped continually.

"I've just been having a word with Mr. Stock and Mrs. Gregory. I don't anticipate any further difficulties for either of you here at the El Garces. Miss Thorson, you will be moved to the dining room immediately, and Mr. McBride, you are always welcome here. You and your friend." He flicked a finger to where Joshua hovered behind them. "I'll be back through this way soon. I imagine I'll find everything as it should be." Though he smiled, there was no real warmth in it, and his tone was such that Caleb had no doubt he expected to be obeyed.

He left, and Mrs. Gregory's face went from white as a blister to red as a bloodstone. "What have you been telling him, Miss Thorson? It's shameful of you to take your complaints to Mr. Harvey instead of coming to discuss them with me first."

"Here now." Caleb stepped forward. "She didn't know who he was any more than I did. And she didn't complain about you. Not a word." Though he might've mentioned something about her difficult personality.

Mr. Stock wrung his hands. "The damage has been done. Rehashing it won't help. I wanted to warn you, Mrs. Gregory, but he forbade me from saying anything about his being here. And you were in the dining room the whole time. I can't imagine why he didn't want to dine with Mr. Chaplin and Miss Pickford." He mopped his forehead again.

"It seems trouble follows you wherever you happen to be, Miss Thorson." Mrs. Gregory's back stiffened. "I will move you to the dining room as he requested, but if you so much as spill a drop of coffee into a saucer, I'll fire you." Her eyes bored into Meghan before switching to Caleb. "And if you persist in hanging around here panting after one of my waitresses, I'll set the sheriff after you."

She wheeled and marched away.

Mr. Stock took a deep breath. "We must make some allowances for her. She's under a great deal of stress. She hasn't heard from her son since he arrived in Europe, and she's been so busy with all the preparations for the celebrity train. Mr. McBride, I hope you won't think me churlish, but it might be best for all of us if she doesn't find you here when she returns."

Caleb nodded, wishing he could stay and spend more time with Meghan, but knowing, as he'd known all along, that his being with her would only cause her trouble and himself pain. He wouldn't wait around to be thrown out. A man had his pride, after all.

"I'm sorry my presence seems to get you into difficulties."

Meghan shrugged. The train whistle sounded, and she glanced over his shoulder to where Mr. Chaplin and Miss Pickford stood in the doorway to the dining room. "I don't have any problem getting into trouble. Like Mrs. Gregory said. It follows me to wherever I happen to be."

"That might be true, but I don't want you to face censure because of me. I'll stay away from the hotel. That will make Mrs. Gregory happy—or at least as happy as a woman of her disposition can be." He hadn't realized how much he had looked forward to seeing Meghan when he came to town. A hole tore open in his chest. Still, it was for the best.

She turned those wide, green eyes on him. "Will I see you again?" Her pretty, pink lips parted, and his breath hitched, but he forced himself to take a firm grip on his resolve.

"No. It's for the best." Settling his hat on his head, he touched the brim and walked out into the sunshine, careful to make sure he didn't show even a trace of a limp.

Chapter 9

Doc washed his hands and wiped them on the roller towel beside the sink. One last patient waited in his front parlor before he could escape to the river for a little sunset fishing. A small practice might not be very exciting out here in the California desert, but it sure gave him plenty of time to stalk record-breaking pikeminnows.

"Miss?"

The pretty blond perched on the edge of one of his wingchairs jumped. One of the girls from the hotel. He remembered seeing her in the dining room. Wedgewood blue eyes fringed with pale lashes met his. Her pale pink dress hung on her slight frame.

"Won't you come in?" He studied her as she rose and entered the examination room. Slight, pale, with dark smudges under those pretty eyes. She had the bone structure of a bird, and her skin was so translucent he could see the blue lines of her veins on the backs of her hands and at her temples.

He motioned toward the chair beside his desk and took his own seat, leaning back, propping his elbows on the arms of his chair, and steepling his fingers under his nose. "What brings you in to see me today?"

She swallowed, staring at her hands in her lap. A single tear splashed onto her thumb. "I don't know where to start," she whispered.

"How about we start with your name?"

"Natalie Daviot."

"There, that wasn't so hard, was it?" He smiled, but she didn't look up. "And how old are you, Natalie?"

"Twenty-two."

Older than she looked. He'd have wagered she wasn't a day over seventeen.

"Are you feeling ill, Miss Daviot?"

The cuff of her dress seemed to fascinate her. She plucked at the lace edging, smoothing it and scrunching it by turns. "I'm just so tired. I thought I'd pick up once I got used to the work, but I'm dragging around like a hound dog's chew toy."

Doc scratched the word *fatigue* on his notepad. "You're a Harvey Girl at the hotel, correct?"

"Yes."

"For how long now?"

"Almost three months."

"From what I've seen, Harvey Girls work very hard. Lots of time on your feet and lots of lifting and carrying. Fatigue after all those long shifts is natural. Any other symptoms?"

She shook her head. "I had a little stomach bug a few weeks ago that hung on for a while, but that's gone now."

Sitting on the very edge of the chair, she looked ready to take wing at any moment. And she had yet to meet his eyes since coming into the exam room. Her slender shoulders bowed, and she wore an unmistakable air of guilt. He began putting all the pieces together and formed a preliminary diagnosis.

"I'm going to have to ask you some fairly pointed and personal questions, I'm afraid, if we're going to figure out what's going on with you."

She took a deep breath as if fortifying herself. "Doctor, I'm afraid I know what it might be, but I really don't want it to be." This time her chin came up and she blinked, sending a fresh pair of tears tracking down her cheeks.

He raised his eyebrows and laid his pencil down before digging in his pocket for a clean handkerchief.

"Are you in trouble?" He kept his tone as kind and nonjudgmental as he could.

She nodded, dabbing at her eyes. "But not the way you think."

"Oh?"

"I think I'm having a baby."

Which confirmed his initial thoughts based upon her symptoms. Poor girl. She had a hard road ahead of her. This wasn't the first time he'd been called upon to make such a diagnosis, and it was never a happy occasion. He wouldn't wish being an unwed mother on anyone, and this fragile girl seemed less able to bear it than most. With as much tact and understanding as possible, he asked a few pertinent questions.

"I'll need to examine you to make sure, but from what you've told me, I suspect you're right. What about the father? Is there any chance he will marry you?" Doc ran his hand down his face. He'd have to get his address book from the desk in his study. That's where he kept his contact information for the girls' home over in Barstow. Marjorie Banks ran the place, and she'd take good care of Miss Daviot during her confinement, and if the girl so desired, she'd find a home for the child.

"But I *am* married." She reached for the back of her neck and slid her finger under a chain, tugging it out from the collar of her dress. A circlet of gold dangled from the links. "My husband is a soldier. I didn't tell anyone about my marriage because if they found out, I'd have to leave my job. The Harvey Company only hires single girls who can live in the dormitories to be Harvey Girls. And I need the money."

The story she spilled out had him shaking his head, both in sadness and admiration. Her husband had answered his country's call to serve, her mother-in-law had suffered an apoplectic attack, her father-in-law was frail, and she'd taken a high-paying job halfway across the country in order to help out. He listened to every word, knowing she needed to talk as much as she needed a diagnosis. What a burden for her to carry. Her pent-up emotions rushed out, and a torrent of tears followed.

"I'll be back. Don't go anywhere."

He went to the kitchen and got a glass of water. Returning to the exam room, he pressed it into her hand. She'd stopped crying, but her chin quivered, and the occasional hiccup jarred her.

"Sip on this. It will help."

"Thank you."

He resumed his seat and put his forearms on his knees, leaning toward her. "Miss Daviot, or should I say Mrs. Daviot? When you're ready, I'd like to get the examination out of the way so we can confirm your suspicions. Then we'll talk about what to do."

Fifteen minutes later, he went to the kitchen to brew some tea, leaving Natalie in the exam room to gather herself and come to terms with his findings. When the tea had steeped, he put everything on a tray and carried it to his study. They'd both be more comfortable there than in the exam room.

She eased into one of his wingchairs and sipped her tea, some color returning to her face.

"I'm sure you can give in your notice without saying why you're leaving. Your husband's family will be glad to see you. You can be with them by the end of the week."

Her eyebrows rose. "I can't go back yet. My mother-in-law's doctor bills aren't paid, and she still needs the district nurse visits. And with the added expense of a baby next year, I need every penny for as long as I can earn."

"But, my dear, you can't conceal your condition forever, and you should be at home with your family."

"I can serve my family best by staying here as long as possible. Every dollar I earn pays for past bills and future expenses." She let her hand drop to her abdomen. As frail and delicate as she was, a determined light gleamed in her eyes. "Working won't hurt the baby, will it?"

Disquieted by her determination, Doc turned his cup in its saucer. "I'd like it better if you could spend more time with your feet up. An unborn child places quite a burden on its mother, and with your demanding job, you'll have to expect that the fatigue will continue."

She sighed. "Is there anything else I can do?"

He rattled off his standard expectant-mother spiel. "Drink plenty of fluids, especially milk. I will caution you against becoming overtired. You have a rather taxing job, and you're not yet used to the climate out here. Dehydration comes on quickly."

Her lower lip disappeared, and she nodded.

"Avoid heavy lifting. I know you sometimes have to carry loaded trays, but try to minimize that. Make extra trips if you have to. That's better than carrying too much at once. What part of the restaurant do you work in?"

"I'm a waitress in the dining room."

"Perhaps you could get yourself transferred to the soda fountain instead. That would be much easier on you. No heavy lifting, no walking miles between tables and the kitchen."

For the first time, a smile curved her pretty mouth. "I could probably do that. I know my roommate, Meghan, just got moved up to the dining room. Mrs. Gregory will be looking to move the girls around to make room for her. I can volunteer for the soda fountain, and Barbara can move to Meghan's spot in the lunchroom. That will be perfect."

"I want to go on record here as saying it would be better in the long run if you were to go home to your family. It would be best all around if you came clean to Mrs. Gregory about your marriage and your coming child."

"I wish I could. And I know I won't be able to hide it forever, but I have to stay as long as I can. If there was any hope of me getting a job at home that would come close to the wages I get here, I'd do it in a heartbeat, but there just isn't. And no one would hire me in my present condition anyway. I need this job, and I plan to stay until they kick me out." Again that determined blue light gleamed in her eyes.

"Then I'm going to caution you. You're going to be tempted at some point to bind yourself up to conceal the fact that you are with child. Don't do it. That's the worst possible thing you could do to your growing baby and your own internal organs. Loosen your apron and let out your dresses to conceal your shape, but don't, under any circumstances, bind yourself. You can do irreparable harm."

She set her teacup down, and the slender column of her throat moved as she swallowed. "I understand. And I can rely on your reticence? You won't tell anyone?"

"You can trust me."

He showed her out, but a heaviness he couldn't dispel hung over him. Nothing good would come from her hiding her condition. It put him in mind of Caleb, also hiding a medical issue. She would be condemned for revealing hers, while his would exonerate him. Hers was a reason to celebrate, and yet she couldn't risk it for fear of losing her job. His was a reason to commiserate, and yet he wouldn't reveal the truth for fear of losing his pride.

But secrets had a way of coming out. He could only hope to minimize the consequences when they did.

"What did the doctor say?" Meghan gathered her sewing supplies into the basket she'd rounded up for the purpose. Blocks of red and white fabric, red embroidery thread, white quilting thread, red yarn for tying the quilt. She mentally checked off her list.

Natalie unpinned her hat and set it on the dresser. "He said to drink plenty of fluids and to get as much rest as I can. There's nothing whatever wrong with me."

"So he thinks it's just taking you some time to get accustomed to the climate and the work?"

A soft smile, as if she were privy to an inside joke, quirked her lips. "Time will solve all my problems. He said for me not to worry so much, but I don't know that I can help it, not with Derek on the front lines like he is."

Meghan nodded. "I think about Lars every day. I can't imagine what you must be going through. A brother isn't the same as a husband."

Natalie shook her head. "It's hard on everyone. Think of Mrs. Gregory with her son gone. She mentioned that she hadn't heard from him since receiving his disembarkation card. I know she worries something terrible. Parents miss their sons, siblings miss their brothers, wives miss their husbands, and children miss their fathers. I don't know that you can rank people's pain as more or less dear. We're all in this together."

"We'd best get downstairs together before Mrs. Gregory comes hunting us."

"Has she gotten over the shock of Mr. Harvey's visit?"

Grimacing, Meghan hefted the basket handle over her arm. "I try to make allowances for her. I mean, like you said, her son has shipped out and she hasn't had word from him in a while, and she is in a position full of responsibility looking after all us girls and the restaurant and all, but I am in danger of getting frostbite every time she walks by me these days. She said I'm supposed to start in the dining room on Monday. She still hasn't figured out how she's going to shuffle everyone around."

Natalie closed the door behind them, and they headed to the Red Cross meeting. "How is the quilt coming along?"

"Okay. I need to get out and about to get more signatures. Though I did manage one rather big coup." A burst of excited warmth spread through Meghan as she remembered.

"Oh?"

"I ran to the celebrity train just before it pulled out, and I managed to get donations and signatures from both Charlie Chaplin and Mary Pickford, and. . ." She paused and wrinkled her nose. "Mr. Ford Harvey made a donation to have his signature put on the quilt, too." She squeezed Natalie's arm. "Isn't that great? More people will want the quilt knowing three famous people donated to have their names embroidered on it."

"That's wonderful. I imagine folks will be eager to put their names on the quilt alongside Mr. Chaplin's and Miss Pickford's."

"I only wish I had been able to canvass the crowd while the train was here. Folks were in a very enthusiastic, supportive mood. I would've been able to get a bunch of donations, I bet."

They reached the bottom of the staircase and turned toward the screened porch. The sound of chattering women reached them through the open doorway.

"Do you want some help with the quilt, or should I go over to the knitting machine?"

"You go make socks. I want to do the quilt myself." She couldn't explain it, but she wanted this project to be all hers. Having help would somehow diminish the effort she was making, or make the project somehow less impressive. Meghan scouted out an empty table. She began laying out her supplies, creating neat stacks of red and white squares and rectangles. When she had laid out all the fabric and threads, a shadow fell across the table.

"How is your project coming along?" Mrs. Gregory, still in her white uniform, stood beside the table with her hands on her hips. "Are you sure you don't want me to assign you some helpers?"

Meghan read the challenge in her eyes and tone, and her chin shot up. "That's quite all right, Mrs. Gregory. I've got everything under control here."

One of the laundresses entered the room, spotted Meghan, and raised her eyebrows in a silent question. Meghan stood and motioned the woman over.

"Mrs. Lassiter."

"Are you ready? I found a couple of boys to bring it in." Mrs. Lassiter twisted her work-reddened hands in her apron, darting looks from the corner of her eye at Mrs. Gregory.

"What's this?" the head waitress demanded.

"I am ready. You can put it right here by my table. And thank you." Meghan put her hand on the laundress's arm for a moment before turning to Mrs. Gregory. "I've arranged for a sewing machine to be brought in from the laundry area. Using a machine will speed up the piecing of the quilt."

Mrs. Gregory's mouth puckered. "Do you know how to use a sewing machine? I can't have someone inexperienced messing around with company property."

"I can use a sewing machine. My mother has had one for years, and she taught me to sew when I was a child. The machine will come to no harm." Meghan did her best to sound appeasing and reasonable, but waves of disapproval flowed from her supervisor, and the woman's lips pressed so hard together, they disappeared.

Two of the bellboys carried in the treadle sewing machine, its tabletop scratched and the gilded scrollwork on the black machine almost worn off.

Mrs. Gregory inspected the battered machine. "Oh, it's the old treadle. You can't do much harm there. I was afraid you wanted to use one of the new electric ones. Very well. Carry on." She turned on her heel and marched away to check on one of the other stations.

Meghan settled in to work, pinning, sewing, snipping threads. She'd have a mountain of ironing to do on all the seams, but that could be done later. For now, she wanted to finish the piecing she'd begun by hand so she could start the embroidering.

All around her, Red Cross volunteers chatted and worked. Some cut bandage materials, others rolled them up. Some, like Natalie, knitted scarves and caps, others turned cranks on two of the knitting machines that created socks lightning fast. At another table, women sorted through the buckets of peach, cherry, and apricot pits saved over from the kitchen for the making of gas mask charcoal. One of the girls had brought in a phonograph. Songs like "Pack up Your Troubles in Your Old Kit Bag," "It's a Long Way to Tipperary," "Keep the Home Fires Burning," and "Just a Baby's Prayer at Twilight (For Her Daddy Over There)" reminded them all of why they were working so hard and who they were working for.

Several of the ladies stopped by to see what Meghan was up to, and though many offered to help, she refused. She couldn't wait to hand the money over to the Red Cross, knowing she'd accomplished the entire task by herself.

Natalie drifted over after a while. "How are you coming along?"

"Fine. How's the knitting going?" She barely looked up from her sewing.

"The knitting's fine, but I thought I might give you a little warning."

The treadle stilled. "What?"

"I know how much this quilt project means to you, both the actual assembly of the quilt and the money you are hoping to raise before Mr. Gibson returns, but you're not making any friends here. A lot of these women would like to help you, but you've rebuffed every offer. You're coming across as selfish and standoffish."

"I'm not being selfish. There's plenty for everyone to do. I don't need any help. Anyone else would just be in the way." Meghan snipped a thread and finger-pressed the seams of a completed block.

"Maybe it's not about you needing their help as much as it's about them needing to help you."

"You're not making sense." Meghan laughed. "Anyway, after I finish this last block, I've gone as far as I can with the sewing. Now I just need to gather the names and collect the donations. I'll embroider the squares before I put them together." With a final snip, the square was done.

Sighing, Natalie shook her head. "I've been talking to Mrs. Gregory." She helped Meghan gather and stack the pieced quilt blocks and pick up stray threads.

"What about?"

"Since you're moving to the dining room day after tomorrow, she needs to do some shuffling of positions. I volunteered to work at the soda fountain."

"You what?" Meghan dropped her scissors onto the table with a clatter that had conversations pausing and heads turning. She lowered her voice. "But I was so looking forward to finally working with you. Now you're moving to the soda fountain? You won't get nearly the tips there. That's one thing that Barbara is always complaining about, the paltry tips people leave when they order a soda or an ice cream cone."

"I know, but I've been so tired lately, and the doctor said I should find a way to conserve my strength. Working the soda fountain will do just that, and Barbara can move to the lunchroom to take your vacant position. See? It all works out."

"Mrs. Gregory went along with that?"

"She did. I mentioned that I wasn't acclimating to the heat too well and that I'd been to see the doctor. She was actually very nice about it. I understand they had a girl pass away from heatstroke a couple of years ago, and she takes that kind of thing very seriously." Natalie shrugged. "I think somewhere under all that starch and protocol lurks a lonely, hurt woman who just wants a friend."

"And I think you're a very nice girl, Natalie Daviot. You see the good in everybody."

Jenny passed their table, her arms full of bandage rolls. "Hey, ladies, how's it going? We're just about done with bandages for the day."

Natalie took the rolls, one-by-one, out of Jenny's arms and lined them up on the end of Meghan's table. When she finished, she pressed her hands to her lower back. "I'm beat. I think I'll go lie down before we have to go back on duty."

"I'm about done, too. I'll be up to our room to drop off all this stuff before I head into town to go door-to-door for signatures." She mounded fabric into her basket. "When I have a good list going, I can get started on the embroidery."

Natalie gave a small wave and left the sunroom. Hopefully, she'd get some good rest in spite of the heat.

"Your quilt's an awfully big project." Jenny leaned against the table. "Are you sure you can get enough donations just from town?"

"If I have to, I'll drive around the county and up toward Bullhead City. I'm sure Mr. Stock would let me borrow the hotel's automobile."

"You can drive?" Wonder and admiration colored Jenny's tone, and her eyes widened. "You can drive an auto?"

Meghan nodded. "My father has an Oldsmobile. He taught me to drive."

A mischievous glint came into Jenny's eyes. "Then you'll be able to drive out toward the river, right?"

"I imagine so."

"Then you could take some of us girls swimming." Jenny grinned. "We wouldn't have to wait for one of the bellboys to drive us out to Mr. McBride's place."

At the mention of Caleb's name, Meghan's heart bobbed. She was so conflicted about him. On the one hand, he was kind and interesting and intriguing. Something in him called out to her, as if he had some secret, hidden hurt that she could ease for him. And yet, from other sources she'd heard nothing good. He was a coward, a profiteer. How could she be drawn to him and repelled at the same time? Which was true, or was it all true? All she knew was that she couldn't stop thinking about him. And yet, he'd made it clear they wouldn't be seeing one another again.

Jenny must've sensed something, because she pounced. "Speaking of Caleb, isn't he handsome? All the girls think so. Don't you? Mrs. Gregory has warned us all against him. To hear her talk, you'd think he was the Kaiser's brother or had the typhoid or something. Though there wasn't much danger of any of us girls coming under his influence, at least not until you came along. He never used to come in here, hardly even came to town, but he's been in the hotel a bunch of times since you showed up. I heard Mrs. Gregory a couple of days ago telling the bellhops and maids to let her know if he came into the hotel again. She said he'd been 'sniffing around' one of her girls, and she wasn't going to stand for it. I figured she must mean you, since you're the one he heads for when he comes to town." Jenny blinked innocent eyes that invited Meghan to share a confidence.

Meghan's cheeks betrayed her, growing hot. "Sniffing around" had such bad connotations, she felt she had to put Jenny right.

"He's done nothing of the sort. I've served him a couple of times in the hotel, and I saw him at the dime-a-dance. That's all."

Jenny raised one eyebrow and crossed her arms. "Uh-huh. Tell that to the horse marines. Caleb McBride has given the cold shoulder to this town ever since he arrived. I bet he wasn't in Needles more than a handful of times ever, but in the last couple of months, he's been hanging around town and coming to the hotel. He never came to any of the Harvey Girl Friday Night Socials, and he sure never ate in the lunchroom before your arrival. And not only did he come to the dance, but the minute he arrived, he snatched you away for a stroll under the stars. Folks are talking. Small town and all, everyone knows everyone else's business."

Snatching up her basket, Meghan propped it on her hip. "Well, people should mind their own business instead of poking their noses in where they don't belong."

Jenny blinked at her tone, but she persisted. "Then there *is* something going on with you two?"

"Of course there isn't. I barely know the man. Anyway, Harvey Girls aren't supposed to court. I signed a contract."

"Fiddlesticks. What do contracts have to do with courting? Do you know how many Harvey Girls have gotten married the day after their contract expires? Half the girls working here are being courted by railroad men. The joke is that The Fred Harvey Company is actually a matchmaking service for the Atchison, Topeka & Santa Fe." She linked arms with Meghan. "Anyway, enough about that. If you can get the hotel car, let's get up another swimming party or two, okay?"

Meghan let Jenny prattle on as they headed upstairs, but she gave no firm assurances. With Mrs. Gregory expanding her web of informants, she had a feeling that if she wanted to make a success of her move into the dining room, she'd best steer clear of Caleb McBride's property.

Chapter 10

Meghan wove between the square tables for eight, raising her tray of desserts carefully over her head so as to clear the patrons but not hit the low-hanging chandeliers. Her first week as a dining room waitress had gone well. At least Mrs. Gregory hadn't said anything to her about any mistakes. And the dining room supervisor seemed satisfied with her performance.

She had fallen into the rhythm of the new work. One blessing of being a senior waitress meant she no longer had to polish coffee urns in between train departures. The dining room urns were kept in the kitchen, not out on the counter for all the diners to admire. Everything in the dining room lent a more sober atmosphere, from the rich paneling and coffered ceilings to the linen tablecloths and ornate chandeliers. Though speed was appreciated and necessary, one must never give the appearance of rushing.

"Two queen's puddings and two Muscatine ices." She set the

plates before each person, working counterclockwise around the table. "Will any of you be having coffee with your dessert?" Holding the now empty tray low before her, she gave her most encouraging smile.

Heading back to the kitchen, she scanned the room. Close to capacity. Though she enjoyed the patrons in the dining room, she missed the camaraderie and informality of the lunch counter. Most of the soldiers passing through had vouchers for the lunchrooms, part of the deal worked out between the company and the military. The dining room was reserved for more well-to-do travelers and those looking for a little peace and quiet after the clattering bustle of the train.

"Coffee to table six."

The drinks waitress, Sandra, nodded and lifted her tray where a silver coffee pot rested in solitary splendor. The maître d' showed two gentlemen to one of her tables for two under a window, and Meghan's breath caught. The first man was a stranger who walked with all the military precision she'd expect from an officer in uniform, but the man who took the chair opposite him was familiar from her thoughts and dreams.

Sandra nudged her. "What are you waiting for? Go take their drinks order and give them their menus."

Meghan walked across the dining room as if in a trance. What was he doing here? He'd made it clear he wanted nothing to do with her. Yet, here he was again.

She put on her best smile. "Good afternoon, gentlemen. Welcome to the Harvey restaurant. Today's specials are Viennaise chicken with homemade noodles and beef tenderloin stroganoff.

I can also recommend the fried chicken Castañeda. It's excellent. While you're considering the menu, may I take your drink order? We have coffee, hot tea, iced tea, water, freshly squeezed orange juice, tomato juice, and lemonade."

The man in uniform set his hat on the window ledge. He had pale blue eyes, sandy hair, and a sharply defined nose. "A hot day like today, lemonade sounds good. How about you, McBride? Something cool before we talk business?"

"Make it two lemonades." Caleb kept his attention on the printed menu.

Meghan arranged the cups according to the code to let Sandra know what the gentlemen had ordered and stepped away.

"Miss Thorson." The dining room supervisor crossed the room and spoke softly into her ear. "Please inform Mrs. Gregory that Mr. McBride is in the hotel."

"What?"

"We are under orders to inform the head waitress when Mr. McBride patronizes our establishment. Go and tell her, then return here to take their orders."

Dread coursed through her. "Why does she want to know? Surely she won't throw him out? He's done nothing wrong."

"Ours is not to question the demands of Mrs. Gregory. Go find her and get back here quickly."

"Please, send someone else."

"There is no one else. Go." She made a shooing motion before stepping around a potted fern to man her station beside the kitchen door.

Meghan blew out a breath, trying to tamp down the nasty feeling that she might be betraying Caleb somehow by telling Mrs. Gregory that he was dining in the restaurant. The clock was ticking. She had to find her and get back to the table to take their orders in a timely manner. Maybe that was her out. If she couldn't find Mrs. Gregory quickly, she'd have to abandon the task to get back to work.

Unfortunately, she spotted the head waitress across the lobby standing in the doorway of the lunchroom. "Mrs. Gregory."

"What do you want? Aren't you supposed to be waiting tables? What are you doing traipsing around the hotel?"

Meghan swallowed and grabbed hold of her temper. "I was sent to inform you that Mr. McBride is dining with us today."

Her eyebrows rose and her face hardened. "Really?"

"Yes, ma'am." Meghan turned to go.

"Wait."

"I must get back. I have customers."

"Is he alone?"

"No, Mrs. Gregory. He's with an army officer. A major, I believe."

"Fine. Return to your station. I'm sure your customers are wondering where you've gotten to."

Meghan gritted her teeth. Shooed away as if she were the one dawdling. Her footfalls sounded loudly on the tile floor.

She returned to the busy hush of the dining room and approached Caleb's table. "Have we decided?"

The gentlemen placed their orders, and she went to the kitchen to report to the chef. On the far side of the blistering hot kitchen, Harvey Girls bustled through the flopping doors to the lunch counters. They chatted with the sous chefs and busboys, cheerful and busy. The dining room staff proceeded with pleasant but serious expressions. No jocularity, the ultimate in professional service behavior.

She missed the lunchroom.

Carrying the first course to Caleb's table, she couldn't help but overhear part of their conversation. Her curiosity surged, and she slowed her pace to linger without being too obvious.

"I'm going to have to have at least one more carload of hay. What I can get around here is so thin and light, it hardly puts any meat on their bones. And half a carload of grain. When can I expect the next shipment of horses?" Caleb leaned back, staring somewhere over the major's shoulder and giving no indication that he knew Meghan or even realized she was there.

She set their salads before them, noted both needed refills on lemonade, and motioned to Sandra. Unable to think of a reason to hover, she moved away. Unbidden, she looked back over her shoulder and caught Caleb watching her leave. Their gazes meshed, and a stab of guilt pierced her. Why had Mrs. Gregory wanted to know he was in the hotel?

When they'd finished their salads, Meghan cleared their plates and served the main courses. She couldn't help but notice the strong backs of Caleb's hands, the way his muscles played beneath his white shirt, and the crisp springiness of his sun-bleached hair. She had to force herself not to touch his shoulder to test the warmth of his skin.

The major picked up his fork. "I've made the rounds of several ranches in central California and purchased fifty new mounts. They'll be coming on the train in just over a week. I'll send several handlers along with them. They'll deliver them to your place so you don't have to come into town."

Meghan bit her lip. If he didn't have to come to town for horses, when would she see him again? She served her other customers, but Caleb's table received more than its fair share of her attention, for she couldn't stay away. With each course she caught snippets of their conversation, adding to what she knew about Caleb. The major's commendation of Caleb's training warmed her through with pride.

"The last group you sent to Fort Riley, the commandant was especially pleased. They were certainly in tiptop shape, and very well trained, ready for learning battle maneuvers. He wanted me to pass along his thanks."

"Fifty head is the most I can handle out at the ranch. I wish I had a better place. It's pretty stark out there. Without getting feed hauled in, I couldn't even support fifty head."

"We'll head out there after the meal and we can go over any equipment you might need."

"Gentlemen, your dessert." She set the plates before them and opened her mouth to offer coffee, but she stopped as a large woman she recognized from their Red Cross meetings stormed into the dining room.

"There you are. I heard you were in town again." Red-rimmed eyes blazed, and a quivering chin jutted high. With hard steps, she marched across the floor. She wore black, unusual in the high desert heat. She even had a black hat with weepers trailing down her back.

The maître d' flapped behind her ineffectually, with small cries of "Madame Babineax, please."

Coming to a halt before Caleb, she clutched her purse. Both he and the major rose, placing their napkins on the table. Meghan, frozen by the righteous indignation in the woman's pose, stood slack-jawed, a sense of foreboding wrapping around her like a cloak, the dessert tray forgotten in her hands.

"Excuse me, ma'am?" The major bowed. "How may we be of assistance to you?"

"I don't want to talk to you. It's this yellow coward I want to address." She scrabbled in her purse and pulled out a large white chicken feather. "My son is dead. Killed in France, while you sit here dining in comfort without a worry in the world. But no more. This entire town is going to know you for the coward you are. I hereby bestow upon you the Order of the White Feather."

A gasp went up from the diners. Meghan's skin prickled as Caleb went white under his tan. The woman tucked the feather into his shirt pocket and slapped it hard.

"Any man who would refuse to enlist, then calmly sit in the nicest restaurant in town plotting how to profit off the very war he is too cowardly to fight in, well, that man deserves a chicken feather and much worse. You should be thankful I didn't bring tar with me. The people of this community are patriotic and proud, and we know a flat-out coward when we see one. You, sir, are a coward." Her face quivered with emotion, her eyes blazing.

Caleb said nothing, his lips pressed into a thin line.

The major couldn't hold his tongue, however. "Madam, please. You are mistaken. You judge him unfairly. Why, this man—"

"Sir, please. Let it go." Caleb shook his head.

"But, you can't let her go on thinking—"

"Please." There was a hard edge to his voice, and his eyes went steely.

A lump formed in Meghan's throat. He wasn't even denying it. In spite of all the evidence to the contrary, she'd held on to a shred of hope that the whispers and accusations of his cowardice weren't true. And yet, when faced with this humiliating debacle, being called out in front of the town and this fine army officer, he put up no resistance. He just stood there mute, letting his accuser win.

He *was* a coward.

Blinking back tears of disappointment, she turned away. She couldn't bear to look at him, so shameful and weak. How had she ever imagined him to be fascinating and interesting? Mrs. Gregory was right.

He deserved that chicken feather.

"Why didn't you explain to that woman? Why just stand there and take it?"

Major Alexander's questions hung in the air as they bounced along the rutted road leading to Caleb's place along the river. Caleb turned the wheel to avoid a rock.

"Aren't you going to answer me? You had every right to throw that feather back at her." The major's mustache jerked. "A distasteful custom if there ever was one, handing out chicken feathers to those deemed too cowardly to enlist. Started over in Britain, Admiral

Fitzgerald rousing the press and then silly girls continuing it to spur young men to enlist. Ridiculous."

Caleb glanced down at the tip of the feather protruding from his shirt pocket still. A writhing ball of humiliation twisted in the pit of his stomach. Bad enough to be humiliated in front of the major and the entire complement of customers in the restaurant, but to have Meghan witness his disgrace. The horror in her eyes, the confusion at first, and then the distaste. It gnawed at him like a hungry pack rat. He'd known the instant she went from incredulous to disillusioned. All the light had gone out of her, and she'd turned away from him just as the rest of the town had. She'd held out longer than most, but in the end, things had gone just the way he had expected from the first.

"What are you going to do with it? You should've thrown it away or left it at the table. Why keep it?"

He grunted. "Believe I'll hang on to it. The way this town is riled up against me, I figure in a week or two I'll have enough to make a fan. It gets powerfully hot here most days. I could use a fan."

"McBride, I don't know how you can joke. I checked up on you, and I'm very sorry about your. . .well, your infirmity, shall we say." He cleared his throat and stared out the windscreen, as uncomfortable as everyone was who learned about Caleb's foot. Not knowing what to say, not knowing where to look. And unconsciously treating him differently than normal men. Some behaved as if he were a freak, something to be ashamed of, like his father had. Others seemed to consider that it was his mind that was twisted and warped, that a weak foot meant a weak intellect. And then there were those like the major, who tried to bluff, to act as if the notion didn't bother them, but subtly, they behaved as if Caleb were fragile. They were so embarrassed by the whole notion, they walked on eggshells, trying not to let him know they were uncomfortable.

"Fifty horses will really stretch us. Is there any money to hire another wrangler or two?" Caleb changed the subject, freeing both himself and the major from awkwardness.

The major grabbed onto the new topic, relief coloring his voice. "I'm afraid there isn't at the moment. The truth is, this war has made the higher-ups have to rethink their strategies. This newfangled tank, airplanes, trench warfare. The mounted cavalry is becoming obsolete. The War Department is putting more money into mechanizing our troops than it is into acquiring and training horses. We've only got about six of these operations like yours going across the country. At the start of our involvement, we had close to fifty."

Caleb pondered this as the house and barn came into view. If the war went on long enough, he'd be out of a job. He could leave the Needles area. When he'd first been approached about taking on the job of training horses for the cavalry, the idea had appealed, even though they'd sent him to this inhospitable region—both the climate and the people as it turned out. He'd thought of little else than doing what he'd been hired to do, knowing that when the war ended, he would shake the dust of this town off his boots and not look back.

But that was before he met Meghan. Before she erupted into his life and made his heart spin wild dreams. Dreams where he had someone special who loved him, in spite of his flaws. Someone who knew the real him, the real Caleb who lived inside his less-than-perfect shell. Someone who would believe in him in spite of what everyone else thought or said.

He pulled to a stop before the porch and killed the motor and his foolish thoughts. Joshua came out, letting the screen door slap closed behind him. His brows arrowed toward each other, and distrustful lines formed on his forehead. Joshua hated strangers. Like a dog who had been beaten, he would circle warily, sniffing things out before he formed a judgment as to whether to trust the newcomer. Caleb had a fair idea of how the boy felt.

The major hopped from the truck, shading his eyes and surveying the property with as close a scrutiny as if he were a prospective cash buyer. He was silent for a long time.

"You should be proud of yourself. I can't imagine how you turn out such fine horses on such a barren spit of land." His piercing blue eyes met Caleb's. "Only the best trainers are still in business. Those near fifty other trainers I mentioned before? One by one they've been shut down as demand decreased. But we let them go in order of their abilities as much as for their geographical locations."

Joshua's dark expression lightened a bit, and Caleb shrugged and nodded. Again he wished the townsfolk could hear the major's praise, though precious little good it would do.

The boy clomped down the wooden steps and pointed to Caleb's pocket. "What's that?"

"Nothing."

"It doesn't look like nothing. It looks like a chicken feather."

"Your keen powers of observation are staggering. Yes, it's a chicken feather."

"Why do you have it in your pocket?"

The fiery shafts of humiliation returned, and Caleb swallowed hard. "Did you finish the chores while I was gone?"

"Yeah, but that sorrel mare's getting worse. I think she's got a case of the wobbles."

"I'll check on her."

"He staying to supper?"

" 'He' is Major Alexander to you, and no, I'll run him back to town before then. Major, this is Joshua Hualga, my assistant. Joshua, this is Major Alexander, the man who buys the horses we train."

The major sized up the boy, stuck out his hand, and gave Joshua's reluctant hand a brisk shake. "Good to meet you. You're doing good work here. McBride's horses are consistently the best turned-out mounts coming into Fort Riley. You should be proud."

"Yes sir." Joshua tucked his hands into his back pockets and lost a little of his wariness.

"I'd be interested in seeing your training methods, McBride."

The major had a reputation as a fine horseman, and his experienced eye missed nothing. He ran his hands down forelegs, stood back and watched the animals both on the long line and under saddle, and gave some practical advice on what to do with one little bay with a tendency to bite.

They finally worked their way around to the last pen and the sorrel mare Joshua had mentioned, alone in the small pen. Joshua climbed the fence and dropped lightly into the corral. The mare turned her head to look at him but stayed under the shade shelter. Her legs splayed at odd angles, her stance wide as if bracing herself on a rolling ship deck.

"Hmm, I think your wrangler's diagnosis of the wobbles might be correct." The major tapped his trim moustache.

"Lead her around, Josh." Caleb folded his arms on the top rail. He lifted his lame foot to rest it on the bottom rail and missed the slat. Lurching, he let out a surprised grumble, mentally smacked himself for being so careless, and looked down at his boot as he lifted it again to make sure he got it placed right.

The major had clearly noticed Caleb's stumble, but he turned his attention back to the horse as if nothing had happened.

Caleb studied the mare. "At first I thought she got into some loco weed, but now I think it's more serious."

The mare swayed and lurched, keeping her head low and walking as if she couldn't quite feel the ground.

"She's worse under saddle." He pushed his hat back and swiped at the sweat on his forehead. "I haven't put a saddle on her in a week, hoping she'd come out of it, but I think she must've injured her back somehow."

The major climbed the fence and slowly approached Joshua and the horse. He ran his hand under her mane, patting and murmuring. "See if she'll back up for you, Joshua." He kept his tone low and soothing.

Though Joshua pulled back on her halter, and even put his hand on her chest, all the while commanding her to back up, the mare stood still. Her brown eyes appeared bewildered, as if begging them to help her, to tell her what had gone wrong.

"That's enough, son." Concentrating, Major Alexander started at the withers and pressed along the mare's spinal column. Bone by bone, he worked his way toward her hips. Just back of where the saddle would sit, he pressed and the mare's head came up, her eyes widened, and she skittered away from him with a neigh. Joshua hung on as she slewed around, her legs going in all directions.

Somberly, the major joined Caleb. "There's a back injury there all right. Maybe a tumor, maybe a compression fracture, but something." He fisted his hand and banged it on the top rail. "A shame. I remember purchasing this mare near Santa Barbara. Big and rangy, and certainly up to carrying an officer through the French mud."

"Nice temperament, too." A weight settled in Caleb's gut.

"Best to get it done soon. Especially if it's a tumor. She's in a bit of pain now, but that will get worse."

Joshua released his hold on the halter and loped over. "What are we going to do?"

"Nothing for it. We'll have to put her down."

The boy gnawed his lower lip, staring at the mare. "Are you sure?" He blinked rapidly. From the bright sunshine or tears? Joshua presented such a tough face to the world. This was the first crack Caleb had been able to detect in his armor. Well, that and the hunger in his voice when he talked about studying medicine.

The major put his hand on Joshua's shoulder. The boy tensed, but he didn't shrug it away. "I'm afraid so. Maybe someday a veterinarian will invent a surgical procedure to help a horse with the wobbles, but for now the only thing we can do is put her down."

Joshua nodded. When the major dropped his hand, the boy tucked his hands into his pockets and moved a few steps away.

"I'll take care of it when I get back from town. You don't have to be here." Caleb gripped the top rail, pushing back until his arms were straight and lowering his head to stare at the ground for a moment. He hated the thought of Joshua being anywhere around when he put the mare down. An idea struck him. "In fact, if you want to, you can take Major Alexander to the depot."

Joshua's head swiveled. "Really?" His eyebrows rose. The truck was Caleb's pride and joy, and though they'd had some driving lessons, Joshua hadn't been allowed off the ranch while behind the wheel.

"I think you're ready for a trip to town." Perhaps a little reward would distract Joshua from the sadness of losing the mare.

Normally stoic features softened, and white teeth flashed. "I'd like that."

"Straight there and straight back, but don't hurry. I'd rather you got there slowly and in one piece, and I'm sure the major would, too."

As they disappeared down the long, dusty lane, Caleb pulled the feather from his pocket. Though he'd joked with the major about keeping it, he had no desire to hang on to the offensive object. The wind fluttered it, and he opened his fingers.

The feather floated, skittered, dropped to the ground, and was borne away on the hot breeze. Just like his hopes and dreams of being with Meghan.

Chapter 11

I sure wish we had mornings off instead of afternoons." Meghan tied a voile scarf over the top of her hat and under her chin. Digging for her gloves, she glanced at Natalie. "Are you sure you want to come with me? You could take a nap. I'll admit you look a little better since you've been working at the soda fountain, but you still don't look any too robust."

Natalie shook her head. "It's much too hot to try to sleep. At least in the automobile there will be a breeze."

Meghan threw her bag on the seat and went around to the front of the car to turn the crank. Getting permission to use the hotel's transportation hadn't been easy. She'd had to prove her driving skills not only to Mr. Stock, but to Mrs. Gregory as well. Only the fact that she wanted to go door to door appealing for Red Cross money swayed them in the end. The engine sputtered to life, and she hurried around to slip behind the wheel.

"Where are we going first?" Natalie raised her voice to be heard above the rattling.

With one hand on the wheel, Meghan dug in her bag for the map Mr. Weeks from Claypool's Department Store had drawn for her. "We'll drive north along the river for about ten miles and stop at places along the way back toward town, then, if we still have time, we can swing south and hit a few places in that direction." Though one place on the map she intended to give a wide berth. No way would she stop at Caleb McBride's. Having his name on the quilt would mean sure disaster when it came time to auction it off. In fact, if folks knew he'd contributed, she likely wouldn't get another signature at all.

That white feather. Why hadn't he stood up for himself, given his reason for not enlisting? At least had the fortitude to. . .what? What did one expect from a coward? It was like asking a lemon tree to produce apples.

Why? Why couldn't she get him out of her head? Even with concerted effort she couldn't eradicate him. He'd said he wanted nothing to do with her, she knew she wanted nothing to do with him, and yet, he occupied far too many of her thoughts and dreams.

Natalie trailed her hand out the window, cupping the breeze. She laid her head back on the seat and closed her eyes. At least the road was fairly smooth, though the dust they raised coated everything. Perhaps Meghan should've taken Mr. Stock up on his offer of driving goggles.

Flat, sandy desert stretched out on both sides of the road, though on their right, a greenish-gray smudge marked the brush that grew along the riverbank. When she'd reached the farthest noted point on Mr. Week's map, she turned in along a narrow, rutted path toward a house in the distance.

"How'd it go at this one?" Natalie poured some water from the jug they'd brought with them onto her handkerchief and dabbed her throat and swiped the back of her neck. Her cheeks bore pink blotches, and the hair at her temples clung to her skin. The car roasted in the sunshine.

Taking the jug, Meghan let some of the lukewarm water trickle into her mouth. She wrinkled her nose, both at the tepid fluid and the reception at the house. "Pass. She's got no money and too many mouths to feed."

At most of the houses along the road the answer was the same with varying degrees of animosity. Some were apologetic, some antagonistic, and in all, she garnered only two donations. Four dollars. With each stop, the temperature rose and Meghan's spirits fell.

"Don't be discouraged. It's four more dollars than you had before." Natalie shifted on the seat and pulled her blouse away from her skin. "Maybe we should call it quits for today. It's hot enough to melt rocks. It's got to be well over a hundred degrees, and there's no shade out here."

A dull headache had started at the base of Meghan's skull. "I'm not ready to give up yet. There's still the south road. Things might be better there."

Natalie passed her the water jug. "There's not much left. Maybe we should be done."

"No." She shook her head, surprised when a wave of dizziness washed over her. "I can drop you off at the hotel if you want, but I can't afford to wait another week to go out again. I don't have many afternoons off between now and when the quilt needs to be done." Lifting the water jug, weakness made her arms tremble, and water sloshed onto her chin and ran down her neck. The momentary coolness jarred her, and she blinked. Almost immediately, evaporation set in, leaving her parched.

She gripped the steering wheel and pointed the nose of the car south. The clock was ticking. They only had a couple more hours before they had to have the car back to the hotel. She pressed on the gas pedal. "When we get done, I'm going to go hide in the basement refrigerator, and I don't care if Mrs. Gregory finds me. If we weren't so rushed for time, I'd do it now."

"Before we hide in the cold store, I think we should stop for some ice cream at the soda fountain. I'd love to get a cold-food headache and shiver a little bit." Natalie consulted the map. "There are six places marked on here."

"So five more stops."

"Six."

"No, five. I'm not stopping at Caleb's place."

"Are you sure? How will he feel if he knows you stopped everywhere else but not his place?"

She shrugged, concentrating on keeping the car in the center of the road. "He said he didn't want to see me anymore, and the feeling is mutual."

"What?"

She squinted. Heat waves shimmered on the horizon, obliterating the distance. The road worsened, bouncing and jouncing them, kicking them from rut to rut. "He won't be hurt if we don't call. He'll be relieved."

None of the first four houses produced any subscriptions. The last one she wanted to visit lay on the far side of Caleb's property. Was it even worth it to go that far? She checked her timepiece against the map. They could make it there and back to town in time if they hurried.

She blinked, trying to clear her eyes. Black spots encroached at the edge of her vision. She shook her head. What was wrong with her? Was she getting sick?

"Meghan?" Natalie gripped the door with one hand and braced her other hand on the dashboard.

She sounded as if she were standing at the end of a long hallway, miles from Meghan. "Huh?"

"There's something wrong with the car. Look." She took her hand off the dash to point at the hood. Steam leaked around the edges and through the vents in the black metal. Slowly, Meghan pulled to the side of the road and the car bumped to a stop. She turned off the motor, though it took her a couple of tries to find the ignition. Wobbly didn't begin to describe how she felt. Maybe it was something she ate?

"I shink. . ." She tried again. "I think we overheated the car." Why did her head feel like it had been stuffed with pillow ticking?

"Meghan." Natalie grabbed her shoulder and shook her. Waves

of nausea sloshed through her middle, and the black spots in her vision grew bigger and closer together.

"Meghan, what's wrong?" Natalie's voice got slower and farther away as darkness claimed her.

Caleb leaned forward in the saddle, relishing the breeze pressing against his chest and fluttering his shirt. Though it was a bit on the early side for his evening ride out into the desert, he'd been so restless at the house he thought he might go crazy. Joshua's mother had come by for a visit, and he'd wanted to give the mother and son privacy. With him in the house, Mrs. Hualga wouldn't say a word.

His mount, a sturdy sorrel with plenty of stamina and very little speed, cantered over the hard-packed sand at a steady pace.

"You'd be better off on a bridle path back east, teaching youngsters at some riding school, old boy." Caleb patted the gelding's sweating shoulder. But in another week or so, he and his corral mates would be on a train headed to Fort Riley and the next stop on their journey to the war zone.

Pulling his mount back to a trot and then a walk, Caleb removed his hat and swiped at the sweat on his forehead. The ground sloped upward away from the river, and clumps of dusty brush dotted the landscape. The temperature hovered somewhere in the midnineties, down a dozen degrees from that afternoon, but still scorching. As they topped out on the rise, he made out the dark, wavering smudge of Needles in the distance.

From here, he could see just how isolated the town was, a small dot on the map, an island in a sea of sand and cactus. Insulated. They protected their own, and they were none too accepting of strangers. If one hadn't been born in Needles, or one didn't work for the railroad in some capacity, inclusion and acceptance into the community was a fairytale wish.

A tumbleweed bounced across the road, and the placid sorrel merely flicked his ears and studied it, never breaking stride. Caleb watched it roll and spin until it disappeared down the far side of a sandbank. He was so much like that tumbleweed. Needles hadn't embraced him, and as soon as the war was over or the need for horse-trainers for the cavalry ended, he'd brush the dust of this town off his boots, climb aboard the train, and head somewhere else. No ties, no roots. . .he shook his head. . .no home.

No Meghan. He'd seen the look of disappointment, of embarrassment, when that woman had handed him that feather. Though Meghan had held out and taken his part longer than he'd thought she would, in the end the opinions and accusations of the people of Needles had drawn her away.

As he had known they would. He'd been a fool to think otherwise. And he'd rather she turned away from him for a reason that wasn't true than to have her know about his shameful secret and reject him because of it. He'd lived through that once with Patricia. He didn't know if he could live through it again.

Enough feeling sorry for himself. Things were as they were, and there was nothing he could or would do about them. He was alone by choice and inclination. Even if the town of Needles had embraced him like a long-lost son, he'd still want to move on, to be alone. It was safer, for his heart and his peace of mind.

On the verge of turning back to the house, something caught his attention out of the corner of his eye. Squinting against the sun and cupping his hands at his temples, he strained to see. A dark object wavered on the road ahead. Big, like an automobile, but no dust plume followed it. Who would be stopping out here in the desert in the late afternoon? It was hot enough to fry a stove lid over easy.

Curious, he heeled the sorrel into a lope. As he approached, the heat waves resolved themselves into a dusty black car at the side of the road. Car trouble? A lost tourist? This road saw about as much traffic as the vegetable tray at a pie social. Only one more ranch lay beyond his, and Wilbur Frame was even more of a recluse than Caleb tried to be, always pottering among the rocks, prospecting for who knew what. Except for Joshua's mother and Major Alexander, Doc was the only person who ever drove this far out of town. This car was much too big to be Doc's battered old runabout, and Joshua's family didn't have a vehicle.

Someone huddled beside the car, and uneasiness tightened the back of his neck. Something was definitely wrong. He jabbed the sorrel in the ribs, wishing now he'd chosen a more fleet-footed mount.

The mass beside the car resolved itself into two people as one of them stood and shaded her—it was definitely a her—eyes. When she spied him, she waved her arm, beckoning him before kneeling beside the other figure once more.

The car was big, and as he approached, he recognized it as belonging to the El Garces. The kneeling girl was Natalie Daviot.

A flash of red hair from the prone figure had his heart clogging his throat. He pulled his horse up a few paces away and swung from the saddle.

"What's wrong? What are you doing out here?"

Natalie, her normally pale face raspberry red in the heat, looked up. "The car overheated then Meghan passed out, and I don't know what to do." She fanned Meghan's face with her hand.

"Where's your water?" He unclipped one of his canteens from his saddle and unscrewed the cap. Kneeling beside Natalie, he touched Meghan's skin. Paper-dry, and her pulse leaped under her jaw.

"We ran out." She pointed to the empty jug on the running board. Her movements were slow, as if the heat had taken all of her energy and will.

"That's all you brought with you?" Cupping the back of Meghan's head, he raised her up, gently bringing the canteen to her lips. "How long have you been out here, and what on earth possessed you to head out into the desert by yourselves without enough water to wet a handkerchief?"

Meghan's eyes rolled, and she sputtered as the water hit her tongue. Mumbles that became words leaked from her dry lips. Her eyelashes fluttered, revealing her green eyes clouded and disoriented. "Lars. Hold on, Lars. I'll get that ambulance. I love you, Lars." She went limp once more.

Lars? Who was Lars? A shaft of jealousy ripped through him. He'd been a double-fool. No way a girl as pretty and lively as Meghan would be unattached, and he'd never asked her, partially for fear of what she would answer. He chose to hide his disappointment behind anger.

"What are you doing out here with no water?" His barking tone made Natalie jump.

"We were gathering subscriptions for the Red Cross. Is she going to die?" Her eyes reddened but no tears leaked out. She was probably too dehydrated. And she had no idea of the danger they had put themselves in.

"I've got to get Meghan back to the house, and I need your help. Get my horse." He lowered Meghan's head once more and tipped the contents of the canteen over her hair and splashed her face and throat. Natalie drew his horse close. He wanted to curse his weak leg as he contemplated the logistics of getting Meghan onto the horse and mounting behind her.

But it had to be done. If he didn't get her temperature down, she was going to die.

"Unhook that other canteen." He tucked his hand behind Meghan's shoulders and scooped behind her knees with his other. Lurching to his feet, he stumbled against the side of the car. Heat from the blistering metal shot through his thin shirt, and he jerked away. "Help me get her into the saddle."

Between them, they managed to get her situated, though she was no help at all. She lolled and sagged, unconscious and unresponsive. Using the running board as a mounting block, he scrambled up behind her, wrapping his arms around her waist and leaning her back against his chest.

Though he hated to leave Natalie behind, he had no choice. His horse couldn't carry three, and he had to get Meghan to help as soon as possible. "Don't leave the car. Stay in the shade and make sure you drink the entire contents of that canteen. I'll send someone back for you as soon as I can. Don't stir a step, you hear me?"

"Just take care of her. I'll be fine."

The ride to his house, though less than two miles, seemed to take forever. Thankful for the sturdy sorrel who seemed not to notice his double burden, Caleb prayed as he hadn't prayed in a long time.

Please, Lord, don't take her. She's so young and full of life. She hasn't hardly even started to live, and she's got such big plans. Please, Lord, don't take her.

His prayer muscles were as atrophied as his left leg. Though he had long ago asked Jesus to be his Savior, he had a hard time not resenting the fact that God had chosen to send infantile paralysis his way and cut him off from the love of a family. Since Patricia's rejection and the move to Needles, there were some parts of his heart that were as dry as the desert around him. His spiritual life had been gathering dust.

A wavy blur appeared in the distance, resolving itself into house, sheds, corrals, and garage as he approached. Thankfully, Mrs. Hualga and Joshua still sat on the front porch. He rode straight to the nearest corral and swung down. Meghan toppled off into his arms.

Joshua pounded across the dirt yard. "What happened? What's Meghan doing out here?"

"Get the truck out of the garage. The hotel car broke down on the road and there's another girl out there. I need you to drive out and get her. Ask your mother to come here and help me with Meghan." He hitched her higher into his arms. "And open the corral gate."

Not bothering to hide his limp, he crossed the corral to the sunshade and lowered Meghan, clothes and all, into the water trough. Getting her cooled off was his first priority. Her hair floated in the water like red seaweed, and her face was deathly pale.

Mrs. Hualga stooped beside him and put her hand on Meghan's chest. "Her heart is racing."

"What else can we do?" He looked up into her brown, impassive face, so like Joshua's.

"Keep her there. I will be back." She padded toward the house.

The truck sputtered to life and rattled out of the garage.

"There's another girl, not as bad off as Meghan, but she's going to need help, too." Caleb called after Mrs. Hualga, who raised her hand in acknowledgment but kept walking.

Something nudged him between the shoulder blades, and he turned on his knee. His horse clopped over and stuck his muzzle into the trough. Caleb grabbed the reins and pulled him away. After running in the heat like he had, the last thing he needed was a bellyful of water. He should be walked until he was cooled off, rubbed down, and brushed. But there wasn't time. Meghan came first.

"Lars?" she whispered.

"Can you hear me?" He cupped the back of her head, wiping her cheeks and forehead with his wet fingers. "Meghan?"

No response. Even her lips were white. Her freckles stood

out, and her skin was as silky as a baby's. His suntanned, work-roughened hand seemed so coarse in comparison. But she was so still. So deathly still.

Who was Lars?

Mrs. Hualga returned. "Bring her to the house."

He lifted Meghan, streaming water and still unconscious, into his arms. He jerked his chin toward his horse. "Please tie those reins to the fence. I'll take care of him when I get her inside."

His leg radiated weakness, and afraid he would stumble and drop her, he shuffled his foot along the ground, not daring to lift it lest it buckle under him. He'd done too much today, taxed his twisted limb too far. Soon it would be a knot of cramps and twitches. If Mrs. Hualga noticed his halting gait, she said nothing. He got Meghan into the house and into his bedroom. Mrs. Hualga had pulled back the thin blanket, and Caleb lay Meghan on the sheet. Joshua's mother bustled in and elbowed him out of the way.

"What can I do?"

"See to the horse. Then bring water and newspaper and thermometer. You have ice?"

"I do." An old-fashioned icebox that went through ice at a ridiculous rate. He usually bought a block of ice when he went into town for groceries, then raced like a madman back home to get it into the insulated compartment in the top of the icebox before it turned to water. Thankfully, he'd gotten groceries the day before. There should be at least half a block left. A block tended to last about three days, and after that, he made do with powdered milk and canned vegetables and fruit until his next trip to town.

"Bring broken ice."

He tended to his horse, stripping the saddle and bridle and haltering the animal. Tying him to the fence in the shade, he left a single bucket, a quarter full of water where the horse could reach it. When Joshua returned, he'd send him out to finish the job. He swung by the tool shed for a hammer.

Working the pump in the kitchen, he filled a pitcher and a bucket with water. The box of medicaments on the linen closet shelf gave up the thermometer. Outside his bedroom, he tapped on the door. "Here's what you wanted. I'll bring the ice as soon as I can."

Please, Lord, don't take her. Why isn't she waking up? Why was she so stupid as to be careening around the desert in that car? It was that quilt. That stupid signature quilt. She was like Don Quixote, charging around, heedless of danger.

He hefted the dripping block of ice out of the icebox and set it on a kitchen towel. Wrapping it tightly, he picked up his hammer and smashed away until he'd reduced the block to manageable chunks.

"I've got the ice." He tapped on the bedroom door once more. A rattling rumble came through the open front door down the hall. Joshua returning with Natalie. Mrs. Hualga called for Caleb to enter. She straightened from the bed, studying the thermometer she'd just removed from Meghan's mouth.

"What does it say?"

She shook her head. "It's bad."

He studied the glass tube. The mercury hovered near the one hundred and four degree mark. His mouth went dry.

"Newspaper?" Mrs. Hualga took the ice bowl from him.

"I forgot it. I'll be right back." Meghan lay swathed in wet sheets. Her bare arms and lower legs stuck out, and her lashes fanned her cheeks. She was so still, he had to concentrate for a moment to make sure she was breathing.

"Go get the newspaper." Mrs. Hualga's sharp voice uprooted his feet.

Joshua and Natalie came up the front steps, the boy with his arm around the young woman's waist. Caleb snatched the newspaper off the front hall table. "Bring her in here. We can treat them together."

Natalie's face was still an alarming shade of red, and more worrisome, she wasn't sweating a bit. Mrs. Hualga tut-tutted, sent the men from the room, and took over.

Caleb leaned against the wall and took his weight off his left leg. "Thank you for bringing Miss Daviot." He scrubbed his hand down his cheek. "I pray they'll both be all right."

"Ma's dealt with heat sickness before." Joshua stuck his hands into his back pockets, shifting his weight. "Anything I can do?"

For a moment Caleb couldn't think. His entire being was focused on Meghan. "I left my horse tied up in the corral. He should be cooled out enough to turn in with the other horses. Then I want you to drive to town and get the doc. Stop by the hotel and let someone know where the girls are and that we'll bring them and the car back as soon as we can."

The bedroom door opened once more. "Come, I need you." Mrs. Hualga grabbed his arm and pulled him inside.

Natalie lay beside Meghan, draped in damp sheets. She gave a weak smile and raised her fingers an inch off the bed. Meghan didn't stir.

"More water." Mrs. Hualga was a woman of few words. She held up the bucket. "And towels."

As Caleb manned the pump in the kitchen, the truck rattled out of the drive once more. Joshua might be prickly and defensive, but he was a young man who could be counted upon in an emergency. What would he have done today without the Hualgas? Balancing a stack of towels in one hand and the bucket of water in the other, he limped down the hall.

She took the towels and bucket and pushed him into the chair beside the bed. "Here." He found himself clutching the newspaper. Did she expect him to read it?

Rolling her eyes, she folded it in half. "Fan." She moved the air over Meghan's face, and then dipped a cloth in water to moisten her skin. "Water, then fan."

Natalie raised her head from the pillow, but Mrs. Hualga pressed her small, brown hand against Natalie's shoulder.

"Lie still." She bustled out and returned with a drinking glass. Ice clinked, water poured. "Drink."

Caleb dipped the edge of a towel in the bucket of water at his feet and trickled it over Meghan's arm. Mrs. Hualga took a section of the newspaper and began fanning Natalie.

After an eternity, a groan escaped Meghan's cracked lips, and she stirred. "My head."

"Shhh." He clasped her fingers and gently pressed them into the mattress. "You have to be still."

Her lashes fluttered, and confused, pained green eyes appeared. "Caleb?" She blinked, squinting. "Where am I?"

"You're at my house. Your car broke down in the desert."

She stiffened. "Natalie?"

"Easy. She's right beside you. Joshua's gone for the doctor."

Mrs. Hualga nudged his elbow. "Make her drink." She held out a glass of water. "All of it. Then more, but slow."

He pressed the glass to Meghan's lips, letting sips of water trickle inside her mouth. Slowly, aware of her headache, he eased wet strands of hair off her cheek and temple. On the far side of the bed, Mrs. Hualga tucked a towel-wrapped bundle of ice behind Natalie's neck. She quickly fashioned two more bundles and slipped them under Natalie's arms.

"Here, like that." Thrusting a bundle at Caleb, she pointed to Meghan's neck and arms. "Keep fanning."

The color subsided from Natalie's face and returned to Meghan's over the next half-hour. Pulses slowed, breathing became more regular, and the knots in Caleb's muscles began to relax. Perhaps they were out of danger.

Meghan didn't mention Lars again. In fact, she said nothing, just lay on the bed, drinking when told and not opening her eyes.

Footsteps clomped on the front porch, and Doc Bates came into the bedroom. "What have you girls been doing to yourselves?" He adjusted his glasses and set his medical bag on the edge of the bed. Opening the bag, he rummaged, making glass clink. Gripping his thermometer, he rounded the footboard and went to Natalie, his brow wrinkled. "Open."

Resentment jabbed his ribs that the doc would automatically go first to Natalie.

"Doc, it's Meghan who was passed out. Don't you think you should check her first?"

Meghan clasped his hand. "Don't. I'm all right."

He leaned close to her ear. "But you were worse off than Natalie was. Your temperature threatened to blow the end of the thermometer right off."

"But then you helped me." Her voice still sounded too weak and slow for his liking. Meghan was a firebrand, a crusader, and righter of wrongs. She was full of life and movement and color. To see her so still and unresponsive had jarred him more than he'd realized. Her fingers entwined with his as her eyes closed.

Doc read the thermometer, shook it down, and stuck it back in Natalie's mouth. "Joshua should be here soon. I came in my own car, and I believe he was going to stop at the hotel. Caleb, step outside so I can do a thorough examination of both these young ladies." Doc took his stethoscope from his bag. He looped it around his neck and lifted Natalie's wrist to check her pulse. "I think, thanks to the good nursing they received from Mrs. Hualga, that they're both going to be just fine."

Caleb leaned against the hallway wall, as drained as a leaky bucket.

Joshua joined him there. "I stopped by the hotel on the way out of town. That French chef fellow sent a block of ice, and Mr. Stock said not to rush back. Make sure the ladies are going to be fine first."

"What did Mrs. Gregory say?"

"I didn't see her, thankfully."

"Probably just as well. What did you do with the ice?"

"Stuck it in the icebox."

"Great. Let's bust it up and make some more cold packs in case Doc needs them. And I could use a cold drink. How about you?" He clapped Joshua on the shoulder and followed him to the kitchen.

Twenty minutes later, Doc and Mrs. Hualga joined them. "Ah, iced tea, just what I need." Doc rubbed his hands together.

Caleb poured. "What's the verdict?"

"They'll be back to their old selves in no time. For now, they need rest, fluids, and no more gallivanting around the desert in the middle of a summer afternoon. What on earth were they doing out there?"

"It's that ridiculous quilt." Caleb rubbed his fingers down his glass. "They were looking for donations for a signature quilt Meghan's making to raise funds for the war effort."

Doc pursed his lips. "A worthy cause, though I'd think they'd be more sensible about their timing. Not even a Gila monster would stir in this heat."

"It might be a worthy cause, but if they'd have died out there in the desert—" He broke off. Now that they were out of danger, the enormity of their folly smote him. Someone needed to explain to them, to Meghan in particular, how stupid they'd been.

Meghan dozed and woke, dozed and woke over the next couple of hours. Doc checked on her, as did Mrs. Hualga, dousing her skin with water, forcing her to drink, taking her temperature. Natalie lay beside her, sleeping peacefully. If only Meghan could drift into a deep slumber and forget the pounding in her head. She ran all the metaphors for headache she could think of through her mind, but none seemed adequate to describe the pain in her skull. At last, some strength returned, and she forced herself to sit up and reach for her dress draped on the foot of the bed.

"You should lie still." Natalie rolled over and sat up slowly.

"So should you." Fumbling with the buttons, she squeezed her eyes shut for a moment. "My head is killing me, and lying there thinking about it isn't helping." Nor was thinking about how little she'd accomplished in the way of procuring donations and signatures for her quilt. The one thousand-dollar goal seemed further away than ever.

"We should be thankful God sent Caleb McBride to rescue us. You could've died out there."

"We both could've." Meghan didn't know how she felt about Caleb's rescue. Part of her got all warm and swimmy thinking of him bearing her away on his horse—if Natalie's recounting could be believed—like some gallant, brave knight of old. Another part of her cringed and skittered about. After what she'd witnessed in town with him refusing to stand up for himself, to give an accounting of why he hadn't enlisted, she couldn't help but be disgusted. How could a man be so brave and yet cowardly at the same time?

A tap sounded on the door, and Natalie finished buttoning up her blouse before opening it. Caleb stood in the doorway, his weight shifted on one leg as it often was. Meghan's stomach muscles tightened, and she looked away.

"Are you sure you two should be up?" He stepped inside, his boots rasping unevenly on the floor.

Natalie balled up the sheets they'd been wrapped in and gathered soggy towels. "I'm fine, but I think Meghan should stay in bed."

"We should get back to town. Mrs. Gregory will be having a fit already. And Mr. Stock must be wondering where his car is."

Caleb took the bedclothes from Natalie and dumped them into a basket beside the dresser. "Don't worry about these. I'll tend to them. There's iced tea in the kitchen. Do you want me to bring you some?"

"No, I'd like to go out and say thank you to the doctor and to that young man who came to get me out on the road. What is his name?"

"Joshua. Joshua Hualga."

Natalie disappeared, and Meghan became acutely aware that she and Caleb were alone in his bedroom. She bent and picked up her shoe, her head throbbing and a bit of dizziness swirling at her temples.

He cleared his throat. "Don't worry about rushing back to town. Joshua told Mr. Stock where you were when he fetched Doc out here. As for the car, Joshua and I will drive out there and refill the radiator once the sun goes down, and we'll see that it gets back to the hotel."

She nodded, her insides swooping. "Natalie tells me you came to my rescue again. Thank you. That's twice you've saved my life."

Shrugging, he leaned against the dresser. "How are you feeling?"

"Better. Thanks to you and Joshua's mother." Weakness flowed through her arms, and her shoe weighed a ton. She forced herself to tug it on and planted her foot on the floor to work her toes all the way inside.

"It was a close-run thing. You were babbling and passing out. You scared about ten years off my life."

She'd scared herself. "I'm sorry. The car overheated, and I guess we did, too."

He rubbed his palm against the back of his neck. "What were you doing out there in the first place? You could've been killed."

"I know. Good thing you came along. We were near to roasting." She tried to keep her tone light, to push away the fear of nearly dying. "It's hot enough to bake a lizard."

His brows slanted downward, and his mouth hardened. "This is no joking matter. As much trouble as you are always in, you need a full-time keeper."

Jamming her foot into her other shoe, she straightened. "I do not." She pressed her fingertips to her temple, regretting her loud tone.

"Yes, you do. You're always leaping before you look, expecting others to pull you out of your troubles and save your neck. When are you going to grow up and realize the world is a dangerous place?"

"I've said I'm sorry. What more do you want?"

He crossed the room and grabbed her by the shoulders, lifting her up and giving her a shake that, while not rough, awakened a new wave of agony in her head. "I want you to promise me you'll never be so foolish again. I want you to stop taking risks. You're so busy tilting at windmills and charging fortifications, you don't stop to think of the danger you put yourself in. And this time it wasn't just you. You could've killed Natalie, too, and what for? For a blanket? Because you want to get in good with the Red Cross and Mrs. Gregory and make a big name for yourself by raising a thousand dollars, you're willing to put yourself and your friend in jeopardy."

Stung by his harsh tone, she spit back. "How dare you speak to me about taking risks? At least I'm not afraid. You won't enlist. You won't even speak up for yourself when someone calls you a coward. You just stand there and take it."

Anger sparked in his eyes, and something else, pain, a deep hurt that had her regretting her harsh words even as they flew from her lips. That is, until he spoke again, wounding her, accusing her.

"You don't know what you're talking about. You rarely do. Instead of getting the facts, you jump to conclusions and leap into the fray. My reasons for not enlisting are my own. I'm entitled to my secrets, just as you are yours. You've kept things from me."

"What secrets have I kept from you?" Surely he wasn't talking about Natalie's marriage. He couldn't know about that, and why would he care if he did?

"What about Lars?" He curled his lip.

Meghan blinked. "What about him?"

"You said you loved him."

"Of course I love him." She bunched her forehead. "Are you sure you aren't the one who had too much sun?" When had she talked to Caleb about Lars? As a rule she didn't say much about him, but she didn't exactly make a secret of having a brother "over there."

"And I bet he's a soldier."

She squared her shoulders and lifted her chin. "He is. He enlisted right away. While I long for him to come home, and I'm afraid for his safety, I'm so proud of him, of his courage, I could burst. He's the reason I'm raising the money for the ambulance. And I don't care what it costs me. If he can be brave and sacrifice, so can I. He's a real man who knows his obligation to his country and those he loves. He'd never shirk his duty. He's no coward."

"Like me, you mean. Why don't you come out and say it? A man like me would never be worthy of a girl like you." A look of tortured anguish twisted Caleb's face, so near her own. His fingers tightened on her arms, and as if he couldn't help himself, his lips came down and claimed hers, hard and insistent, as if his frustration had finally outpaced his normal, tight control.

She forgot about her headache. She forgot about being angry. She forgot about everything. The kiss started out fierce and angry, but in a split-second it changed to something else altogether. His lips were wonderfully warm, his skin raspy as his whiskers brushed against her cheek. He smelled of sunshine and horses and hot desert air. Her hands crept up his shirtfront and edged around his neck. His hands spanned her waist as if to steady himself, and then found their way around her, bringing her tight up against him.

This is wrong. This can't be happening. Stop it! Like a scream, the thoughts echoed in her head.

Balling her fists, she shoved against him, breaking the kiss.

Immediately he pulled away, letting go of her waist and stepping back. His chest heaved, and his eyes glowed hot.

Her own breath came in gasps, and hot shame swirled in her ears and up her cheeks. What kind of woman was she to allow a man who insulted her one moment to kiss her senseless the next? "How dare you? You want me to say right out what I think? All right, I will. Caleb McBride, you disgust me. You avoid going to war when every able-bodied man in the country is answering the call. You hide out here on this barren spit of land training horses to go into battle. Horses that will show more courage in one day of wartime service than you will your whole life. And you take money from the same government you are afraid to fight for. It's despicable. You, sir, are a coward, and I wish I had a whole fistful of white feathers, because you would deserve them all." Her hand rose and smacked his cheekbone. "Don't ever come near me again."

Cupping his offended cheek he stepped back another pace, stumbling and knocking his shoulder against the doorjamb. His face had gone white under his tan, and a bleak, cold remoteness had replaced the heat in his eyes. "Don't worry. I won't. A person can only take so much sanctimonious claptrap, and I get enough from Mrs. Gregory and the rest of this two-bit town. When you get back to Needles, be sure to congratulate your head waitress. She'll be so proud to know you've turned out just like her."

He left her, and she sagged back onto the bed, holding her face in her hands. Her head threatened to split in two. And why shouldn't it? Her heart was already shattered.

Caleb avoided the kitchen and headed to the back porch. What had he been thinking? His cheek stung from the impact of her hand,

and his pride stung from the acidic accusations she'd hurled at him. In spite of all his warnings to himself, he'd allowed himself to spin dreams about Meghan Thorson, about how she would be different from every other woman he'd ever met. About how she might be the one to heal those broken places in his heart and love him in spite of his faults and flaws, his infirmities and insecurities. About how together they could be the family he'd always longed for. And he'd allowed those dreams to override his common sense to the point that he'd actually kissed her. Not just a peck either.

His chest still lurched in breaths of hot summer air, and weakness raced along his limbs. For an instant, for a suspended moment in time, everything had been perfect. Anger had fallen away. They'd stopped being adversaries and melded together in a giving and taking that had started a firestorm of longing raging in his heart and opened realms of possibilities he'd only dreamed of before.

But it had all come crashing down, as it always did when he dared to risk his heart.

She hated him. She thought him a coward. She was so enamored of soldiers and the Red Cross and her cause, she would never see him as anything but a yellow dog.

Not to mention this Lars fellow, whom she admitted outright that she loved. Lars the brave soldier who had enlisted the moment the call went out. Who was probably at this very moment covering himself with glory on a European battlefield.

He leaned against the weathered siding and smashed his heel backward into the gray boards. Pain shot up his leg, but he didn't care, bashing his foot into the wall again and again. He gripped handfuls of hair, gulping in breaths and striving for some semblance of control.

Why? Why, God? Why did you destine me to be a cripple? Why can't I be whole so I can prove I'm no coward? Why can't I be a real man and win the love of a woman? Why won't you let me be worthy?

Sinking to the porch floor, he rested his crossed arms on his good knee and let his useless foot sprawl on the boards, pressing his forehead into his wrists. He never should've kissed her, and yet, he hadn't been able to resist the need to claim her, if only for a moment. And though he might regret a lot of things in his life, he knew he'd never regret giving in to that overwhelming impulse. It changed everything, and yet it changed nothing.

She loathed him. And who could blame her? He loathed himself.

Chapter 12

M iss Thorson, nicely done with table seven. The customers were demanding, but you've managed to satisfy them all very well." Mrs. Gregory stopped beside Meghan clutching her ever-present clipboard. "I'm glad to see you've finally settled into your job."

"Thank you, Mrs. Gregory." Meghan didn't know whether to laugh or cry. From the moment she'd arrived in Needles, she'd longed for any kind word of approval from the head waitress. Now that she'd gotten it, it seemed a hollow victory indeed.

Nothing felt right inside or out. Lethargy and listlessness stalked her. All her normal drive and verve had deserted her, and she went through the motions of her job automatically. The only thing that brought her any joy at all was the quilt project and even that had become burdensome.

She cleared empty plates and removed centerpieces to replace the tablecloths with new, snowy linen before the next train arrived.

Sweat trickled between her shoulder blades. She'd asked a long-time Needles resident when the heat wave would break, and he'd laughed in her face. Maybe around Christmas. She shook her head, realizing Mrs. Gregory was still speaking.

"As soon as you finish setting the tables, go sit down and have some ice water with the others. We can't have you passing out from the heat again."

Though brusque, Mrs. Gregory's voice held a hint of concern, another new facet. She'd been particularly solicitous ever since Doc Bates had returned the girls to the hotel with several admonishments to both them and Mrs. Gregory about all the staff taking care in the heat. He'd ordered Meghan and Natalie to bed for the rest of that day and the next, and to half days of work over the weekend before allowing them to return to normal duties.

Meghan let the batwing doors flop behind her as she carried an armful of table linens to the hamper in the corner of the kitchen. A thermometer beside the back door showed the temperature to be hovering near one hundred five. She resisted the urge to cover up the mercury and numbers. Knowing just how hot it was made things worse.

A mountain of tablecloths and napkins spilled over the edge of the hamper, and with a sigh, Meghan added hers, shoving at the pile to make it stay. Tugging, she pulled the balky cart away from the wall and wheeled it toward the laundry room. The only sound in the darkened laundry was the squeak of the wheels and her footsteps gritting on the tile. In deference to the heat, the laundry staff now only worked at night when the temperature dipped into the eighties.

When she returned with an empty cart, the dining room girls were seated around a plain work table in the kitchen drinking iced tea. Nobody talked much, conserving their energy for the customers to come. The kitchen staff continued to work around them, though without the customary bustle and noise. The chef had altered the menu to suit the temperatures, and most of the dishes were served cold.

Mrs. Gregory motioned to the empty chair beside herself. "Sit down. We've got awhile before the two-thirty rolls in."

Plopping down, Meghan reached for a pitcher and glass. Ice clinked, and when she raised the glass to her lips, the cold tea tasted so good, she almost sighed.

The head waitress looked up from her clipboard. "I'm glad we have a few moments to visit before getting back to work. I wanted to ask you how your quilt project was coming along."

The quilt. For the past week, ever since her disastrous trip into the desert and the fight with Caleb, Meghan had thrown herself into gathering names and embroidering the quilt. She'd even unbent so far as to allow Natalie to help with the sewing. It was as if she had to make a success of the quilt just to prove to herself that Caleb's accusations had been wrong.

"Better now that more donations are rolling in. Mr. Claypool put up a notice in his store along with a sign-up sheet and collection box. And one of the schoolteachers sent home a letter to all the parents at the school. The children made it part of their back-to-school first week activities." Their involvement in the project had greatly encouraged Meghan. She only needed a handful of new signatures and donations to fill the quilt.

"That's good. As the chairperson of the Needles chapter of the Red Cross, I'm responsible to see that pledges are filled. I had my doubts as to your ability to finish the quilt and raise the funds you've promised, but you've made great progress. You're sure you'll have it done?"

"Yes, especially with Natalie's help. Thank you for allowing her to work on it at the soda fountain when she doesn't have any customers." This concession had baffled and pleased Meghan when Mrs. Gregory had offered. "I know the money we raise is going for such a good cause. I haven't heard from my brother in a while, but his last letter spoke so highly of the Red Cross workers over there. He said knowing that medical care is close by gives him and his comrades courage to face the enemy."

Mrs. Gregory patted her pocket, crinkling some paper inside. "I finally heard from Jasper this week. He's working with the quartermaster's department on rations and supplies for the troops. Isn't that wonderful?" The lines in her brow softened, and her lips quivered, losing a bit of their perpetual pucker.

"Wonderful." And it was, for Mrs. Gregory. She knew her son wasn't on the front lines, wasn't in a trench somewhere waiting for the horrifying word to go "over the top." Wondering if the next breath he took might bring with it mustard gas or phosgene. Wondering if he'd die by bullet or mortar shell or sickness.

Her heart constricted. No word had come from Lars in over a month. Mother's last letter had been full of worry and bits of news she'd gathered from the papers, things she couldn't talk about with

Meghan's father. Papa insisted that Lars would be fine. He wouldn't hear any talk to the contrary. But Mama was worried about Papa, too. He'd grown quieter, withdrawn, sitting each evening brooding on the front porch until the mosquitoes drove him inside.

Mrs. Gregory leaned close and patted Meghan's arm. "I have to say, you're a different girl since you had your heat sickness. You've finally lost your impetuosity. You've become levelheaded and devoted to your work in a new way. I asked Miss Daviot if she could account for your new, sober outlook, but she said she didn't know. I have an idea that you've finally come to your senses about that Caleb McBride. If that's the case, I can only say how thankful I am. You're much better off devoting your time and attention to your job and to the support of our soldiers. A man who won't don the uniform and serve his country isn't worthy of your notice."

Every girl around the table listened in and didn't even pretend not to. Heat that had nothing to do with the outside temperature sloshed through Meghan's middle and made its way into her cheeks.

"You are over your fascination with Caleb McBride, aren't you?" The head waitress's eyes pinpointed Meghan.

Her skin prickled, and she didn't imagine that several of the girls leaned in. Dryness invaded her mouth, and she raised her glass, both to drink and to stall for time. Images of Caleb flashed before her eyes, just as they did every night before she went to sleep. His handsome face, his wounded eyes, his gentle care of her.

She blinked, reminding herself to consider the masked look he'd worn when presented with a chicken feather, the anger and fear in his eyes when he'd yelled at her, and the almost loathing twist to his features when she'd slapped his face for kissing her.

And that kiss. The more she told herself to forget it, the more it came to mind. Powerful, earth-shaking, life-changing.

"Well?" Mrs. Gregory's eyebrows drew together at Meghan's hesitation.

She swallowed. "Yes, ma'am. I'm over Caleb McBride."

Later that evening, Meghan leaned against the door and dragged her lace headband off her hair. Closing her eyes, she let her muscles relax.

"Another long shift?" Natalie's rocker creaked.

Meghan dragged herself upright and tossed the headband on the dresser. "Seventy-five for supper. Everyone's temper is frayed to the breaking point with the heat, and one of the girls dropped an entire tray of dirty dishes in the dining room right in the middle of service. China and silverware went everywhere." She slipped out of her shoes and hiked her skirts to unclip her stockings. Rolling them off, she sighed, wiggling her toes against the tile floor. "I thought we'd never get it cleaned up. How about you? How'd the soda fountain go?"

"The usual rush just before the train left. Lots of soldiers. Seems they all wanted some ice cream to take with them. Mr. Stock even came in to help me when the line started snaking out the door." She poked her needle in and out of a quilt block, drawing the red embroidery thread along the penciled-in name. "Between times, I worked on the names. There's only one quilt square left to embroider after this one."

"Really?" A bit of tiredness slipped from Meghan's muscles and she hurried over to inspect the block Natalie held up for her inspection.

"Yes. And it works out perfectly. The only names left are yours, mine, Doc Bates, and. . .one more."

"I can't." Meghan's lips grew stiff and her stomach muscles tightened. "I won't."

"You have to."

"It will ruin the whole project. You've heard what people have said. If I put his name on it, no one will bid for it. I'll fall well short of the thousand dollars I need for the ambulance, and I'll be stuck with the quilt."

"A month ago, you thought his name belonged on the quilt."

"A month ago, I didn't know what he was really like. A month ago, he was a brave hero who had rescued me from falling under a train, a fascinating, handsome man I thought was courageous."

Natalie shook her head. "Nothing has changed. All those things are still true. If you could've seen him riding to our rescue out there in the desert and the tender way he cared for you, you'd know what a kind, gentle man he is." She shrugged. "You can't hold his harsh words against him. He was upset, scared that you might die. If you hadn't run away from his house, you two might've been able to patch things up instead of letting things fester. Trust me, I know. Derek can fly off the handle quicker than you can wink, but his temper never lasts. I'm sure if you and Caleb could just talk things out, you'd change your mind about him."

"That's where you're wrong. He isn't brave and heroic. He's a coward. He won't stand up for himself, won't give anyone a reason behind his actions, and he thinks I'm a brainless flutter-budget who leaps before she looks and always expects someone to rescue her. He thinks I don't care about the consequences as long as I get my way, that I have no grasp of reality, and that I need a keeper." Her ire rose as she recounted his accusations. "You should've heard him."

A snort escaped Natalie's lips. "I did. So did Dr. Bates and the Hualgas. We couldn't help it. You were shouting at each other."

Mortification spilled through her. She sagged onto her bed. They'd heard it all? No way was she asking if they'd heard the slap. Or if they guessed at the kiss. That stupid kiss. Why did her mind insist on returning to it, returning to the iron-hard grip of his hands on her arms, of the heat that had rushed through her—heat she would go to her grave vowing was anger and not attraction—or the way her heart had leaped like a wild thing in her chest when his lips had touched hers?

"Meghan, I don't want you to take this the wrong way, but Caleb does have a point."

"What?" Her spine stiffened.

"Wait. Before you get all defensive, hear me out." Natalie let her handwork fall to her lap and folded her hands over her waist. "You do tend to leap before you look. You see every obstacle as a challenge to be conquered, and you don't know the meaning of the phrase 'can't be done.' Whether it's raising a thousand dollars for an ambulance, becoming the best Harvey Girl on the line, or proving to Mrs. Gregory that you deserve to be promoted, you won't back down. Sometimes this courage and drive are assets for you, and sometimes they lead you to behave heedlessly." Her eyes were filled with warmth and friendship. "The only battle you're not willing to fight anymore is for Caleb. What happened to proving the whole town wrong and standing with him?"

"Even someone as hardheaded and obstinate as I am can recognize a losing battle when she gets hit over the head with it. I was wrong about him. He won't stand up for himself. I can't respect that, and I won't keep hurling myself against that wall."

A bit of starch invaded Natalie's tone, and she shoved the unfinished quilt block into her work bag. "You need to broaden your definition of courage. Caleb McBride isn't weak and cowardly. Everything I know about him, everything I've seen, supports the idea that he's a hardworking, honest, generous man who just wants to do his job and be left alone. If he chooses not to answer a foolish woman who tries to humiliate him in public, I think that shows remarkable self-restraint. He's got the courage to remain true to whatever convictions or reasons he has for not enlisting. Dr. Bates believes in him, and so did that nice Army major who came through. Joshua tries not to show how much he likes and respects Caleb, but he can't help it. The only people who take up against him are the women of Mrs. Gregory's set who are too silly for words. And you. If you could see how you've drooped around here the past week like a battered ragdoll, you'd be ashamed of yourself."

Meghan scowled. "I have not drooped around. I've come to my senses. I can't accomplish my goals when I'm distracted by the likes of Caleb McBride. People tried to warn me about him, but I was too headstrong to listen. You and Caleb have accused me of being impetuous, but when I finally listen to reason and decide to be sensible, you say I'm being silly."

"I think you're being unfair to Caleb and to yourself, and you won't be happy until you resolve your differences." She stood up and pressed her hands to the small of her back, arching and stretching. Her uniform lay across the bed, and she only wore her shift, which stretched tight across her middle.

Meghan's eyes widened. "Natalie?"

"What?"

She pointed to her roommate's waist, clearly outlined by the arch of her back. A suspicious bump pressed against the fabric. "Are you. . . ?" She blinked. "Is that. . . ?"

Natalie glanced down, and her back relaxed. Her hands went to her belly. Sinking down into the rocker, with pink suffusing her face, she let her head fall back, closing her eyes.

Mind chaotic, Meghan knelt beside the chair. "Natalie Daviot, are you pregnant?" Her voice came out with a low intensity that made the air between them vibrate. She shook Natalie's arm. "Are you?"

Her lips pressed together, and her eyelashes fell. A swallow lurched her throat. "Yes."

"Oh, Natalie." Meghan threw her arms around her and hugged her close. Natalie held herself stiffly. "That's wonderful." She pulled back to study Natalie's crumpled face. "Isn't it?"

"How can you say that? With Derek in France and my mother-in-law ill? I'm already hiding the fact that I'm married. This"—she pointed to her stomach—"isn't something I can hide forever. I'll be fired, sent home, and not only will I not have the money from this job, but I won't be able to get another job, and I'll have a baby to support." Her lips trembled, and a heavy sigh heaved out of her chest. "This baby is a disaster."

Meghan grabbed Natalie's hands and shook them. "Stop it. My mama says babies are a blessing, a gift from God." At Natalie's rolled eyes, Meghan tried again. "I know it won't be easy, but if you think of this baby as a little part of Derek. . ." She stopped. If Derek didn't come home, Natalie would at least have his son or daughter. "You're going to be a wonderful mother, and Derek will be so happy when he finds out. Just imagine how proud he's going to be when he holds his child for the first time."

For a moment, a soft, maternal glow invaded Natalie's eyes, but the clouds soon re-gathered there. "But what about Mrs. Gregory? What about my job?"

Meghan's mind raced. "I'm not saying it will be easy, but you've managed so far, and I'll help you. With your uniform on, nobody would guess. I only noticed because you're in your shift. How far along are you, and how much time do you think we have before it becomes really obvious?"

Natalie's blush intensified. "It must've happened right before Derek shipped out. If I had known about the baby, I never would've applied for this job. I'm about four months along."

Meghan's mind whirled. "Good, then we have some time. Our contracts with the company end in mid-November. If we can keep it to ourselves until then, you can finish out your contract, get your bonus for working through a Needles summer, and go home to your family. By that time, maybe Derek will be home."

"You're still a dreamer. The war won't end so soon."

"Well, whichever comes first, the end of the war or the end of our contracts, we'll do our level-best to keep the baby a secret."

Chapter 13

Doc Bates leaned back in his office chair and let the newspaper fall to his desk. Hundreds of soldiers and civilians falling prey to the Spanish Lady, the worst strain of influenza the world had ever seen. Though officials were reluctant to call it such, he had no qualms about naming it an epidemic. From what he could gather in the papers, the big cities were being hit the hardest, Philadelphia, Boston, New York, Minneapolis, but the illness had also spread into rural areas. Nobody was safe.

He picked up the Red Cross literature he'd received that day. Encourage folks to stay home, not to congregate together in large groups, to wear masks, disinfect, clean, wash their hands often. Mrs. Gregory had contacted him about speaking at the next Red Cross meeting. A rueful chuckle escaped his lips. He'd be speaking at a gathering, flying in the face of his own recommendation to steer clear of large groups. Still, word needed to get out somehow, and this was the best way.

A train whistle pierced the evening air. He wiped his forehead with his handkerchief and shrugged out of his waistcoat. Flicking on the desk lamp against the growing dusk, he checked the clock. Those poor folks, trapped on the train in this swelter, and the poor Harvey Girls serving them a meal. Who had an appetite in this kind of heat? And who wanted to be rushed through a meal in order to keep to the AT&SF schedule?

But the train waited for no one.

He hoped Natalie and Meghan were taking it a bit easier. It had been a week since their car broke down in the desert. Once a person had fallen prey to heatstroke, one tended to always have a sensitivity to the heat. Natalie especially worried him. At Caleb's house, she'd been too quick to get up and dressed, and he'd surmised she feared someone discovering her secret. By her calculations, she was about four months along in her pregnancy, and slight as she was, her waist must be thickening. Bounding out of bed and back to her normal routine too quickly could spell disaster. He'd have to call in there and see about scheduling another appointment so he could keep a close eye on her.

Then there was Meghan. A little dynamo most of the time, she hadn't rebounded as quickly as he'd liked. She hadn't met his eyes the entire trip back to town, and no wonder. Everyone in the house had been able to hear the argument she'd had with Caleb, from the opening salvo to the final crack of the slap she must've planted on Caleb's cheek.

Though it was the moment of silence between the fighting and the slap that intrigued him.

When he'd gone into the hotel midweek to check on the girls, he'd been surprised that all the life seemed to have drained out of Meghan. She still worked efficiently, but her smile was automatic, and the sparkle had gone from her eyes. She no longer looked as if life were a grand adventure.

Frankly, he wanted to knock some sense into both Caleb and Meghan. Caleb for being so stubborn and prideful keeping his leg a secret and Meghan for not seeing the caliber of man who stood before her and for listening to harping old gossips with nothing better to do than judge and meddle.

They were making each other miserable, which was a sure sign that they cared for one another. One couldn't be in the same room with them for long without seeing the sparks flying. Before she arrived, Caleb's trips to town had been few and far between. Since her arrival, Doc had practically tripped over him at least once a week.

Not to mention the anguished look on Caleb's face when she lay on the edge of consciousness in his bed and the gentle way he had brushed her hair off her face and smoothed her skin with a damp towel when she'd been delirious from the heat. Caleb had no idea how much he'd revealed in his expression and his actions. If Meghan had been able to comprehend it, she would've known in an instant that he loved her.

And Caleb was fighting it with all he had in him. Of course, with Caleb, Doc expected nothing less. He was too proud and stubborn for his own good. By his own admission, his father had rejected him when he'd contracted infantile paralysis, and Doc had a sneaking suspicion that another similar hurt lurked somewhere in Caleb's past. From the way Caleb was fighting his attraction to Meghan, Doc suspected it had to do with a girl who had let him down.

He hoped Meghan wouldn't do the same. A man could only take so much.

Maybe he'd head out to Caleb's this evening. On the pretense of doing a little night fishing on the river, maybe he could induce Caleb to open up a bit. And a chance to dabble his feet in the river or even wade in up to his neck seemed like a good idea.

Footsteps on the front porch drew his attention. The bell buzzed, and then buzzed again. He was halfway across the foyer when a fist pounded the door. His heart rate picked up.

"Yes?" He swung the oak and glass door open.

Jeremy Peterson, a bellhop at the hotel stood there panting, sweat dripping from his temples. "There's trouble at the hotel." He gasped, pressing one pudgy hand to his chest while gripping the doorframe with the other. "Mrs. Gregory sent me to fetch you."

"What trouble? Is it Miss Daviot or Miss Thorson?" He knew he should've insisted they take the whole week off to recover, especially Natalie.

Jeremy's brow crinkled. "Who? No, they're fine. It's the train. More than a hundred soldiers, and they're all sicker than a foundered mule." He lowered his voice and leaned in. "Mrs. Gregory says it's the influenza."

Doc's heart tripped, and a hollow feeling grew under his breastbone. Lifting his bag from the table beside the door, he made a mental list of everything he would need and where he might procure supplies. "Go roust the druggist and Mr. Weeks or Mr. Claypool from the store. We're going to need help. You said a hundred soldiers?"

"Yep. They started feeling sick right after the stop in Barstow."

"Let's get going then. Tell the pharmacist I'm going to need every bottle of aspirin and rubbing alcohol he's got, as well as whatever he has on hand for coughing, too."

Braking to a stop in front of the hotel, Doc hopped from the car and grabbed his bag. His worst fears had come to life, and now it was up to him to meet the challenge. At least he had some idea what to expect from his brother's letters. But the prospect of a hundred sick soldiers made his insides quake.

A wild-eyed baggage man met him at the door. "Shore glad you got here, Doc." His eyes rolled, showing a lot of white in his black face. "Miz Gregory is shouting at everyone, and Mr. Stock is trying to figure out what to do with all the people. We's all so scared." He looked over his shoulder toward the lobby as if he expected the influenza to reach out and grab him. "I been posted at the door to keep folks out."

Doc brushed past him with a nod. He had too much to do to palaver.

He stopped short just inside the door. Every chair, bench, and several yards of floor in the lobby were occupied by groaning soldiers. A sea of brown uniforms and miserable faces greeted him. Mrs. Gregory rushed up to him. "Thank heavens you're here. What should we do?"

A soldier lying on the floor by the front desk rolled to his side and vomited across the tiles. Several more coughed, their bodies wracked with spasms. Overwhelmed at the sight of so many ill young men, Doc closed his eyes for a moment, bracing himself.

Dear Lord, give us all strength. Guide me through this.

He opened his eyes. "I want these men in beds as soon as possible. If there are any soldiers who aren't ill, put them to carrying men up to the rooms. Send the busboys and bellhops to fetch basins, pans, buckets, whatever they can find. Gather the rest of the staff for a brief meeting."

Mrs. Gregory hastened to do his bidding, proving once again what a capable lieutenant she made, but how unsuited for command she was. Why hadn't she thought to get these men to beds? Though to be fair, the sheer numbers of ill men paralyzed him.

Meghan wove through the soldiers, her face pale, eyes wide. She clasped a stack of towels to her middle. "Doc." She took his elbow and drew him into a corner. "Natalie is going to want to help, and she shouldn't. We have to get her out of here."

He raised his eyebrows. "You know?"

"Yes, she told me. What are we going to do?"

He thought fast. "Tell her to pack a bag and get to my house. She can stay there until this is over. If Mrs. Gregory asks, we'll tell her Natalie is specialing a patient for me. Which she will be doing, taking care of herself."

Lines of strain eased out of Meghan's face. "That's perfect. I'll tell her."

Busboys and waitresses began assisting soldiers to their feet. One of the handymen took a door off its hinges to use as an improvised stretcher. Mr. Stock roped in burly railroad men to help with the moving.

Doc commandeered the south wing of the hotel, turning it into a makeshift hospital. "Move any hotel guests into the north wing. I have a feeling they won't want to stay in any case. Close the dining room and lunch counter for the time being."

When Mrs. Gregory protested that train passengers had to be fed, he said, "Have the cooks prepare boxed lunches. Once folks hear we've got influenza in the hotel, I doubt they will object to staying on the train. I'm going to need the Harvey Girls to nurse sick patients. I can't spare any for serving coffee and sandwiches."

When every soldier had been placed in a room, Doc called the hotel staff together. They met on the second floor loggia. A stiff, hot breeze ruffled aprons and lacy headbands. "There's no pretending this is going to be easy. At latest count, seventy-three of the one hundred soldiers are in the beginning stages of the Spanish Influenza. From what I've read and what my brother, an army physician, has told me, this disease moves fast."

He clasped his hands behind his back. "Mr. Stock, I'm putting you in charge of keeping us supplied with clean basins, hot and cold water, and clean linens. You'll also need to see about moving in more beds. I'm sure these cases won't be the last we'll see. The laundry will need to be going day and night. We must have clean bed linens, and we're going to go through a mountain of washcloths and towels."

The thin, sallow manager nodded. "It shall be done."

"Each waitress will have at least four patients. We've put the men four to a room, with one girl in charge of each room. There isn't a lot you can do, but keeping the patients as cool and comfortable as possible is your first priority. Try to get them to drink, and above all, keep the room clean. We have a limited supply of medicines, and we've wired for more to be sent." He nodded toward Miss Ralston.

"I asked Miss Ralston to break into the Red Cross supplies you've been preparing to send to Europe." He withdrew a gauze mask from the box she offered. "Wear this at all times. This illness is very aggressive and will seek any way it can to infect you. Wash your hands often, and turn your head away if your patient is sneezing or coughing."

He looked out over his allies in the coming war. Some scared, some eager, all unprepared for what was to come, even as he felt himself unprepared. Young, strong, healthy, the exact types who were most vulnerable to this strain of the disease. How many would succumb to the illness over the coming days? How many would survive?

Meghan swallowed hard, tied her gauze mask over the lower half of her face, and opened the door to room twenty four. Two double beds, both occupied by soldiers still in uniform on top of the covers. She braced herself. Unaccustomed to illness, she wasn't sure what she should do. One of the men lay on his side, coughing hard enough to rattle the bedsprings.

His bedmate lay with his arm flung up over his eyes, groaning

softly. The others lay with fever-bright cheeks, coughing or sneezing, moving their legs and arms restlessly. The fan overhead clanked softly, stirring the heavy afternoon air.

Meghan bent over the first man. "Is there anything I can do for you?" She touched his arm, shocked at the heat radiating from his skin.

"Water." His voice rasped.

Relieved at so simple a request, she hurried to the hallway. Mr. Stock had set up a tables there with pitchers of ice water and ranks of glasses. A dishpan sat on the floor to receive used glasses, and stacks of towels, washcloths, and sheets stood ready for use.

Mrs. Gregory went by with her clipboard. "I'll be in to get the names of your soldiers in a minute. Be sure to catalog their belongings and put them into separate laundry bags with a tag."

Meghan nodded, but her heart beat hard under her ribs. She'd have to help them all out of their uniforms and get them properly to bed. Quelling the blush that wanted to soar into her face, she reminded herself not to be silly. Though she'd never performed such personal tasks for men, and strangers at that, she knew her duty and she would do it.

You're a nurse and they are ill. You'll do what you need to do, and you won't be silly about it. You can blush for a whole day after all this is over, but for now, pull yourself together and get on with the job.

She pressed the glass to the young soldier's lips. He drained the contents and let his head fall back as if he couldn't keep it up an instant longer. His eyes closed, and his chest rose and fell rapidly.

Meghan went to the far side of the bed to the soldier with his

arm over his eyes. "Sir, I need to get you out of your uniform. Can you sit up?" The mask muffled her voice and made the air taste and smell like cotton, but she was thankful for it.

He lowered his arm, revealing startlingly dark eyes in his pale face. Even more alarming, the whites of his eyes were no longer white, but red. And the pain in his expression reached out and grabbed Meghan by the throat.

"Please, leave me alone," he whispered.

"I wish I could. Just let me get you settled and you can go back to sleep." She reached for the buttons on the front of his tunic. "Are you thirsty?"

"No." He gave a token protest, pushing softly at her hands before resigning himself. The most difficult part was getting him to sit up so she could remove his blouse. Mindful of Mrs. Gregory's orders, she bundled his belongings into a hotel laundry bag and tagged them.

"What's your name, soldier?"

"Patrick Newton."

Each of the other three did their best to help her, and the last boy blushed hard and insisted she leave the room for a moment, that he could get himself undressed. When she returned, she found him under the light sheet, his eyes focused on the ceiling.

Patrick, Wesley, George, and Harold. All army privates, all from California, all very ill.

"Here, let's put this over your eyes." She folded a damp cloth and set it on Patrick's brow. "It will cool you off and cut the light." She'd drawn the shade, but his headache was so fierce, even the smallest

bit of light seemed to stab his brain cruelly.

Wesley's fever soared, and she sponged him, wringing the cloth over and over, wiping his face and neck and arms.

This is what Caleb did for you.

She forced that thought away. Thinking about Caleb was useless, and she needed to focus on her patients.

George coughed and coughed until she feared he would tear his lungs apart, and Harold lost the contents of his stomach over and over again, leaning over the side of the bed, his head over a bucket. Meghan moved from one to the next in a continual round, seeking to help, her alarm at the speed and severity of this sickness mounting.

Doc came in. "How are they doing?"

She shrugged. "I don't seem to be doing very much for them." Helplessness swept over her. "I'm sponging them off and trying to make them as comfortable as I can, but what else should I be doing?"

"That's about all you can do." He bent over Wesley and placed his stethoscope on the rapidly moving chest. With his other hand, he popped a thermometer into Wesley's mouth. "Get some of the hotel stationery out of the desk, one page for each man, and put their names on the top. I'm going to have you chart their conditions. If you notice any changes, make a note on their paper. Do it every time. If you don't, things are going to blur together. You won't remember when you gave them medicine or when they last had something to drink or when their breathing changed."

He took the vital signs of each man, and she carefully recorded them along with the time.

"I'll send someone in with a couple of bottles of cough syrup and some aspirins. Be sure to mark when you give each man the medicine. And keep the aspirin bottle in your pocket at all times. It's too precious to mislay. In about an hour someone will bring you some chicken broth. Don't be alarmed if they don't want any." He stuffed his stethoscope into his pocket and inclined his head toward the door.

Once in the hallway, he rolled his head as if loosening tight neck muscles. "I want you to watch their breathing and their skin. If they can't fight off the sickness, the next step is petechia, hemorrhages under the skin. The one boy, Patrick, already has bleeding in his eyes. After the small bleeds start, my brother, who has seen quite a bit of this, says the lungs will begin to fill with fluid, causing pneumonia. When that happens, their breathing is going to become much thicker, and might even sound bubbly. Prop them up with extra pillows. If they request anything, try to give it to them. If anything worries you, send someone to find me. There will be a bellhop posted in the hall to run errands and track me down if you need me."

She nodded. The weight of responsibility settled on her, but she refused to bow under it. She could do this. "How are the others faring?"

"Another ten soldiers from the train have come down ill. How are you feeling?"

"I'm fine." She forced some strength into her voice.

"You should still be resting after your heatstroke. You both came back to work too early." He rubbed his hands down his face, disturbing the mask. "You did get Natalie away all right?"

"Yes. She protested, but I threatened to come and find you. She gave in because she knows it's for the best."

"Did Mrs. Gregory give you any trouble?"

"No, she barely seemed to hear me because she was so busy getting sick men into beds."

"It's going to be a long night, and with the way things are going, I expect we'll be seeing more patients. The flu is bound to spread to the town, despite our best efforts. The hotel had townsfolk in it when the sick soldiers arrived, and they carried the sickness to their homes. I've put the police chief wise, and he's going to send his constables around town to check on folks. Those who are the most ill or who don't have anyone to care for them will be brought here."

"What about the trains?"

"For now, they'll stop and refuel, but no passengers will be allowed to get off unless they're sick or live in Needles. The AT&SF will try to keep their schedule, but they'll inform passengers that there won't be any meals or lodging in Needles until we give them the all-clear."

Mrs. Gregory marched past them carrying two buckets, and Meghan nodded to the doctor. "I'd best get back to my patients."

She lost all track of time. Her hands grew red and puckered from wringing out cool cloths, and her back ached from bending over the beds. Her apron bore stains she'd have been chastised for had she worn them into the dining room, and her shoes pinched, her feet swollen and hot.

Harold finally stopped retching and lay still. George's cough grew worse, and he gasped for breath, his face turning purple with each prolonged spasm. When Patrick's breathing changed for the worse, the hairs on Meghan's arms lifted. She sent the bellboy for more pillows and with his help, got Patrick propped up. It seemed to do little good. And most alarming, Wesley's nose began to bleed. She sent for Doc Bates.

His hair seemed to have gone grayer, and new lines had appeared on his kind face. He lifted the sheets and checked his patients' feet. Patrick's and Wesley's were both an odd bluish color.

She wiped the trickle of blood off Wesley's upper lip once more. His eyes moved behind his eyelids, but his lashes remained closed.

"So fast." Doc's murmur was barely audible over the labored breathing in the room. "My brother said it moved fast, but I've never seen anything like this. Yesterday morning, these boys were hale and hearty."

Meghan wrung out yet another cloth and swapped it for the one on Harold's brow. "Tell me these are the worst, that the other soldiers are faring better."

Doc's breath puffed out his mask, and he shook his head. "I wish I could. Step out in the hallway with me for a moment."

Once in the hall, he tugged down his mask. "Jeremy, watch this room while Miss Thorson takes a break."

The bellhop put down the tray of glasses he carried and nodded. Meghan dropped onto a bench and leaned back. Red streaks of light showed through the filmy curtains on the balcony doors, harbingers of sundown. She'd spent all night and all day in the room and beyond noting times of medication, the hours had blurred together.

Had it really been more than twenty-four hours since the train had arrived full of sick soldiers?

Doc sat next to her, pinching the bridge of his nose. "We've already lost two of them, and a score more are critical. The one that's bleeding from the nose. . ."

"Wesley." A lump formed in her throat.

"Don't be surprised if he starts coughing blood soon."

"What's happening to them? This isn't like any flu I've ever heard of."

"Smarter doctors than I seem to think it's a reaction by the body's immune system. The flu is a respiratory disease, and when it attacks, the immune system attacks back. Fluids build up in the lungs, and the patient begins to drown. They cough so hard trying to expel the fluids they end up damaging their lung tissue and bleeding into their lungs. They ultimately die of pneumonia. You saw the blue feet on a couple of those boys? The body is starving the limbs of oxygen in an effort to keep the internal organs alive. Once the illness reaches this stage, death is almost certain."

He heaved out a sigh. "You need to go downstairs and get something to eat. It's going to be another long night, and you will need all your strength. When you've eaten, take a few minutes to walk along the platform and stretch your legs. Jeremy will watch over your patients."

With leaden legs and a heavy heart, Meghan dragged downstairs toward the kitchen. Mrs. Gregory sat at one of the tables, her face in her hands, her shoulders shaking. She raised her head when Meghan entered.

"Miss Thorson." She straightened and smoothed her hair, swiping at her eyes and gathering her composure. "Did you need something?"

Meghan noted her blotchy cheeks and the extra starch in her voice that repelled any comment about her appearance. "Doc sent me downstairs to have something to eat and to get a little fresh air."

"Fine. Chef's got sandwiches and cake in the cooler. I'd best go see that the laundry is keeping up." She pushed away from the table and marched away, her heels tapping briskly.

A yellow piece of paper and an envelope fluttered behind her as she passed, and Meghan stooped to pick it up. A telegram. Without really meaning to, her eyes scanned the brief missive.

WHILE ADVANCING AGAINST THE ENEMY, PRIVATE JASPER GREGORY WAS STRUCK BY SHELL FRAGMENTS IN THE TORSO AND LEG. PRIVATE GREGORY IS RECUPERATING AT THE ARMY FIELD HOSPITAL NEAR THE CITY OF ARRAS. HIS CONDITION IS CONSIDERED CRITICAL. AS SOON AS POSSIBLE, HE WILL BE EVACUATED TO BRITAIN THEN TO THE UNITED STATES.

Meghan's hand shook. Mrs. Gregory's son was supposed to be safe behind the lines working for the quartermaster, not advancing against the Germans on the Western Front. She folded the telegram and replaced it in the envelope, unsure what to do. Poor Mrs. Gregory. Her son was all she had.

Her thoughts went to her brother, Lars, praying he was still alive, praying her parents wouldn't receive a telegram like this. She sank onto a chair and put her face in her hands. Her appetite had fled. Hot tears flooded her eyes, for Mrs. Gregory who held people at arm's length even in her most sorrow-filled moments, for the soldiers on the front lines, and for the poor soldiers upstairs fighting for their lives. She blinked hard, forcing down her fear and despondency, knowing that if she gave in to her tears now, she'd be useless.

"Ma'am?" The whisper barely penetrated the big empty kitchen. She turned. Joshua Hualga opened the batwing door wider.

"Joshua, what are you doing here?"

"I've been all over this hotel looking for you." He stuck his hands in his pockets and hunched his shoulders. "What's going on upstairs? Why isn't the restaurant open?"

"Does Caleb know you're here?" She braced her hands on the table and stood.

"No, and I figure he'd skin me alive if he did know. He let me borrow the truck to go visit my family on the reservation, but I figured somebody better come talk to you."

"Why? Is something wrong with Caleb?" She cast a quick glance over her shoulder. "You're not supposed to be in the hotel. Let's get outside before someone sees you."

His face hardened. "Because I'm an Indian? We went all through that with the man who owns the hotel. I have as much right to be here as anyone."

"Oh, my stars and garters, boy." She grabbed his arm, exasperated and tired. "I don't care if you're Indian, Greek, or the King of the

Cannibal Islands, you can't be in the hotel. It's under quarantine."
She hustled him out of the kitchen, through the dining room and
foyer, and out onto the railroad platform. "Some passengers came in
yesterday who weren't feeling well. They're staying here until they get
better, and Doc put the hotel into quarantine as a precaution." She
downplayed the severity of the situation, not wanting to scare him.

"Doc's here? Does he need help?" Light leaped into Joshua's eyes
and he took a step back toward the lobby doors.

She put her hand on his chest. "Doc's got plenty of help. Now
go home."

"No, ma'am, not till you've heard me out. I risked my job to
come find you, and I intend to say what I've got to say before I go
back and own up to what I've done." His jaw stuck out, and his eyes
glittered in the dusk. "You were pretty harsh on Caleb when you
were out to his place, and it cut him up pretty deep. He's been like
a badger with a boil all week. He was sweet on you, and he thought
you were woman enough to stand up to the opinions of this town
and take his part. He's so disappointed in you, he can hardly think
straight."

"He's disappointed in me?" She gaped. "I'm not the one who
earned herself a white feather. I'm not the one who's so afraid that
he won't enlist."

Joshua snorted and scowled. "You're talking through your hat.
Caleb isn't afraid of anything or anyone. Spend just a minute and
think back on what he's done. He threw himself practically under
a train to rescue you the first day you met. He hired me when he
knew lots of folks in this town wouldn't spit on an Indian if he was

on fire. He stood up to Mr. Stock when he would've thrown me out of the hotel for being Indian. He faces down bullies and gossips every time he sets foot in this two-bit burg. He even braved a dance here at the hotel, one hosted by a bunch of cow-faced old gossips who'd like nothing better than to roast him on a spit, just because he wanted to spend more time with you. You don't know what courage looks like if you think it can only be found in uniform."

Stung by the vehemence in his tone and the fire in his eyes, she fought back. "Then why won't he enlist? Why won't he stand up for himself?"

"His reasons are his own, I reckon, and when he's ready he'll tell you. Until then, you should have faith in him. Caleb McBride holds everything in, even his temper, when most men would've punched someone or struck back somehow. He's patient and careful and private, and he tries not to let anything show. He must care for you an awful lot to be so hurt by you turning against him. The whole town has turned against him, and he hasn't cared a cup of sand what they thought, but you're different. He let himself care, reached out to you a little, and you bit him like a rattler."

Before she could respond, Mrs. Gregory called out. "You there, boy. Get away from here. Miss Thorson, you're needed upstairs."

"Think on what I said." Joshua stepped back. "And tell Doc that I'd be happy to help out with the sick if he needs me."

Meghan returned to the hotel under the watchful eye of the head waitress.

"What did *he* want?" Mrs. Gregory's voice was loaded with animosity.

Mindful of the terrible news the head waitress had just received, Meghan softened her reply. "He offered to help with the sick if we needed him."

"Did you tell him we had the influenza here?"

"No, just that some passengers had fallen ill and Doc quarantined the hotel as a precaution against the illness spreading to the town."

"Fine. Good. Hopefully he'll stay away. You do need to get back upstairs. We've lost two more soldiers, and a couple of the hotel staff aren't feeling too well." The lines had deepened around the head waitress's mouth, and her eyelids were still pink.

Meghan nodded. "You dropped this in the kitchen." She handed over the yellow envelope, giving no indication she knew the contents. When Mrs. Gregory was ready, she'd let people know of her son's condition. Until then, Meghan would guard her privacy.

With her chin held high, Mrs. Gregory took the envelope, but the storm clouds of fear gathering in her eyes belied her outward calm.

Meghan returned to room twenty-four and relieved the bellboy. Her patients clung to life by tenuous threads, and she settled in for a long night of nursing care and thinking over what Joshua had said.

Chapter 14

Y ou did what?" Caleb let his saddle *thunk* to the ground and wiped his forehead. After a day of dust and wind and heat and stubborn horses, his fuse was short. All he wanted to do was get the weight off his leg and drink about a gallon of cool water.

"I went to see Meghan last night." Joshua tucked his hands into his back pockets and stared at Caleb from under his hat brim, defiance in every line of his thin body.

"I thought you were visiting your parents."

"I did. But afterward I stopped in town. That's why I was so late getting back. I'd have told you then, but you'd already gone to bed. And this morning you were in too bad a mood."

"You had no call to see Meghan." The initial explosion of surprise in Caleb's chest grew and rippled outward into anger.

"Didn't I? You've been hissing and snapping around here like a cornered Gila monster all week, ever since she smacked your face.

You're miserable, and you're taking it out on me. Somebody had to do something about what's wrong between you two."

"I have not been a Gila monster, and how I feel has nothing to do with Meghan Thorson. There's nothing wrong between us."

"Then why haven't you gone to town and talked to her?"

"I've been busy, and there's nothing to say."

"That hasn't stopped you all summer. How many trips to town did you make just so you could see her? You're eating your heart out for her, and you're too stubborn to admit it."

"Is that what you told her?" He jerked his hat off and thwacked his thigh, lifting his face to the sun. "Somebody save me from interfering friends and gabbity employees." Curiosity ate at him, and he couldn't help asking, "What else did you tell her, and what did she say?"

Joshua mopped his face and grimaced. He rolled his neck and shoulders and blinked against the glare. "I told her you were more courageous than anyone I had ever met and that she was a fool to let other people define courage for her."

He stilled, leaning against the corral rails. Pleasantly surprised, he didn't know what to say, so he busied himself by coiling and recoiling his rope.

Joshua continued. "I have eyes in my head. I told her to remember all the courageous things you've done that you didn't have to do. About how you do things without thinking about the cost to yourself and that you held onto your temper better than anyone I knew. I just wish you'd tell her the real reason you haven't enlisted."

The rope dropped from his hands. "What do you mean?"

Joshua shrugged. "I told you I have eyes. Why don't you tell her about your leg?"

Cold swept through him. "What about my leg?"

"Can we go sit down in the shade to talk about this? I'm weak as a cat today. Guess staying out late last night didn't agree with me." Joshua turned and headed for the porch.

Snatching up his rope, Caleb made sure the corral gate was latched before following him. When they were both seated in the ladder-back chairs on the porch, he stared hard at his employee. "What do you know about my leg?"

Joshua let his head rest against the top slat and closed his eyes. "I know that you limp on it when you think nobody's looking. I know it pains you, especially after a long day. I figure that's why you've gone to see Doc a few times this summer, and I know that your boots are special made. So what's wrong with it anyway?"

A lifetime of silence on the issue clamped Caleb's lips shut. He got up and went into the kitchen, pouring two glasses of water before returning to the porch. Joshua cracked one eyelid and accepted his glass, drinking it in small sips. Caleb returned to his chair and drained the contents of his water glass.

"You done stalling?"

He glared at Joshua, but the gesture was lost on his hired hand. He had his eyes closed again.

"I had. . ." He could hardly bear to say the words, he loathed them so much. "I had infantile paralysis when I was a kid." He braced himself for a reaction.

Joshua let out a long breath through his nose and raised his eyelids. "That's rough. I've been reading those books from Doc. I guess it's a blessing you can walk at all. But why hide it? It's not like getting sick was your fault."

The words jammed in his throat. It was so hard to explain, how his damaged leg made him feel less than a man, how he'd been judged and found wanting by the very people who were supposed to love him, who should've loved him, infirmity and all.

"I don't like to talk about it. This bum leg has cost me too much. When people know about it, they treat me like I don't have any brains, that my head must be as withered as my foot."

"People like who? Doc knows about it and he treats you just fine. I imagine that major who came to buy the horses must've known something about it, and he looked you in the eye and commended your work."

"They're the exceptions, trust me."

"So who treated you bad because of your leg? Nobody else in town knows, or word would've spread and they'd have laid off all the coward nonsense." Joshua was like a crow picking corn off a cob, peck, peck, peck.

"My father stuck me in an asylum for crippled kids and never spoke to me again." Caleb sucked in a breath and barely avoided putting his hand on his chest. How could a wound so old still hurt like it had just happened?

A phantom smile crossed Joshua's face. "Your dad and mine sound a lot alike. Mine barely speaks to me and was only too glad to see me leave the reservation to work for you. He doesn't know what to do with me. I had the audacity to be different."

Caleb remained silent, leaning forward and bracing his forearms on his thighs, rolling his empty glass between his palms.

"You should tell Meghan at least. She deserves to know. Then she can quit thinking you're a coward. I bet she'd pin the ears back on any of those nosy biddies in town who wanted to run you down. She's a sure enough go-getter and smacker-downer when she gets the bit between her teeth. She'd fire up so quick in your defense, she might burn down the town with her words alone."

"I doubt that." Her outraged face swam in his memory, her hand lifted to strike his face.

"I have a feeling that once you had Meghan on your side, she'd take a bullet for you."

"But if she knew about my leg, she wouldn't *be* on my side. I can live with her thinking I'm a coward because it isn't true. I can't stomach her turning away from me because I have a crippled leg."

"What makes you think she'd bail out on you?"

"Bitter experience."

Joshua raised his eyebrows and took a sip of his water. With the back of his sleeve he mopped his forehead once more. "How so?"

"Nothing to be gained by talking about it." If there was one wound he didn't want exposed, it was his failure with Patricia.

"Nothing to be lost either." Joshua sighed and closed his eyes. "Man, I feel like the dog's dinner."

"I'd best go start supper." He braced his hands on the arms of the rocker and rose.

A grimace twisted the boy's features. "None for me. I'm going to go to bed."

Caleb stopped halfway to the door. Not hungry? That wasn't like Joshua. He reversed direction and laid his hand on the boy's forehead. Heat radiated from his skin.

"You're burning up."

"I think I might've done something stupid."

"What do you mean?"

"When I went to see Meghan. . .the hotel was under quarantine. I went inside anyway, slipped past the bellhop they had manning the front doors."

"Quarantine? For what?"

"Meghan didn't say, but it must be pretty serious if they locked down the hotel and closed the restaurants. From the little bit I saw, I'd venture to say there are a lot of soldiers in the hotel. One of those troop trains. Now I'm thinking going inside wasn't such a great idea. I feel terrible."

Sick soldiers. It didn't take a genius to guess that the Spanish Flu had invaded Needles. The papers had been full of the epidemic for weeks, especially in the military camps.

And Joshua had come into contact with the sickness.

"Let's get you to bed. Maybe it's just a touch of heat or something. If you don't perk up after a good night's rest, I'm taking you to town."

Meghan stood in the hallway, her shoulders bowed, tears stinging her eyes and throat, trying to hold on to her self-control. Within a half hour of each other, Wesley and Patrick had succumbed to the dreadful illness. A pair of hotel porters bore Wesley away on a stretcher, just as they had Patrick only a little while before. George and Harold clung to life, racked with coughing and fever, but still alive.

Patrick had slipped away quietly, his labored breathing becoming more and more shallow, until he'd sighed his last. His face lost its tension, and all movement ceased. Meghan called for the doctor to confirm her fears, and when he'd completed his cursory examination, he'd pulled the sheet over Patrick's face and summoned men to carry the body away.

Wesley had left this world hard. At the end, he'd turned dark, purplish blue, fighting for air, clutching her hand, his eyes pleading with her to help him. Finally, he'd coughed up a great cloud of blood and passed away, his hand growing limp and his eyes unfocused.

Nothing had prepared her for the speed, and in Wesley's case, the violence of death. One moment they'd been alive, and the next, dead. She leaned against the wall, trying to summon the courage to return to the sick room. She'd need to strip the bed and disinfect every surface. George and Harold needed her.

And yet, her stomach quivered at the thought of going back in there. She hadn't known those men at all, but they had been under her care. Had she failed them somehow?

"Miss Thorson?"

Mrs. Gregory pushed a laundry cart down the hallway. She stopped beside Meghan. "I heard you lost another one." She adjusted her mask. "So fast. They've been here less than three days and we've already lost seventeen men."

"Are there any new cases?"

"Nine hotel workers, including Mr. Stock. And a handful of folks from town. They were in the hotel when the train pulled in. And a couple of railroad men have come in, part of the group that helped us transfer patients from the train to the hotel." She shook her head.

A creepy, crawling feeling skittered across Meghan's skin. Such slight contact was enough to catch the illness? Her mask seemed less than adequate to shield her from something so pervasive. And she couldn't get the image of Wesley, drowning in his own blood, out of her mind.

"Do you have any bedclothes that need to go to the laundry?" Mrs. Gregory jarred her back to the present.

"I do. I'll get them." Forcing herself away from the wall, she slipped into room twenty-four. A quick check told her nothing had changed in either George or Harold's conditions. Early morning light seeped in around the edges of the window blind. While the rising sun of a new day usually filled Meghan with optimism and energy, today it just filled her with dread.

With hasty jerks, she tugged the sheets loose from the empty bed, trying and failing to ignore the bright red splotches staining the once-white fabric. Taking the pillows as well, she balled everything together and carried them to the hamper.

Mrs. Gregory gathered fresh bedding from the table a few doors down and brought it back. "We're running out of clean pillows, but Doc insists we not reuse them until they've been washed and dried and sprayed with bleach. The next westbound train is supposed to have more pillows, sheets, towels, and other supplies."

"What do I do about the mattress? Blood soaked through the sheets."

"We'll spray it with that new Lysol stuff the hardware store sent over, flip the mattress, and hope for the best."

"Meghan." Doc's voice called from the head of the stairs. "I have a new patient for you." Doc and Caleb held Joshua up between them. "Hurry and get that bed made."

Meghan wasn't sure which jarred her most, the sight of Caleb standing in the hotel or Joshua, hanging limp, his arms stretched across the shoulders of his boss and the doctor. She stood rooted to the floor. The last time she'd seen Caleb, she'd practically thrown herself at him then slapped his face. Her shocking behavior still had the power to send shame shivering down her spine.

"Miss Thorson?" Mrs. Gregory shoved the stack of sheets into Meghan's hands. "You heard the doctor. Get to work."

Out of habit, she leaped to obey the head waitress, her mind spinning. Joshua had come to the hotel to see her. If he hadn't, surely he wouldn't have fallen ill. Together, she and Mrs. Gregory got the mattress sprayed and flipped. Meghan snapped open sheets, tucked in edges, shoved pillows into slips, and folded a clean blanket across the bottom of the bed. Mrs. Gregory worked on the other side, mirroring Meghan's work.

A wry twinkle lit Mrs. Gregory's eyes. "We'd have made decent chambermaids, wouldn't we?"

Doc and Caleb shuffled through the door with Joshua and lay him on the bed.

He moaned and squeezed his eyes shut. "Why don't you leave

me alone?" The words came out slurred but discernible.

Doc stuck a thermometer under Joshua's tongue and lifted his wrist to check his pulse. "Caleb, you'll get him undressed in a minute, and you can stay and help Meghan since you've already been exposed to the sickness. Mrs. Gregory will give you a mask, and Meghan can show you what to do for Joshua."

George and Harold slept on, and Meghan took a moment to feel their foreheads and straighten the sheets. The water pitcher on the bedside table held only a half a glass, so she picked it up. "I'll step out while you get him settled."

When she returned with fresh water and a stack of cloths, Joshua lay under the sheets, undressed down to his small clothes and restless. Caleb had donned a mask, his eyes watchful and serious, and his skin tanned against the stark white of the cotton gauze. She looked away, unable to meet his gaze for long.

Doc had gone, leaving them alone.

"What should I do for him?" Caleb stood beside the bed, his hands in his pockets, his weight resting on one leg.

She checked the notepaper on the desk to decipher Doc's scrawl, trying to put some distance between her chaotic thoughts and what needed to be done. Temperature 103.9. Pulse 126. Aspirin and cool cloth treatment for fever and aches. Encourage fluid intake.

"There's a basin of water on the bedside table. Wet this cloth." She handed him one of the clean washcloths. "And bathe his face and chest and arms. If that doesn't help lower his temperature, we'll use alcohol. Until the next train comes, there's not much ice left, so we'll use what we have sparingly."

Harold groaned and turned his head on the pillow. A spasm of coughing caught him, and Meghan hastened to his side to help prop him up until it passed. She held a cloth under his chin as he coughed, praying he wouldn't bring up any blood. After a minute or two the coughing ceased, the redness subsided from his face, and he fell back limp on the pillow once more. She smoothed the hair on his forehead and offered him a drink.

"Shhh, just rest. You're going to be fine." His skin felt paper-dry, and his fever-bright eyes disappeared behind his eyelids once more. She wrung out a cloth and passed it over his face and neck.

"What else can I do?" Caleb pulled the chair from the desk and dragged it to Joshua's bedside. She couldn't miss the helpless note to his voice. It resonated with her own feelings of trying to hold back a sea surge. All her efforts were futile in the face of such a rushing, relentless foe determined to take what it wanted.

She withdrew the precious bottle of aspirin tablets from her apron pocket, her only real weapon in the fight. "Try to get him to take two of these. If he can't swallow them, we'll crush them up and give them to him by spoon in some water."

"Is that all?"

"I'm afraid so. Keep them comfortable, write down everything you do for them and when, and pray."

Pray. Pray. Pray. How many prayers had she uttered for the men under her care in the last three days? She closed her eyes to compose yet another imploring, beseeching plea.

When she opened her eyes, Caleb stared at her above his mask. "When was the last time you slept?" He squeezed water from the cloth and pressed it against Joshua's forehead. She handed him a half glass of water and the two tablets.

"Here, kid. You have to swallow these then you can rest."

Thankfully, Joshua opened his mouth for the pills and swallowed them down. A chill rippled through his lean frame, and Meghan tugged the sheet a little higher around his bare chest.

"You didn't answer my question. When was the last time you slept?"

Blinking hard against the grittiness in her eyes, she shook her head. "I've dozed in the rocker at night."

"Why don't you rest for a while? If all we can do is change wet cloths and watch them, I can do that."

"You're sure?" The thought of sleep beckoned like a powerful dream.

"I'll wake you if anything happens."

She eased down into the rocker in the corner of the room and let her head rest against the high back. As disturbing as having Caleb here made her feel, she had to admit not being alone was comforting. Weariness tugged at her limbs and eyelids, and sleep claimed her.

"Meghan." Something shook her, but she ignored it. "Meg—" The sound broke off, caught in a maelstrom of coughing.

Her weighty lashes parted. Cotton-wool filled her head, and pillow-ticking coated her mouth.

"Meghan. Are you awake?" The hand shook her shoulder again.

Caleb's voice. She blinked, sitting upright.

"Meghan, I'm so sorry." More coughing. He put his hand to his chest, his mask puffing in and out with the jagged coughing. Fever brightened his cheeks and eyes. "I think it's got me. So fast. I felt fine awhile ago—" More coughing obliterated his words.

Dread surged through her, yanking her to her feet. She put her hands on his shoulders and then felt his forehead. Heat seared her skin. "Oh, Caleb."

"I'm sorry." Another racking spasm of coughing grabbed him, and he yanked down the mask, gasping for air.

"You need to lie down." She turned him to the double bed where Joshua lay. "I'll send someone for Doc."

The last bit of sleepiness drained from her as she hurried down the hall. Where was that bellboy? The clock at the head of the stairs told her she'd slept for almost four hours. From the open doorways of the rooms she passed the sounds of coughing and sneezing, wheezing and moaning emanated. She checked each room for Doc's reassuring presence, but couldn't find him.

She finally ran into him downstairs in the kitchen, seated at a table, his head pillowed on his crossed arms, snoring softly. Poor man. Should she wake him? What could he do, really? She settled for leaving him a note.

Caleb is sick now. I've put him to bed with aspirin and liquids. I'll wake you if things look bad for him.

She hurried back to the sickroom. Caleb had undressed and climbed into bed next to Joshua. He coughed, holding his chest. Red suffused his face, and he fell back against the pillow gasping.

"Feels like I'm being stabbed." His voice rasped.

Dosing him with aspirin, bathing his face and neck with cool water, encouraging him to drink. All things she'd done a hundred times for her patients and yet, this was Caleb. Just being near him set her nerves to jangling, jerked her thoughts in every direction, and made her wonder if she was coming down with the flu herself. Her breath hitched in her throat, her heart beat erratically, and heat warmed her through. How could he have this effect on her when she'd done everything she could to put him from her mind?

"Check on Joshua." He grabbed her hand, his eyes bright and insistent.

"I will. Lie still. If you try to talk, the coughing will get worse."

She checked on all her patients. Resting her hand on each brow, she tried to determine if their fevers had abated any. George stirred and rolled to his side, his breath slow and even. A spark of hope for him lit in her chest. For the first time since she'd first laid eyes on him, he appeared to be resting naturally.

Harold's head tossed on his pillow, his cheeks still red. She pressed a fresh cloth to his brow and consulted her notes and the clock. Time for more medicine. Every ministration came by rote, all her thoughts on Caleb.

"Meghan," he called.

A quick check on the sleeping Joshua, and then she rounded the bed to Caleb's side. He reached for her hand.

"What can I do?"

"Sit." His throat lurched, as if he fought against a cough. "I need to tell you something." He gave in to the cough, his chest heaving, the bed lurching with each racking spasm.

She moved to sit beside him, holding his shoulders as he curled in a half sit-up against the tearing coughs. "Don't talk. It will be all right."

"Don't leave." The worry in his eyes pulled at her heart. "Promise me you'll take care of Joshua."

Her fingers moved of their own accord, smoothing back the hair on his forehead and letting her finger slide down his cheek. The beginnings of a beard prickled her fingertips. "I'll take care of you all. Rest now."

His lashes lowered, but his grip on her hand remained tight.

Caleb wandered in a strange land. In moments of lucidity, he knew he was very sick, but between times, he drifted and dreamed. His bones ached deep in the marrow, and his joints radiated pain. Sharp-clawed beasts tore at his chest with every breath, and his head throbbed with every heartbeat. He staggered across a parched desert wasteland in search of water to quench his raging thirst, tripping, falling, fighting the thorns and sliding sand, the scorching heat and wind. In the distance, standing beside a waterfall, surrounded by trees and grass and cool mist, Meghan stood with her hands outstretched, a ring of yellow flowers gracing her hair. Her lips stretched in a beckoning smile, and she waved him on, but no matter how many sand dunes he stumbled over or cactus thickets he forced his way through, he could never narrow the distance between them. In time, her image began to waver and fade, and he clawed his way up yet another slippery slope, calling to her, begging her not to leave him. The wind sucked his words away, and she disappeared from view.

"He's so restless." Meghan mopped Caleb once more, holding down his arm when he tried to swat her away. "Half the time he's fighting me, and the other half, he's squeezing my hand so hard, it goes numb."

Doc Bates bent over Joshua on the other side of the bed, listening to his breathing while he waited for a thermometer reading. He straightened, his back cracking. "I sent word to Mr. and Mrs. Hualga at the reservation to tend the horses until Caleb and Joshua can go home. I told them under no circumstances to come here. They wouldn't be allowed into the hotel anyway, and I don't want them taking the sickness back to the reservation. I have enough patients as it is." He held the thermometer up to the light.

"How is he doing?"

"No better, no worse." He pressed his hands to the small of his back and kneaded. "I want you to get some rest. Mrs. Gregory is working out a schedule so we can spell everyone."

She wanted to protest that she couldn't leave her patients, but she was too tired. "What about you? Who's going to spell you?"

He rubbed his eyes, pinching the bridge of his nose. "There's a doctor coming from Flagstaff on the next train. As soon as he gets here, I'm going to fall into bed."

Meghan checked the clock, though the temperature in the room told her it had to be nearly noon. Four days since the train had come bringing the sick soldiers. Caleb stirred again, a soft moan escaping his lips. She smoothed the hair off his brow.

"At least we haven't lost anyone in the last few hours." Doc removed the thermometer from Joshua's mouth and squinted at the glass tube. Shaking it down, he swabbed it with alcohol before slipping it into its metal case and returning it to his pocket. After jotting a few notes, he swiped his wrist across his forehead. "Keep a close watch. From what I've been able to observe, the first sign of a patient heading toward real complications from this sickness is a bluish tinge to their extremities. From now on, I want you to check your patients' feet and check them often. I'll add it to the patient notes." When he'd finished writing out his instructions, he turned to leave and staggered, grabbing the edge of a dresser to steady himself.

Meghan rounded the bed to his side to grasp his elbow. "Are you all right? You're not feeling ill, are you?" Worry tightened her throat.

"No, just tired to the bone, like everyone else." He smiled and patted her hand. "You get some rest just as soon as someone comes to take your place."

She crossed her arms at her waist and bowed her head, leaning against the dresser. Sandpaper coated the insides of her eyelids, and her hands and shoulders ached from wringing out wet cloths. The room, in spite of her best efforts to keep it clean and fresh, smelled of sickness and heat. Lead weights pulled at her limbs, and sand dunes of tiredness invaded her head.

George shifted, drawing her attention. His eyes opened, and he stared at her. "Water?" His voice was weak as a whisper. She gave him a drink and went to check his patient notes to see when he could have more medicine.

Check all extremities for discoloration at least once an hour.

Doc's note swam before her vision, and she blinked, focusing once more.

She blew out a breath and went to George first, girding herself for the task. "George, I need to have a look at your feet. I'll get you tucked back in as soon as I can." He nodded and closed his eyes.

Tugging the bottom sheet out from the end of the mattress, she laid it back, exposing first George's feet then Harold's. Pink, and warm to the touch. Satisfied, she retucked the sheet and made a note of the time and condition.

Moving to the beds where Caleb and Joshua lay side by side, she took a deep breath and turned up the bottom of the sheet. Her hand stopped in midair, hovering, trembling, and the sheet dropped from her numb fingers.

Her breath clogged her throat. With her mouth hanging lax and her mind clanging and clamoring, she shook her head, blinking away what must be an exhaustion-induced hallucination. Her eyes roved to Joshua then back to Caleb.

Dizziness overtook her, and she clutched the footboard, closing her eyes against the nausea and vertigo. Realization smashed through her surprise. Her heart cried for Caleb, breaking into small pieces for all the wounds he'd suffered in silence, for the way he guarded his secret, never telling the truth about why he wasn't a soldier.

Many of the disjointed puzzle pieces, the things about Caleb that seemed to be in conflict, fell into place. The withered, buckled, wizened calf and foot explained so much, and yet filled her mind with questions. A tear splashed onto his twisted foot, and she reached out to brush it away. His skin was cool to the touch, and she swallowed against the lump in her throat.

Shame and guilt pounded hard on the heels of understanding. Of all the wounding insults the people of Needles had inflicted, hers had been the most grievous. For she had given him hope and offered friendship and more before snatching it away, giving in to the pressures of those around her, siding with the ignorant and judgmental. Every accusation she'd hurled at him smacked her in the face.

After a quick check of Joshua's straight, strong limbs, she re-tucked the sheet, covering Caleb's secret and vowing to herself never to mention it to anyone. She was finished betraying Caleb's trust.

"Meghan?" he mumbled.

With a guilty start, she sought his face. His eyes remained closed, but he frowned, his hand grasping the air at his side.

She returned to her chair beside him and took his hand, rubbing the back of it with her thumb. His fingers closed around hers, fever-hot and rough, but his body relaxed a fraction, as if her touch brought him comfort.

He was the bravest man she'd ever known, and she'd called him a coward. He bore his burden in silence, never using it as an excuse, never giving in or giving up. He supported himself, even contributing to the war effort in spite of his leg. How did he manage to even walk without a limp? How had she and everyone else in this town missed the signs?

Her mind cast back to the clues she should've seen. How

he usually stood with his weight on one leg. The strange way he mounted his horse. The fact that he'd come to the Dime-A-Dance but refused to dance. She'd taken his slow, even steps as a sign of his easygoing temperament, but now she could see he had to have been measuring his strides, concentrating on not letting his limp show.

And the chicken feather. Humiliated in front of a crowded dining room, in front of that army major, in front of her. Every word that bombastic virago had said to him pierced Meghan's heart. He'd bravely stood before that silly woman, taken her insults without firing back, and refused to fight. At the time, she'd thought he'd lost all dignity, but in truth, he'd preserved his honor, even if he was the only one who knew it.

Doc entered the room, his brows knit and furrows on his forehead. "I thought I'd just relieve you for a few moments and check your patients' feet myself, all right? Why don't you go get some fresh air on the balcony?" He took her elbow to lift her out of her chair.

Meghan tugged away, shaking her head. She kept hold of Caleb's hand on the white sheet. "You don't have to bother. I checked them already." Another tear leaked out of her eye, and she swiped it away.

The doctor slumped, hanging his head. "Then you know." A huge sigh heaved his white coat front. "If I hadn't been so tired, I never would've made that slip up." His hands balled at his sides. "Caleb is going to kill me when he finds out."

Swallowing against the lump in her throat, Meghan took a steadying breath. "Then we won't tell him, but I have to know what happened to him? Why is his leg like that?"

Doc sighed and scrubbed his eyes with the heels of his hands.

"Let's go out into the hall where we can talk and not disturb anyone."

She followed him out of the room, blinking at the sunlight pouring in the hallway windows. With the blinds drawn and curtains pulled in the sickroom, she felt like a burrowing owl coming out at the wrong time of day.

Doc leaned against a windowsill, checking up and down the hall to make sure they were alone. "What you saw there is the result of poliomyelitis, otherwise known as infantile paralysis."

Meghan bit her lower lip. Poor Caleb. "Is it painful?"

"The initial illness certainly is. I'm told it's like the worst cramp or charley horse you can imagine. The muscles seize up and lock, and the nerves become confused. The body refuses to obey signals from the brain. The most severe cases result in permanent paralysis, atrophied muscles, and in some cases the bones get twisted and malformed because of the muscles pulling on them. Caleb was very young when he contracted the disease, and his legs didn't grow evenly afterward. The pain eventually subsides, but it can come back. Caleb's leg aches and is weak, especially when he overdoes the work, which is pretty much every day."

"Why didn't he ever tell anyone? Why let everyone think him a coward and profiteer? He has a perfectly legitimate reason not to enlist. In fact, the army wouldn't take him."

"Because he's proud and stubborn, that's why. He doesn't want any pity." Doc rubbed the back of his neck. "I suppose, now that you're his nurse, I can tell you a little of his history, the little bit he's shared with me, but it must go no further. We must guard his privacy in this matter."

Hearing how Caleb's family had turned against him when he'd contracted the disease broke her heart afresh. No wonder he'd said he had no family that claimed him. How could anyone turn their back on their own child? It wasn't as if he'd gotten ill on purpose. But to put him into an asylum, to refuse to even visit him. Fresh tears stung her eyes.

Doc waited as a busboy pushed a laundry cart down the hall before continuing. "He's so sensitive about people judging him because of his leg, he refuses to tell anyone. He won't wear a brace, even though it would help him, and he won't slow down. His leg gives him quite a bit of pain these days, but he keeps on. And I have a suspicion that somewhere in the not-too-distant past, a girl disappointed him, but he backs away from talking about it."

Meghan crumpled, leaning against the balcony railing. "And I haven't helped matters at all. Joshua was right when he said I'd let Caleb down."

"I've watched you two together. I had high hopes that you two might make a match of it. You care for him very much, don't you?"

"I did." She pressed her lips together. "I do. And I thought he cared for me."

"I think he still does."

"No, not after what I said to him. He'll never forgive me. He let himself be vulnerable, let himself show some emotion, and what did I do? I smacked his face and called him a coward."

"So that's it? One little setback in your relationship and you're going to quit on him?" Doc's voice flicked like a lash. "Who's the coward now?"

Meghan's backbone stiffened, and her hands fisted. "I'm no coward. It's just. . ."

"Just what? Caleb has had nothing but a raw deal for about as long as he can remember. But if you stand by him, you two can do anything. I've never seen anyone so willing to take on a challenge as you. Whether it's becoming a first-rate Harvey Girl—oh yes, I've heard from several sources what a fine waitress you've become, a credit to the company—or sewing that quilt and raising money with it, or being the best nurse we've got in the hotel right now. You never back down from a challenge, so why start now? If Caleb means anything to you, if you care for him at all, then get in there and fight for him. Fight first for his life, and then, when he's better, fight for his heart."

In spite of her exhaustion, the flame of ambition flared in Meghan's heart, the quickening of her pulse, the explosion of ideas, the call to the crusade.

"Do you think he'll forgive me? Do you think he'll have me?"

"You'll never know if you don't try." Doc stood, yawned, and checked his watch. "You'd best get back to your patients. Until Caleb is better, don't broach the subject. Between the two of us, we should be able to care for him without letting on that you know. I'm here if you need me."

He headed down the hall to check on more patients, and Meghan took a deep breath, girding her mind and heart for the battle of her life.

Chapter 15

The week passed in a blur for Meghan. For days, she left Caleb's side only to eat or change into a clean dress. Caleb's fever soared, his chest racked with coughs, and he writhed as if trying to escape his own aching body. The only time he lay still was when Meghan held his hand and bathed his face and neck with cool, damp cloths. She prayed long and often for both him and Joshua, dozing in the rocker, starting awake every time one of her patients moaned or moved, and refusing to budge, even when Mrs. Gregory offered to send someone to replace her.

On the fifth day, Caleb's fever finally broke. Meghan, so tired she could hardly raise her arm, touched his forehead. Cool and slightly moist as a fine sheen of sweat appeared on his brow. Tears of thankfulness sprang to her scratchy eyes, and she bit her lip, sending up a prayer of thanksgiving. For the first time in what seemed forever, Caleb looked at her with clear eyes.

"Meghan? How's Joshua?" His voice croaked from dryness and lack of use.

Meghan pushed him gently back against the pillows when he tried to sit up. "Shh, he's fine. We moved him to the other bed." She poured a glass of water and held it to his cracked lips. "His fever broke two days ago, and he's resting comfortably, though he's so hungry all the time, I can barely keep him fed."

He lay back with a sigh. "The soldiers?"

"A special train with army doctors arrived. They loaded all the recovering soldiers onto litters and put them on the eastbound. They're at an army base by now, recuperating."

"And the town?" His eyelashes fluttered, as if he had to work to focus. After nearly a week of delirium and fever, he'd lost weight, and no doubt would take weeks to recover fully. But her heart still soared. Once the fever broke, if he took care, he should be on the road to recovery.

"There have been a lot of cases, but most are being treated in their own homes now that the soldiers are gone and Doc can take the time to visit house to house." She straightened the covers, careful to keep from looking toward the foot of the bed. "You and Joshua are the last patients in the hotel. The trains are running again, and the dining room and lunchroom are operating once more, though all the waitresses wear their masks while they serve."

"What about my horses?" He struggled up to his elbows. "And how long have I been sick?"

She pressed her palms against his shoulders, conscious of warm, male muscles and solid bone. "Lie still. Your horses are fine. Joshua's parents are looking after them. You've been very ill, and it's going to take awhile before you regain your strength. I'm going to send down to the kitchen for some broth and hot tea." As she made to move away from the bed, he grasped her hand.

"Have you been here the whole time?"

Shrugging, she withdrew her fingers from his. "Mostly. Doc spelled me sometimes. Now, you rest. You need to build up your strength."

He was asleep again before he'd finished half the broth, but this time it was a peaceful slumber. Meghan drifted to sleep watching the steady rise and fall of his chest.

Doc gently shook her awake. "I see we've made some improvement since this morning."

Blinking and shaking her head, she chased the muzziness from her brain. "Yes, his fever broke just before noon. He's been sleeping ever since."

Caleb's eyes opened. "I'm awake now."

Lifting Caleb's wrist, Doc stared at his watch. "How are you feeling?"

"Like last week's leftovers." He coughed, holding his chest and scrunching his eyes.

"That's to be expected. The cough will most likely hang on for a while. We'll try to get you propped up a little more now to help you clear your lungs. Don't want you developing pneumonia after all the fine nursing you've had."

After satisfying himself as to his patient's welfare, Doc sent a no-nonsense look Meghan's way. "Okay, young lady, I've humored you because it really did seem as if Caleb rested more comfortably when you were nearby, but now that he's on the mend, I'm putting my foot down. You're going to return to your room and go to bed. Natalie came back to the hotel yesterday, and she'll look after you."

Now that Caleb and Joshua were both out of danger, she longed to fall headfirst into her pillow and not resurface for a week, but she couldn't just abandon her post. "Who will take care of my patients?"

"I will. I'll get them shifted to my house where I can see to them myself. Mrs. Gregory wants her hotel back, and I quite agree. It appears the worst of the epidemic is over for the time being, so I can more than take care of two convalescent patients in my own home. Now get." He shooed her toward the door. "Natalie's waiting for you."

Meghan stumbled along the hallway toward the staff quarters, dragging at her apron strings and yawning. For more than ten days, she'd survived on catnaps and quick meals. She hadn't slept in her own bed for such a long time, everything seemed strange as she opened the bedroom door.

"There you are. How are Caleb and Joshua?" Natalie rose from the corner chair and laid aside her handwork. Tired as she was, Meghan noticed Natalie's thickened waist. She wouldn't be able to hide her condition much longer.

"Caleb's fever broke at last. Doc is going to take both of them to his house. He's ordered me to bed." Boat anchors tugged at her eyelids, and she couldn't stop yawning as she slipped out of her black dress.

"I'm glad he did. If you'll forgive me for saying so, you look like you've been dragged through a knothole backward." Natalie turned back the sheets and went to draw the drapes. "You sleep. We'll talk later."

Meghan fell into bed and fathoms deep into sleep.

"You can stop pretending now, Doc." Caleb eased down onto the mattress and let Doc help him swing his legs up off the floor. Tiredness seeped from every pore, and he didn't protest when Doc pulled the sheet up for him.

"Pretending?" Doc felt Caleb's brow.

"That she didn't see my leg."

"You need to rest. The move from the hotel to my place took a lot out of you."

"You're doing it again."

"What?"

"Changing the subject."

"Why can't you lie back and go to sleep like Joshua? He isn't giving me half as much trouble as you." Doc lowered the window shade. "We can talk about this later, when you're stronger."

In spite of his weariness, Caleb pushed himself upright. His arms trembled, and the room swam. "Doc, I need to know the truth. How did she react? Was she repulsed?" He hauled in a staggering breath, his chest muscles aching from so many days of coughing. "Of course she was repulsed. Forget it. I don't know why I even asked." Arms buckling, he flopped back onto the pillows.

"If you must know the truth, then, yes, she did see your leg, several times in fact, and not once did I get the impression she was repulsed. Sorry and sad that you had to suffer? Yes, but most of all, I got the impression that Meghan was remorseful. She feels bad about how she and the town have treated you. Poor girl."

"Poor girl?" Caleb scowled.

"That's right. She feels bad, and so do I about you contracting polio and suffering long-term consequences, but you are the one who set the rules for this game. You chose to keep your infirmity a secret. You chose to let this town believe a lie. You chose to let Meghan believe a lie. I can only guess you wanted to protect your pride. You built a wall around yourself and rejected the people of this town before they got a chance to reject you. But Meghan got in, didn't she? She snuck around or over that wall, and when she got too close, you chased her away because you were afraid. Instead of telling her the truth, you used the lie to fend her off." Doc rubbed his hands down his face. "That girl cares for you a great deal. She told me so, but what does it matter if you're too afraid to accept her? In that respect, the town of Needles has it right. You *are* a coward."

Caleb's hands fisted on the sheet, and waves of weakness flowed over him. His one ally in this town, and he'd been betrayed. His mind swam with crashing thoughts, and he clamped his lips together to keep from saying all the words that crowded into his throat.

Doc shook his head. "I'm sorry. You're in no condition to deal with all this right now. I should've held my tongue." Lines deepened on his face, and sadness invaded his eyes. "It's just that I see how good you and Meghan could be together. She'd never let something like a bum leg come between you. I hope, if she comes to visit, you can finally be honest with each other."

He closed the door behind himself, leaving Caleb alone.

She won't come. And I don't want her to. Doc's bald statements reverberated in Caleb's head. *Doc doesn't know what it's like. He's a whole man. Nobody would pity him or reject him. When you aren't whole, all you have is your pride. If I gave that up, what would I have? A man had to have his pride, didn't he? And if he couldn't be proud of his abilities, then at least he could be proud knowing he had right on his side when others accused him of dodging the draft.*

"Pride goeth before destruction, and a haughty spirit before a fall."

Caleb's eyelids fluttered open. Where had that come from? As a man who had spent the past twenty years living in mortal terror of falling, the Bible verse hit hard at his very core.

If you let go of your pride, you'll have nothing, Caleb McBride. You'll be nothing, a nobody, just like you were when your father looked right through you as a kid. He clutched the sheet, trying to find a hold as the walls around his heart began to quake.

"If you let go of your pride, you'll have Me. I am your Father, and I know you. I always see you. I'm just waiting for you to finally see Me."

But what can I bring to You that You will accept, if I have nothing left of myself, nothing that makes me worthy of Your love? Had all his striving been for nothing? Bits of rubble fell from the barricade he'd erected around his pride.

"The sacrifices of God are a broken spirit: a broken and a contrite heart, O God, thou wilt not despise.

"There is nothing you can bring to make yourself worthy. I am the

one who makes you worthy. Your worth isn't determined by your physical body or your intellect or your pride. Your worth isn't determined by how others see you or by how you see yourself. Your worth is established because I died for you. Because I have called you worthy. You are mine. Abandon your pride, humble yourself."

A rock-hard lump formed in Caleb's throat as his soul wrestled with the truth he had known from a child but constantly fought against. If he abandoned his pride, he would be vulnerable. He would have to be open about his leg, about his life. He couldn't hide anymore.

And that meant facing the people of Needles.

Even worse, it meant facing Meghan.

"I thought you were over this nonsense." Mrs. Gregory snapped open a tablecloth and let it float onto the dining room table. "I thought you had come to your senses and finally seen Caleb McBride for what he is. You told me you were finished with him."

"It isn't nonsense, and I was wrong. I judged him unfairly, and so have you and the rest of the town. He's a fine, upstanding man, and he deserves to have his name on the quilt alongside everyone else." Meghan rolled a cart of china and cutlery across the floor and began setting the places. Her first shift back and the fireworks were already beginning. She tried to remind herself about the stress Mrs. Gregory was under, the worry that dogged her steps as she waited to hear about her son's fate, but the injustice of her claims made it difficult.

Meghan could tell, in spite of the mask covering the lower half of Mrs. Gregory's face, that the head waitress's mouth was pinched in a persimmon pucker. The next tablecloth snapped open with more force. "I won't have it, and what's more, the people of this town won't have it. If you persist and include Caleb McBride's name on that quilt, I assure you no one will bid on it."

"That's not fair. He's done nothing to deserve this treatment." Meghan's indignation burned hot and bright in her chest, all the more because of her guilt in the matter. But she wouldn't back down. It was too important. "If you really knew him, you'd see that." How could Meghan convince her without betraying Caleb's secret?

"Poppycock. I've known him longer than you have, young lady, and I have to insist that you stop this. Against all initial indications, you've become a valued member of this serving crew and one of the best waitresses I've ever trained. I would hate to see you throw it all away on a wastrel like Caleb McBride. If you persist in seeing him and in putting his name on that quilt—making him the equal of everyone in this town who has sacrificed and prayed and labored for the cause when he's nothing but a coward with no sense of duty, I will be forced to make an adjustment that I don't want to make." She straightened the chairs at the table. All around them girls bustled in and out of the kitchen and dish room and linen store preparing for the incoming train passengers. Though they continued with their work, they couldn't help but overhear. The longer Mrs. Gregory talked, the louder her voice grew.

Meghan adjusted her mask, gulping. Sent home in disgrace to face her father with yet another failed escapade. She couldn't let that happen. He'd never let her do anything ever again. "You'd dismiss me?"

"I would." Mrs. Gregory pulled herself up to her full height, several inches taller than Meghan. She crossed her arms at her waist, formidable and every inch the boss.

"You can't fire me for putting Caleb's name on the quilt. I donated the money in his name. If you fired me for that, I would be forced to go to Mr. Ford Harvey himself." Her knees quaked as she played her ace card.

All work in the dining room had ceased, and the girls didn't even pretend not to be listening anymore. Even Natalie poked her head around the corner of the soda fountain door.

Mrs. Gregory's eyes blazed and her face hardened, but it was the chilling calm, the razor edge to her voice that froze Meghan to the core. "The quilt is yours, and you can certainly choose which names you put on it, and I would not fire you for that. I would, however, fire you for having an improper relationship with a man while in the employ of the Harvey Company. You don't deny that you've been seen in Caleb McBride's company upon several occasions. I myself caught you consorting alone and unchaperoned the night of the benefit dance. You've been out to his property more than once, and when he fell ill here in the hotel, you refused to leave his side. Those are just the times I know about. Consorting with men, especially men of Caleb McBride's type, is forbidden. I've warned you before, and I'm warning you now. If his name goes on the quilt and you choose to make public your feelings for him, I will dismiss you from the company."

Meghan gasped. "I've never had an improper relationship with a man in my life."

"I know what I know." Her hands settled on her hips. "Now, unless you wish to have your employment terminated for insubordination, I suggest you finish setting these tables and learn to hold your tongue." She glanced at the clock over the doorway and clapped her hands, raising her voice to encompass all the wait staff. "The train will arrive in less than ten minutes. I expect a flawless service, girls."

Meghan slapped plates and cutlery on the table, ignoring the curious, sympathetic, and speculative glances being sent her way. Now she knew how Caleb felt, being falsely accused. At least Caleb had the sense to keep his mouth shut.

"It's the right thing to do." Meghan picked at the seam holding the binding to the quilt. Her heart thudded in her chest, and her mind raced. Was she making the biggest error of her life or redeeming her biggest mistake?

Natalie ran the iron over the bib of an apron. "I know it is, but what about Mrs. Gregory? She was very clear."

"But she's wrong, and I've given in for too long. It isn't that I don't feel for her. Her son is fighting for his life, all shot up in some foreign hospital. But that doesn't mean she should be allowed to bully people. Your husband and my brother are on the front lines, and we're not slapping down ultimatums and threatening people with unfounded accusations." She freed the corner of the quilt block and picked up her embroidery thread. The need to hurry made her fumble-fingered.

"Mr. Gibson will be here this afternoon for the rally tonight. What are you going to tell him if no one bids on your quilt? How are you going to explain the shortfall in your pledge?"

She shrugged, though a heavy hand pressed her shoulders at the thought. "I'll give him the money I raised from the signatures, and I'll tell him the truth. I made the quilt in good faith, and if no one bids on it, then I will have to admit defeat in that quarter." She swallowed the bitter lump in her throat and jerked her chin up. "But I don't care. I'll be victorious in a more important battle. The battle of right and wrong." Her needle poked in and out of the white fabric.

"What about the ambulance? What about Lars and Derek and the other soldiers? You've been on a crusade all summer long, and you're so close to your goal. Not to mention what will happen if you go through with this. Mrs. Gregory will fire you quicker than you can say American Red Cross. Then where will you be?"

"I'll be on the side of right." Meghan set her mouth and drew the red embroidery thread through the cloth to form a capital *C*.

With a sigh, Natalie set the iron upright and hung the apron on a hanger. "You're the most stubborn person I've ever met. I'm going out for a bit. Do you need anything from Claypool's?"

"No. I have to finish this, and then I'm on duty in the dining room until the rally starts."

"I'll be back before then." She picked up a basket and held it in front of her. For the past week, she'd been carrying things with her to shield her middle from speculative eyes. How long before someone noticed and started whispering? "I hope you know what you're doing."

"So do I."

Caleb pushed his good foot on the boards and set the rocker into motion, studying the view from Doc's front porch. For the first time in nearly three weeks, he felt almost normal, and he sighed, flexing his hands and rolling his shoulders. Tomorrow, he and Joshua would head home. It was time to get back to the horses. The Hualgas had urged them both to stay in town until they were fully recovered, and Caleb knew the horses were well looked after, but a man needed to shoulder his own responsibilities. He'd been laid up long enough. Besides which, if he went home, he'd stop hoping and expecting Meghan to walk over from the hotel. In spite of Doc's prediction that he'd see her again, she'd stayed away, causing doubt and uncertainty and all the old feelings to come crowding back. His chest pinched. *Stop thinking about her.*

Forcing his mind away from Meghan, he considered his other dilemma. How to make known to the people of Needles why he hadn't enlisted. It wasn't as if he could just put an advertisement in the newspaper, could he?

He picked up the copy of the *Desert Star* from the side table and scanned the front page. The entire top half under the masthead was devoted to tonight's Red Cross rally at the El Garces Hotel. Below the fold, more news from the war front about the desperate fighting. But this time there was cause for hope. Only days before, the Allied troops had broken through the German fortifications at the Hindenburg line. Surely, with such a huge victory, the end of the war must be drawing near.

"Here." Joshua edged open the screen door, carefully balancing a tray. Ice clinked in a pitcher of lemonade. "It's going to be tart. I stirred in the last of the sugar, but it wasn't much."

Caleb sipped the pale yellow liquid and winced. "Whew."

"Yeah, but at least it's cold."

"You up to going back to the ranch tomorrow?" He set the glass down.

"I'm ready." Joshua took the other chair, stretching his legs out before him and resting his glass against his lean stomach.

"Doc said half days to start with for both of us. Last thing we want is a relapse."

"At least all this laying around has given me a chance to read." Joshua withdrew a slim volume from his hip pocket. *Diseases of the Pancreas* in gold letters on a clothbound cover. "I think I've read just about every medical book Doc has."

"You've made up your mind to go to medical school then?"

He nodded. "Doc says I can do it, and that he'll help me. He's already started putting out some feelers. Maybe I can start at the new year."

A small figure in black and white hurried toward them, and for a moment, Caleb's heart leaped, but as the woman drew near, his pulse subsided. No red hair, no flashing green eyes. Not Meghan. Caleb laid aside the newspaper and pushed himself to his feet as Miss Daviot turned in at the gate. He cleared his throat and frowned toward Joshua, who snapped his book shut and scrambled to his feet.

She mounted the steps, and Joshua offered her his chair. "Ma'am. I'll get another glass."

Wiping her brow, she took the chair and set her basket on her lap. "Thank you, Joshua. Mr. McBride."

"Caleb, please." He resumed his seat. "What can we do for you? Doc's not here. He walked up the street to the Sawyer place. A couple of their little ones had the influenza pretty bad, and he wanted to check on their progress now that they're on the mend."

"Actually, it's you I wanted to see." A flush decorated her cheeks, though he couldn't tell if it was from the heat or some other reason. "It's about Meghan."

His heart did a hiccup, and his mouth went dry. In spite of the tartness, he swigged a mouthful of the lemonade, screwing up his eyes as the sourness bit deep. "What about her?"

"She's about to commit Red Cross membership and career suicide. Since you're the cause, I thought you should know the sacrifice she's willing to make for you."

"What?"

"It's this quilt. She informed Mrs. Gregory this morning that she intended to put your name on it. Mrs. Gregory told her in no uncertain terms that if she did, not a soul in town would bid for it. Meghan was hoping to raise several hundred dollars from auctioning the quilt in order to reach her pledge of one thousand dollars to purchase a Red Cross ambulance. If no one bids, she will be humiliated in front of the town, disgraced before the Red Cross, and even worse, Mrs. Gregory said she will fire Meghan."

A squirming ball of worms took up residence in Caleb's gut. Sick, clammy weakness washed over him. "She can't fire Meghan for something like that."

"She says she'll fire her for breaking the company's rules against fraternizing with gentlemen while in the Harvey employ. In short, Meghan will lose her job because she has fallen in love with you."

Caleb blinked, as stunned as if she'd hit him with a baseball bat. He said the first thing that popped into his mind. "Meghan's not in love with me."

The screen door creaked, and Joshua emerged with another glass. Right behind him came Doc. Their snorts of derision mingled, and Joshua rolled his eyes.

Doc sauntered to the porch rail and leaned against it. "I came in through the back, and just in time, too."

Joshua sank, cross-legged onto the planks and leaned against a post. "How come everybody in town knows Meghan's in love with you except you?"

"Then where has she been the last week? Stands to reason if a girl loved a fellow, she'd come and see him, wouldn't she?" Caleb set his glass on the table and leaned forward, bracing his forearms on his thighs.

"She slept straight through the first day, and on my orders." Doc poked his chest with his thumb. "I told her to stick to her room and do no work at all for the next couple of days to recover from all that nursing."

Natalie toyed with the handle on her basket. "And ever since then, she's been either working flat stick in the dining room, or she's been sewing like crazy to get the quilt finished on time. As it is, she didn't have time to quilt it. Just ended up tying it with red yarn. Meghan's barely had a moment to herself. And if Mrs. Gregory found she'd snuck out to see you, she'd have been fired on the spot, quilt or no quilt. Her not coming to see you doesn't mean she doesn't love you. Perhaps it means she's trying to protect you from more of this town's scorn raining down on you." Her eyes narrowed, as if she were wondering if he were good enough for her friend, and he wasn't exactly coming up to scratch. "If she didn't love you, why would she risk her job and being humiliated in front of the whole town?"

"We've all tried to tell you." Joshua drew his knees up. "That girl is in love with you, and even a blind mule with his head in bucket could see you're in love with her. The question is, what are you going to do about it?"

"What about this Lars fellow she said she loved?" Caleb grasped at another straw.

Natalie rolled her eyes. "Lars is her brother. Of course she loves him."

Shocked relief made his face go slack. Her brother?

"Well," Joshua asked, "what are you going to do?"

Their eyes bored into him, and he wanted to squirm like a first grader caught putting a frog in the teacher's desk. And yet, Meghan loved him? Was willing to stand up to an entire town on his behalf, even knowing he was a cripple?

"Well?" Doc prodded.

"My truck is still at the hotel, isn't it?"

"Right where you left it when you brought Joshua in. Why?"

"I need it if I'm going to get out to the ranch."

"What?" All three spoke in unison. Joshua's mouth flopped open, and disapproval invaded Doc's eyes. Natalie bit her lower lip and shook her head.

"I need to go home."

Natalie's mouth dropped open, and a look of pure disappointed disgust locked Joshua's features. Doc shook his head and pulled his hands from his pants' pockets. "I don't want you driving out into the desert by yourself. I'll take you." His voice sounded leaden with defeat.

Caleb stood, bracing himself for what was to come and praying he had the courage to see it through.

Chapter 16

Meghan hurried to change out of her uniform and into the new dress she'd ordered from the Sears Roebuck catalog just for tonight's occasion. A beautiful green voile with lace trim, it was as up to the minute as the wide-brimmed hat she'd ordered to go with it. The satin sash on the dress and the ribbons on the hat matched perfectly. As she donned it, she felt she was gearing up as a knight to go into battle.

She set the hat at a cheeky angle and winked at her reflection to give herself courage. "We who are about to die salute you." She snapped a salute, picked up the carefully folded quilt, and went to meet her fate.

Citizens of Needles trooped upstairs for the festivities. Jenny Ralston had delivered the news that Mr. Gibson had arrived and that Mrs. Gregory had fallen over herself to make him welcome. With no evening train scheduled, the entire hotel staff had been pressed into service preparing the north loggia with lights and bunting, tables and streamers.

It seemed as if the entire city had turned out, as if to celebrate after laboring under the threat and burden of influenza for so long. Perhaps a little light gaiety would offset some of the sorrows.

Meghan skirted clusters of chatting guests, her quilt tucked under her arm. All around the perimeter of the room, auction items had been set out. Jars of jam, baskets, lace collars, breads and cakes, needlepoint pillows. A small card marked the place where her quilt should go, the last item, and the supposed highlight of the auction.

Feeling the eyes watching her, noting the stilling of conversation, Meghan laid the quilt out on the table, draping it to show off the red crosses on the white fields. From the curious craning of necks and the way people crowded around when she stepped back, Meghan could only surmise that word had gotten around about her confrontation with Mrs. Gregory.

Someone linked her arm, and Meghan turned. Natalie squeezed her elbow, her cheeks bright and her blue eyes brilliant. "You did it then?"

Meghan couldn't speak, so she nodded. Mrs. Gregory sailed into their sphere of vision, parted the onlookers and reached for the quilt. Shaking out its folds, she scanned name after name until she came to the bottom right corner.

Caleb McBride.

In the same square as Doctor Bates's, Mr. & Mrs. Weeks's, Natalie's, and Meghan's.

There could be no mistaking Meghan's intent. Where every

other square bore four names, one in each corner, this square bore six. Meghan had embroidered Caleb's name just under hers.

They would rise or fall together.

And from the glare in Mrs. Gregory's eyes, it would be a spectacular fall.

She and Natalie found seats near the quilt and not too near the front. "I want to be able to make an escape if they come after me with torches and pitchforks." Meghan tried to make a joke, but it fell flat.

"Doc should be here soon." Natalie fussed with her handkerchief, twisting it into a knotted mess.

"Did you see him? Did he say how Caleb was?" All week her thoughts had centered on Caleb, praying he was recovering, hoping Doc would come to the hotel, eyeing the calendar waiting for her next half day off so she could at least go to Caleb and apologize face-to-face.

"Shh, they're starting."

This time it was the mayor of Needles who made the introductions as people settled into their seats. Jenny Ralston slid into the chair next to Meghan and bumped shoulders.

"Did you do it?" Her whisper carried at least three rows back.

"Shh. Yes."

"Girl, you are either really brave or really stupid."

At the moment, Meghan felt more the latter than the former.

Mr. Gibson stood and moved to the podium as applause rippled through the group. His florid face glistened in the evening heat. Someone grunted behind her and nudged her chair. Meghan glanced over her shoulder. A black-clad matron leaned forward. "How could you?"

In an instant Meghan recognized her. She was the woman who had given Caleb the white chicken feather. A shiver raced across Meghan's shoulders, and she turned to face the front. She knotted her fingers in her lap, pressing her knees together to stop them from quivering.

"Ladies and gentlemen, thank you so much for coming out tonight. I hope you've brought your generosity as well. We have a fine lineup of items for the auction." Mr. Gibson yielded the podium to the auctioneer for the night, Mr. Stock.

The hotel manager, thinner than ever after his bout with the flu, smiled and held up the first item, a hand-crocheted dresser scarf. "What's my bid for this fine piece?"

The bidding began sluggishly, and Meghan kept her eyes on her hands. As the auctioneer worked his way around the perimeter of the balcony, the tension in the room grew. Or was it just the tension in her own middle?

Jenny bid for a couple of small items, but neither Natalie or Meghan raised their hands. Finally, Mr. Stock approached the quilt. Meghan raised her chin and took a deep breath. The way Mr. Stock tugged at his collar, he acted as if Mrs. Gregory herself were holding the leash. He darted a glance at the head waitress as if to ask what to do.

Mr. Gibson stepped in. "I'm so pleased with this fine quilt. When Miss Thorson declared her intention of tackling such a large project by herself, I had my doubts." He lifted the quilt and motioned for a man on the end of a row to come help him hold it up for all to see. "Look at this. Every square filled. I see some familiar names here. Mrs. Gregory, Mr. Stock, Mr. Claypool." He nodded in the direction of Needles's most prominent businessman. "And some very famous names as well. Charlie Chaplin and Mary Pickford? And the distinguished Mr. Ford Harvey. Surely such wonderful additions to the quilt add greatly to its value. I can't wait to see how much money such a beautiful item will bring in. Proceed, Mr. Stock."

A ripple went through the room and through Meghan's body. Though she tried to take deep breaths, all her air crowded into the tops of her lungs and didn't satisfy her need for oxygen at all. This was it. Her final, glorious stand at the El Garces Hotel.

Mr. Stock cleared his throat. Meghan dared a look at some of the faces in the crowd. The hard eyes and pinched lips boded no good.

"What's my opening bid for this quilt?" His voice squeaked a bit, and he modulated it.

Silence.

"Shall we open the bidding at one hundred dollars?"

Nothing.

Heat rushed into Meghan's cheeks. Several women smirked and crossed their arms. Mrs. Gregory's lips flattened.

"Shall we say, fifty?" A hint of pleading tinged the question.

The night breeze riffled the palm leaves just over the balcony rail, the only sound in the room. Hot tears burned the backs of Meghan's eyes, but she blinked hard, refusing to let on how much she hurt inside. If Caleb could bear this town's disapproval and scorn, she could, too. Natalie reached over and patted her arm.

Mr. Gibson frowned and tugged at his moustache. "Not a single bid? For this fine quilt?" His frown deepened, and he sought Meghan's face.

"Five hundred." A deep voice from near the staircase had every head turning.

Meghan's heart jumped right up to her throat and stayed there. That was the voice that filled her dreams, a voice she would know anywhere.

Her eyes met Caleb's, and her mouth went dry. Intense, locked on hers, and challenging her to rise to the occasion. She could only see him from the waist up as the people seated between them blocked her view. It was all she could do not to run straight to him, to throw her arms around his neck and beg his forgiveness for judging him so unfairly, to express her thankfulness that he'd come tonight, and above all, her shock at him bidding on the quilt.

Step, *clank*, step, *clank*. He came toward her.

A murmur started in the back—gasps, grunts, questioning tones.

Step, *clank*, step, *clank*.

The tears she had fought now won the war and tumbled over her lashes as he came into full view.

He was wearing his leg brace, the one Doc said he refused to ever wear again. Wide buckles held it to his thigh, knee, and ankle, and a steel frame ran down each side and under his boot. He ignored the reactions around him, making a beeline for Meghan. Jenny scooted out of her chair and into an empty one in the row ahead, turning to stare along with everyone else.

Without taking his eyes from Meghan, he spoke again. "I believe the bid was five hundred dollars, Mr. Stock."

He held his hand out to Meghan. Her own shot out to grasp his fingers.

"You don't have to do this." Her whisper strangled on all the emotions running through her as she took in his features. Paler and thinner, he still looked wonderful to her.

"I want to."

Mrs. Gregory snapped upright out of her chair. "Miss Thorson—"

"Six hundred dollars."

The balcony deck seemed to sway beneath Meghan's chair. Heads swiveled again, and Mrs. Gregory gasped.

A man stepped out of the shadows, hands in his pockets. A man Meghan recognized, and from her pale expression and slack jaw, a man Mrs. Gregory recognized as well.

"Sorry. You don't mind if I bid, too?" His lips twitched beneath his moustache.

Mr. Stock sagged against the edge of the table and mopped his brow. His Adam's apple lurched. When he'd finally composed himself, he managed to utter, "The bid is six hundred. Will you raise to seven, Mr. McBride?"

"No, thank you. I believe six hundred is enough. I wouldn't want to bid against my good friend, Mr. Harvey." He flashed a quick smile and nodded at Mr. Harvey. Meghan's heart swelled until she thought it might burst.

"Sold to Mr. Harvey for six hundred dollars." Mr. Stock drew in a deep breath. "I'd like to thank you all for coming. That concludes our auction for this evening, ladies and gentlemen. There are refreshments laid on in the dining room downstairs. If you will all make your way down there, and don't forget to pick up your auction purchases and pay for them before you go downstairs."

Everyone remained still for a moment, and then the room burst into movement and voices. Meghan hardly dared believe in the warmth surrounding her heart and mind, all caused by the tender glow in Caleb's eyes. She swallowed and twisted her fingers through his. He squeezed her hand and winked at her.

"Caleb."

Someone jostled her, and he steadied her, holding her elbow. She tried again. "Caleb, I—"

Before she could say another word, Mr. Gibson descended on them.

"My dear, so happy. Delighted. The quilt is wonderful. Six hundred dollars." Mr. Gibson shook her hand hard enough to rattle her teeth. "Mr. Harvey has agreed that I should take the quilt with me on my travels. He thinks—and I quite agree—that having it to display as I speak would certainly inspire other Red Cross groups to make their own signature quilts. You'll have an impact on not just this group, but many others as well." He clasped her shoulder, beaming.

Reluctantly she withdrew her hand from Caleb's and fumbled with her handbag, withdrawing a receipt. "I don't want to forget. If you give this to Mr. Stock, he will get you the money from the signature subscriptions. It amounted to almost five hundred dollars, and I thought it best to keep the money in the hotel safe. That, along with Mr. Harvey's generous bid on the quilt should be enough for that ambulance."

"Splendid, splendid. I shall chase down Mr. Stock forthwith." He drifted away, beaming and accepting congratulations.

Mrs. Gregory took his place. Her cheeks blazed with color. "Miss Thorson, what is the meaning of this?" She raked her gaze over Caleb's leg brace. "What sort of charade are you trying to pull?" She turned to Meghan. "And how dare you go behind my back and summon the head of the company." Her face went from red to dull purple.

Doc Bates, hitherto unnoticed by Meghan, tapped Mrs. Gregory on the shoulder. "Perhaps you'd like to sit down somewhere? You look a trifle flushed. I'm sure we can have a reasonable discussion without any unnecessary accusations."

"I quite agree." Mr. Harvey's voice dropped onto the conversation like a blanket smothering a fire. "Might I suggest the principle parties wait here until the rest of the guests have drifted down to the food?"

Natalie rose, but before she could leave, Meghan grabbed her hand. "Please, stay."

And so, in a very short time, only a few people remained under the bunting and paper lanterns: Meghan, Caleb, Natalie, Doc Bates, Mr. Harvey, Mrs. Gregory, and Mr. Stock, who came puffing up the stairs after seeing the reception was well underway. Caleb took possession of Meghan's hand once more.

Mrs. Gregory fired first. "Mr. Harvey, you should be advised that I'm firing Miss Thorson. In spite of multiple warnings by myself and others, she has persistently defied me in regards to seeing Mr. McBride. As you know, it is against company policy for Harvey Girls to have romantic liaisons while in the company's employ." She glared at Meghan and Caleb's linked fingers. "On more than one occasion I've found Miss Thorson in Mr. McBride's company including finding them in an embrace right here in the hotel."

Caleb's fingers tightened on Meghan's, and heat crept up her cheeks. That magical night by the fountain was forever burned in her mind and on her heart. If Mrs. Gregory hadn't interrupted, they very well might've shared their first kiss under a felicitous moon rather than that anger-prompted kiss that ended in a disastrous slap.

Mrs. Gregory wasn't finished. "I'm also appalled that she would bother you with this situation. Contacting the head of the company?" She rolled her eyes. "Insubordination, failure to follow the chain of command, improper behavior with a member of the opposite gender, and now this."

"But I didn't—" Meghan's protest was cut off by Mr. Stock clearing his throat.

"Mrs. Gregory, I was the one who notified Mr. Harvey. I received a bulletin that he was traveling on the westbound that came in at noon today, and I asked if he could stay over to deal with one or two things that were likely to crop up tonight." He tugged at his collar and rubbed his hand down the front of his white jacket. "You see, I heard you were planning action against Miss Thorson, and while I can appreciate your sympathies, what with your son off to war and all, I felt perhaps you were allowing personal prejudices to cloud your otherwise impeccable judgment."

Groping for a chair, Mrs. Gregory plopped down. Her face took on the hue of ashes, and Meghan's chest squeezed. She sent Mr. Stock a grateful look. Imagine the fussy, standoffish hotel manager going out on a limb for her like that.

Mrs. Gregory seemed to rally a bit. "Well, that doesn't excuse her behavior, consorting with the likes of this charlatan and coward, and openly defying me when I ordered her not to include his name on that quilt." She was like a cornered animal, spitting and snarling, and trembling with fear.

"Perhaps I can shed some light on this subject. With your permission, Caleb?" Doc Bates raised one eyebrow.

"No, Doc, I best do it myself." Caleb's thumb brushed the back of Meghan's hand, and an uprush of love for him welled through her. She squeezed back.

"I know it looks fishy, me wearing this brace, but the truth is, I should've worn it more often up to now. But I was too proud. I didn't want anyone pitying me. I could take disdain, anger, even disgust, but I couldn't stomach pity." His other hand strayed to the leather wrap around his thigh. "When I was a kid, I came down with polio. My leg"—he patted the steel brace—"isn't as strong as it should be. I would've liked nothing better than to enlist and go defend my country alongside fine soldiers like your son. But the army wouldn't take me."

"So," Doc butted in, "he's helping the war effort in another way. He trains horses for the military. They hired him, they ship the horses to him, and he turns them into cavalry mounts. He won't brag on himself, so I will. He's found ways around his—infirmity—

to turn out some of the best mounts the army has ever seen. When Major Alexander was here to look over the operation, he was very impressed. Caleb is one of the best trainers the army has."

Mrs. Gregory's eyebrows bunched, and she glared, first at Caleb, then his brace, then at Doc. "Why didn't he say so in the first place? Why let us think he was a coward?"

"I didn't think it was any of your business. I've never asked you about your childhood illnesses or your past. I wanted to be judged for what I am—a man, a horse trainer, a good citizen, a patriot— not for what I'm not." He squared his shoulders. "And, because I want to be honest, I have to admit it had a lot to do with pride. I was ashamed of my leg, and I didn't want people to know about it. The pain of being shunned as a coward was nothing to the pain of being shunned as a cripple. But it's time to put that behind me. I am what I am. Folks can take it or leave it, but I'm not hiding it anymore." He shot Meghan a look that sent sparkles all through her veins. His eyes held a promise that soon they'd be alone.

Meghan swallowed against the lump in her throat. She was so proud of him she thought she might break right down and cry.

"As to firing Meghan. . .I hope you'll rethink that. I know, and she does too, that Harvey Girls aren't supposed to keep company with men, but I want you all here to know that we've never been out on a date together. Every time we've seen each other, it's either been here at the hotel or in the company of others, like when she came with the other girls out to my place to picnic at the river. And the time, circumstances forced her into my company when her car broke down in the desert. We had a proper chaperone all the time, and Doc can vouch for that."

Mr. Harvey shook his head, easing his hands into his pants' pockets. "I don't think Miss Thorson needs to worry about being dismissed. I'm sure, now that Mrs. Gregory has heard the facts of the matter, she'll be more than willing to reverse her decision—about a lot of things. War and epidemics bring about special circumstances, and we need to be flexible and understanding with one another."

Meghan looked down, away from the shock and hurt and bewilderment on Mrs. Gregory's face. She had to feel as if the ground had fallen away from beneath her. "Thank you, Mr. Harvey. In any case, my contract is finished soon, and I don't believe I'll be staying on. I've learned so much the past few months, and I'm grateful for the job, but I think—I hope—there are some changes coming in my future that will make staying on at the El Garces impossible."

"I have something to say." Natalie rose from her chair. Her pale, hollow cheeks and wide blue eyes made her look so vulnerable. "I'm so proud of Caleb for what he did here tonight, braving the scorn of this town to stand up in public for Meghan by sharing his deepest secret. It's given me the courage to face you all with my own secret."

"Oh, Natalie, no," Meghan whispered.

"I have to. I can't lie anymore. It's dishonoring to God, to Derek, to Meghan and Dr. Bates whom I asked to keep my secret and lie for me." She folded her hands in front of herself. "Mr. Harvey, Mrs. Gregory. I wasn't truthful when I applied for this position. The truth is that I'm married. My husband, Derek, is fighting in France. I took the job because we needed the money to provide care for my mother-in-law. But I shouldn't have lied. I should've trusted God to provide for our needs."

"Married?" Mrs. Gregory put her hand to her throat.

"And I'm expecting." Rosy tint ebbed and flowed in Natalie's cheeks. "I should've come to you the minute Dr. Bates confirmed it, but I was too afraid. But no longer." She lifted the chain from around her neck and removed her wedding ring from the gold links, slipping it onto her finger and raising her chin. "I was afraid to trust God to meet our needs. His way never includes lying and deception. Caleb and Meghan have given me the courage to trust Him to take care of me and my baby."

Meghan turned to her and hugged her. "I'm so proud of you. But I'm sorry, too. I'm going to miss you so much."

Mrs. Gregory seemed at a loss for words. She blinked, looking from one face to another as if she didn't recognize anyone. Mr. Stock took the head waitress's elbow and led her toward the stairs murmuring something about getting her something to drink.

"Miss, or should I say Mrs. Daviot? That was a very brave thing you did. I'm sure we can come to a reasonable agreement about your employment." Mr. Harvey smoothed his moustache. Natalie nodded and gave a tremulous smile.

Doc took her elbow. "How about we go get some punch and cake and find a place to sit down?"

He escorted Natalie away, leaving Caleb, Meghan, and Mr. Harvey.

"Sir, thank you for all you did for me today. Thank you for bidding on the quilt. I hope you won't be too harsh with Mrs. Gregory. She's under so much pressure. Her son has been wounded and she's waiting to hear how he's faring." Meghan bit her lip.

"She's been a longtime faithful employee. I'm sure we can resolve things." He smiled. "Though I am not happy to hear that one of my best waitresses is planning on abandoning us at the end of her contract. How much time do you have left?"

"About six weeks. I should be home with my family before Thanksgiving."

His moustache twitched. "If I read the signs right, Mr. McBride might have something to say about that." Sketching a small wave, he sauntered toward the stairs and the murmur of conversation drifting up from the reception below.

Meghan found herself alone with Caleb at last. Shyness swept over her, surprising her. He released her hand.

Clink, step, *clink*, step, he walked over to the balcony rail and turned, leaning back against it. She moved to stand before him. His finger under her chin raised her face.

"Well, Meghan Thorson, it seems we have a few things to talk about."

She nodded.

"First, I want to apologize. I had no call to lay into you like I did when you were out at my place. I had no business kissing you against your will—"

"It wasn't against my will." The words tumbled out of her mouth before she could stop them.

He grinned and reached for her, cupping her shoulders and drawing her to him. "Is that so? Then maybe you won't mind this one too much. I've been wanting to kiss you all night." His lips came down on hers, familiar and yet so fresh and new and strange. Everything she remembered about their first kiss came rushing back before being drowned by feelings she'd never felt before. Stars burst behind her eyelids as she melted into him. His arms came around her, giving her an anchor in the storm of emotions and happiness and exhilaration. For the first time, she felt as if this was the real, unguarded, Caleb, free from his fears and his past, free to love and be loved. She murmured his name against his lips.

"Caleb."

A growl came from his throat, and he deepened the kiss as if he wanted to devour her. His fingers tunneled in her hair, dislodging her hat, and she clung to him as the world spun around her.

She loved him. With all her heart. She wanted her love to help heal him completely, to help him forget the pain of the past and reach toward a brighter future, together.

He lifted his lips from hers and peppered her face with kisses. "I know we have so much to talk about, but I could stand here with you in my arms forever."

Turning her face, she rested her cheek against his chest. His chin came down on top of her head, his arms still around her. She sighed. There was nowhere on earth she'd rather be. His heart thudded under her ear, in time with her own.

"I love you, Meghan. I've tried to fight it. I've tried to hold you at arms' length, but I just can't anymore. I think I fell in love the first time I looked into your eyes. You knocked the wind out of me, literally."

She hugged him tighter and looked up into his face. "I love

you, too, Caleb McBride. And I'm so sorry for everything. I wish I had been true to my first instinct about you instead of letting Mrs. Gregory and her friends sway me. I let what they *said* override how you acted. You were courteous, brave, self-sacrificing, understanding, caring—"

"Whoa, whoa, whoa, I'm no saint. God had to have a pretty stern talk with me about my pride and about the anger and bitterness I was carrying around about this town. We haven't really started to work on how I feel about my family yet." He grimaced. "Nor the jealousy I felt toward someone named Lars that you claimed to love." Giving her a little shake, he kissed the tip of her nose. "That was naughty of you."

"I do love Lars." She put on her most innocent expression. "But not the same way I love you."

"My leg doesn't matter?"

"Not to my love for you. Not one single bit. I love you."

"You're sure, because it isn't going away."

"I certainly hope it isn't." She noted the tired lines around his eyes. "Let's sit down. You're still recovering from the flu."

Once seated side-by-side on the folding chairs, Caleb took her hands. "Thank you for taking such good care of Joshua and me when we were sick. I was scared that I would die before I got to tell you how I felt about you. Then, when I knew you had seen my leg and you didn't come to see me at Doc's place, I thought maybe you were so repulsed you couldn't bear it." He swallowed hard, his vulnerability blazing in his eyes. "That happened to me before, a woman I thought I loved and was going to marry found out about my leg and she couldn't handle it. She broke things off. That's when I left Kentucky and headed out here. The desert seemed to mirror how I felt inside. I didn't intend to keep my leg a secret here, but somehow, when someone asked me why I hadn't enlisted, I just couldn't make myself say the words." He shook his head. "I could've kept you from a lot of trouble if I'd just have been honest up front."

She stroked his cheek, reveling in the freedom to touch him and not be rejected. "No recriminations. The past is the past and we can't change it. Our job is to do the right thing here and now."

"I guess the right thing then is to ask you if you will marry me. I'd get down on one knee, but. . ." He waved toward his brace. "I might not be able to get up again."

He'd taken her breath away. "This will do me just fine. And if you're asking, I'm accepting. Yes, Caleb McBride, I will marry you. But I warn you. I don't do anything by halves. I'm going to love you with everything I have."

He leaned in and kissed her again, this time with a hunger and power she hadn't anticipated but reveled in. Ending the kiss, he put his forehead against hers. "I'm counting on it."

When he'd caught his breath, he asked, "What about your job? Harvey Girls aren't supposed to be engaged."

"I think it will be okay. I know a guy." She gave him a saucy grin. "Though I suppose we should be circumspect for the next few weeks. I don't want to flout Mrs. Gregory's authority completely. If they let me stay on, I'll be respectful, though it won't be easy."

He laughed. "Now why doesn't that surprise me?" He kissed her again. "I don't think I will ever get tired of that. Who would've thought the beautiful redhead with the amazing green eyes—the girl I rescued from falling under a train—would be the one to take on this town on my behalf? Not only that, but she stormed the walls and barriers I had put up around my heart. She snuck in when I wasn't looking and healed parts of me I didn't even realize were broken. How could I not love her?"

"And the man labeled a coward took on that same town on my behalf." She rested her head on his shoulder. "And he sacrificed his privacy, exposed his most vulnerable secret in order to stand up for me. How could I not love him?"

His chest heaved in a sigh. "I suppose we should head downstairs to the reception. We have to face the town sometime."

"A shame. I'd love to stay right here in your arms forever, just you and me."

"We'll do it together." He rose and offered his hand. "You and me."

Epilogue

T wo days before Meghan's contract ended, she stood in the dining room, tears streaming down her face, reading the headline of the *Desert Star*. Caleb stood beside her as people cried and hugged and yelled.

The Armistice had been signed. The war was over. Lars would come home. Derek would return to Natalie and his family to await the birth of their baby. All of America's doughboys would come home.

Harvey Girl rules notwithstanding, Meghan dropped the paper and flung herself into Caleb's arms. "It's over. It's over. It's over," she chanted happily into his ear, squeezing his neck.

He held her tight as chaos reigned around them. Mrs. Gregory sat at a table and openly sobbed. Word had come the day after the auction that her son would recover from his wounds, but he had lost his right arm below the elbow. Broken, the head waitress had apologized to Meghan and Caleb, developing a whole new respect for what Caleb endured every day.

Joshua burst into the dining room. "Did you hear? Did you hear?"

"Yes. Isn't it wonderful?" Meghan reached out and drew Joshua into their hug.

"It won't change any of our plans, will it?" he asked when he'd extricated himself. "We're still going to Minnesota, right?"

"Right. On the Saturday afternoon train. You, Caleb, Doc Bates, and me. You're going to love Minnesota. I wish we were going in the springtime, but you'll get to see snow."

"I can't wait. I still can't believe he got me into college. Who would've guessed that Doc Bates had gone to medical school with Charlie Mayo?"

"Doc's going to miss you when he comes back here. He says you're underfoot all the time asking questions and trying to learn everything before you even start school."

Joshua grinned, so confident and excited, no longer the hunch-shouldered, resentful, haunted boy he'd been when Meghan first met him. His parents had given their consent to his leaving with them, and his father had even managed a rough hug of good-bye.

"Well, since you delivered the last batch of horses to the train, there hasn't been anything to do at the ranch." Joshua shrugged. "I'm going to go find Doc. He's probably heard the news by now."

That evening, Meghan and Caleb walked beside the fountain in the open-air lobby, holding hands. "It's going to be a long road ahead, isn't it? The world is going to have to find its way back to peace."

Caleb nodded. "But we'll do it. Time will heal the wounds, dull the hurt." They walked slowly to the musical accompaniment of the splashing water and the *clink* of Caleb's leg brace. He didn't wear it all the time, but by day's end, he usually had it on. She never mentioned it unless he did, still finding her way with how much he wanted to share about his leg and how he was feeling about it. Time would help with that, too.

"I'm just glad it's all over. Healing can't start until the fighting ends."

"That was certainly true for us, wasn't it? You're a little firebrand when you get riled up." He brushed his fingers along her temple, his eyes soft.

"Papa would say it was my Celtic heritage that makes me volatile, and Mama says it's my Viking blood."

He wrapped his arms around her and rested his chin on her hair. "Whatever it is, I'm glad it's mine."

"Me too, Caleb. Me too."

Even though **Erica Vetsch** has set aside her career teaching history to high school students in order to homeschool her own children, her love of history hasn't faded. Erica's favorite books are historical novels and history books, and one of her greatest thrills is stumbling across some obscure historical factoid that makes her imagination leap. She's continually amazed at how God has allowed her to use her passion for history, romance, and daydreaming to craft historical romances that entertain readers and glorify Him. Whenever she's not following flights of fancy in her fictional world, Erica is the company bookkeeper for her family's lumber business, a mother of two terrific teens, wife to a man who is her total opposite and yet her soul mate, and an avid museum patron.